The Finish Line

A Novel by

Christine O'Connor

Order this book online at www.trafford.
com or email orders@trafford.com

Most Trafford titles are also available at major online book retailers.

This novel is a work of fiction. The situations are fictional. No character is intended to portray any person or combination of persons living or dead.

Printed in Victoria, BC, Canada.

ISBN: 978-1-4269-2360-9 (sc)

Our mission is to efficiently provide the world's finest, most comprehensive book publishing service, enabling every author to experience success. To find out how to publish your book, your way, and have it available worldwide, visit us online at www.trafford.com

Trafford rev. 1/21/2009

www.trafford.com

North America & international
toll-free: 1 888 232 4444 (USA & Canada)
phone: 250 383 6864 • fax: 812 355 4082

For Shelby Cartier.
Dream big little one.

&

In memory of
Grandma (Bette) Beattie.

"It's gonna hurt every now and then.
If you fall get back on again.
Cowgirls don't cry."

-Ronnie Dunn, Terry McBride-

Acknowledgements

Thank you to my daughter Shelby for your perspective. It is amazing what a little one can teach us about love, laughter and life while quietly growing up all at the same time.

I wish to recognize the support of my family. Thank you for having faith that I am on the right path no matter where the path may be taking me. I love you guys.

Chapter One

A hush fell over the crowd just before the horn sounded to signal the start of the race. The race of all races had commenced at the *Greatest Outdoor Show on Earth*, the *Calgary Stampede.* The crowd came to life as the four drivers each raced toward their top barrels to complete the traditional figure eight pattern. There was no room for error in this race and a grimace streaked across the face of many-time champion Dave Southern, as he creased his top barrel and it crumpled on the ground like a wad of useless paper. Dave was all smiles only minutes ago when he drew the number one barrel position for this race but the smile was now gone. He knew the race was over for him. It is hardly necessary for the announcer to scream this confirmation over the sound system. For some people in the crowd, Dave's misfortune was an even better opportunity for a driver that they want to see bring it all home. The crowd cheered even louder.

Garret made a textbook turn off of his bottom barrel in position number two and headed for the track. He was a long way from the finish line on this track deemed the *Half Mile of Hell* by anyone who knows chuckwagon racing but already he had the feeling that this race was all his tonight..

The world famous *Rangeland Derby* Chuckwagon Races run each year during the *Calgary Stampede* bringing the top thirty-six drivers in the world together for one elite competition. The derby runs nine heats of races, with four teams competing in each heat. Each team consists of the chuckwagon driver and his four outriders. Competition is fierce as no less than thirty-two thoroughbreds speed around the track in each race. Many races are lost and won based on the success or lack thereof in the figure-eight barrel turn. It is exciting, it is chaotic, it is fun and in the wrong circumstances, it can be dangerous and even deadly.

In comparison to the more veteran drivers, Garret was still a junior at this game. As Garret crossed the finish line he looked back to see that his outriders had successfully made the journey with him. A lot of pressure is placed on everyone involved, especially in the *Calgary Stampede's* World Famous $100,000.00 *Dash For Cash.*

Dave followed Garret in second place. He knew his fate long before the finish line. The other two drivers completed the race in third and forth. They were veterans of the track but even they felt good for the kid on this night. It really was his turn. The crowd was deafening at this point. Garret did it. He was the new *Calgary Stampede* Champion.

"Garret, wake up. We've got a lot of work this morning, remember?" Cara gently jostled him from his dream.

Cara's long, wavy auburn hair cascaded over her shoulders as she looked down at him with her riveting green eyes. She was already dressed in her jeans and a dark pullover. He grinned up at her, begging her for a kiss as he gestured with outstretched arms. She responded, finishing the kiss with a slight pull on his arm.

"I'm up, I'm up," Garret groaned. "I was just having the best dream."

"Oh, well it must have been about me then," Cara teased.

"Well sort of," Garret replied. "Because when we finally win Calgary this summer, it will be about us and all of our hard work finally paying off."

Cara smiled at Garret. "It's a great dream Garret and who knows, maybe this is your year for everything to come together, but we'll never know until we get those horses in and see who's going to be in the lineup for this year, so let's go!"

"All business all of the time. That's my Cara. That's what I love about you the most." Garret ran his hands through his short blond hair and stretched before rising from the bedside. Seeing the sun begin to stream through the window brought him to his feet more eagerly.

Cara smiled at the remark. Many times Garret bragged to their friends and family members about what a great team they were and how hard she worked. She was so proud to be a part of the team and proud to be Garret's wife.

As Garret crossed the soft beige carpet of their bedroom, his thoughts turned back to the dream. He was entering his sixth season of professional chuck-wagon driving and he felt like everything was on the cusp of coming together. He was excited about the season but at the same time, none of it would matter to him without his wife and son. The dream of capturing the *Calgary Stampede* championship was a nice dream to have but it paled in comparison to the life he was already blessed with. There was nothing more important to Garret than the love of his family and friends; no championship could ever take the place of that. The McCormack's worked hard together as a family and they played hard in the time they had away from the racetrack. If they were to find victory in Calgary, it would be the whole McCormack team that would enjoy it. Garret was long past the youthful days of wanting only for himself.

Cara took a quick peek into the bedroom where their four month old son Corby slept soundly, surrounded by horse figures and prints throughout his room. She smiled at the way he was sleeping. His body position and the way he slept with one arm above his head reminded her exactly of how Garret looked when he was sleeping. Father and son both had matching sharp blue eyes and blond hair, but the soft wave in Corbyn's hair was definitely from his mother. It was hard to believe that Corbyn James McCormack, affectionately known as Corby, was now in their world.

Cara closed Corby's bedroom door and quietly crept down the hallway of their four bedroom ranch home. At the rear entrance, she gathered her warm clothes. Although it was April in Alberta, the mornings were still quite chilly, especially in the foothills of Alberta where they lived near the small town of Spruce View. This part of the country was beautiful and from the McCormack ranch, the Canadian Rocky Mountains stood tall only a short distance to the west. It was the perfect land for race horses. The pastures grew lush and green and the water coming from the creeks, fed by mountain springs, was plentiful.

Mary Hartman lived directly across the gravel road from the McCormack ranch and came over each morning by seven to watch Corby while Cara helped Garret with the horses. Dan and Mary Hartman ran a small cattle operation but they loved chuckwagon racing and often travelled along with the McCormack's to help out wherever they were needed. Spring training was a crucial time and Garret relied heavily on any extra pair of hands to help with the horses. Cara was often able to lend a hand in the morning while Mary watched Corby.

Garret was already at the large white and green hip roofed barn gathering lead shanks when Cara arrived. He usually hit the ground running during spring training so it came as no surprise that he beat her to the barn. She continued past the barn to the grain bin to scoop some oats into a bucket. It would be impossible to bring in all of the horses without something to persuade them a little. With spring in the air, the horses all had a little extra pep in them.

Garret and Cara walked out to the big pasture behind the barn. It was a crisp beautiful morning. The ground was still fresh with morning frost which made the surface slippery. They swung open the large metal gate which would allow the horses entrance into a smaller area where they could be caught and led into the barn. Garret and Cara could barely make out the horses at the far end of the field. As Cara began to shake the bucket of oats, the horses raised their heads to the familiar sound. One by one they walked towards the twosome, slowly working their way into a gallop. It always seemed as though the animals could sense that race season was near. Their excitement could almost be felt. Thoroughbreds are bred to run. It is what they love and live for, much like the people who tend to own them. After a long winter, they were as eager to start the season as their owners.

In a matter of minutes, twenty-eight race horses were gathered into the smaller pen by the barn, eagerly reaching at the bucket of oats in Cara's hand. As each horse allowed a lead shank to be snapped onto his halter, he was rewarded with a taste of oats.

The real feast awaited them in the barn where precise rations of oats were dished out.

Cara kept the horses occupied with the oat pail while Garret continued to catch them. Garret led the horses into their stalls, giving each one an affectionate scratch as he tied him up. For Garret, just working with the horses at home in preparation for the season was rewarding for him.

As the last horse was led into the barn Cara could hear the echo of Mary Hartman's voice over the barn intercom which connected to the house.

"The youngest McCormack is up," Mrs. Hartman chimed. "I'm going to start breakfast for you okay?"

Cara grinned as she pressed the intercom button down. "That would be wonderful Mary." She was always such a thoughtful and caring woman. Mary Hartman was sixty-two years young with three grown children of her own, all living in big cities. She also had five grandchildren to brag about, but she did not see them as often as she would have liked. When Cara told Mary they were expecting their first child, she was as excited as if it were one of her own grandchildren. Mary vowed right then and there that she would be available to watch the baby as often as they needed. She understood the demands the horses could put on a family.

Cara had a very difficult birth when their son was born and the doctors told her soon afterward that she would never conceive another child. At the time, it was enough of a miracle that they had Corby but sometimes Cara felt a little emptiness at the thought of never having a baby brother or sister for him to grow up with.

With the horses eating contently in their stalls, Garret and Cara went to the house for breakfast. The morning frost was quickly dissipating and it looked like it would be a beautiful day to get some training and exercise done.

"So how is everything out there this morning?" Mary spoke as Cara entered the kitchen. She carried on with the breakfast preparations as she chatted with Cara. Her bob length silver hair was tidy as usual and the slender woman worked as though she were in her own kitchen. The kitchen was as familiar to her as her own and she rifled through the oak cupboards, pulling out the items she needed. The dark granite counter tops gleamed in the early morning sunshine. The kitchen was cheery and anyone who stopped by for a visit felt welcome around the large oak dining table.

"Everything is just great," Cara answered with a smile. The smell of bacon and eggs danced through the kitchen. "Thank you so much for this," said Cara as she washed up at the sink before grabbing some bread to begin making the toast.

"It's my pleasure," answered Mary. "I know how busy things get for the two of you at this time of the year.

As soon as Cara popped the bread into the toaster she moved toward the living room where she could hear Corby cooing happily. He lay on a blanket on the floor, merrily kicking his feet as he batted at some toys on a plastic bar that straddled him. Cara knelt down and played with her son until she heard the sound of the toast popping up. She returned to the kitchen to help finish with breakfast just as Garret was entering the living room to watch Corby; his morning entertainment.

Normally, at this point in the day, Cara would be rushing to get herself out the door to school. As an elementary school teacher, there was plenty to do before the school year ended in June but right now Cara was on maternity leave with her new son.

Teaching school was the perfect career for Cara. It allowed her to work with children and it also allowed her the time off in the summer that she needed to travel the race circuit. Children and horses, particularly race horses, were Cara's two passions in life after that of her husband and son. Teaching and horses were after all, how Cara had met Garret in the first place.

Growing up near Vancouver, British Columbia most kids did not have the exposure to horses the way that Cara had, but Cara's father Lee Beaton loved the track and often took Cara and her brother to *Hastings Park* for the races. Cara was only thirteen when her father decided that family life was not nearly as interesting as his drinking, womanizing and gambling.

One day he agreed with Cara's mother that Cara could come to the racetrack in Seattle with him for an overnight trip. Cara was thrilled to go to the races in a place like Seattle. In all of the excitement at the track she lost sight of her father's whereabouts. After the races, Cara wandered through the paddock area where she was sure she would find her Dad catching up with old friends. What she found instead was her drunken father, his pants down to his ankles, in a paddock with one of the young trainers pressed firmly against the wall. The woman could not have been more than five years older than Cara.

Lee turned around when he heard Cara's gasp but by the time he had his pants pulled up, Cara was gone. That day Lee decided it was time for him to move on. He never contacted his family again. Cara caught a bus back to Vancouver and never told her mother what she had witnessed. She told her mother that she simply lost track of her Dad and came home. Why put her mother through any more than that. The last image of her father was the one that remained with her ever since. She vowed never to waste her time trying to find him later in her life. Looking back, she was sure that her mother knew all about her dad but denial was a less painful avenue to take than the truth.

Their father left a large hole in the hearts of his wife and their two children however Cara's mother Karen was a strong person and refused to allow her children to wallow in pain or self-pity. What the children's father did to their family was not their fault and Karen never let them hold onto any guilt for his actions. Cara and her younger brother Jason grew up strong and competitive, taking after their mother. The only thing Cara really took from her father was his last name and a keen interest in racing horses.

Although Karen Beaton was less than enthused about Cara's attraction to the racetrack, she felt it was the one thing that she could let her daughter enjoy on their limited income from her small catering business. Cara continued to hang around the track long enough to get noticed by some pretty impressive names in horse owners and trainers. She was young but she was tough and it did not take long for Cara to pick up a job as groom and later as a trainer's assistant, working the horses out in the mornings. Cara earned her stripes around the track and when it came time for her to leave for University to pursue her chosen career as a teacher, she chose *Simon Fraser University.* It was as close to the racetrack as she could get, allowing her to continue to work at the racetrack to help pay her way through school. With *Hastings Park* only a few miles from downtown Vancouver, it was the perfect arrangement.

During Cara's final year at *Simon Fraser,* she was working on a race day like many others at *Hastings Park* however on this day, Garret happened to be at the track as well. He was a horse trainer and a chuckwagon outrider from Alberta with an interest in purchasing some race horses for the future he was planning as a chuckwagon driver. Cara had heard of chuckwagon racing, but she never heard anything good about it. She was not impressed with Garret as soon as she learned what he was there for.

Garret first noticed Cara as she carefully wrapped the legs of the race horses that would be running that day. He was not shy and introduced himself immediately. Of course Cara had to express her opinion about what she thought of chuckwagon drivers but Garret simply challenged her further. It was not long before he convinced her that if she really wanted to know what it was like, then she should come back to Alberta and work on the chuckwagon circuit for the summer herself. The one thing Cara was not afraid of was a challenge. At the first opportunity, she signed on for employment with one of the wagon drivers and she was off to Alberta for a summer.

Cara was pretty sure that these people racing horses on this ever-mobile circuit would be no match for the luxury of a regular racing stable. When Cara arrived in Grand Rapids, Alberta for her first show, she hated to admit it but she was pretty impressed with what she saw. Of course, there was no way she was going to admit this to Garret. He later told Cara that he thought she was pretty stubborn which usually annoyed him, but this time there was something different that made him want to get to know her.

As the summer wore on, the two were soon spending a lot of time together. They teased one another mercilessly and they fell in love slowly. A summer of racing turned the pair into soul mates. Cara and Garret were married two years later. The same year, Garret began professionally racing chuckwagons.

Cara smiled as she remembered what brought her to small town Alberta in the first place. She could not have chosen a better life for herself if she had dreamt it all up. It was hard to believe that six years had already passed since their May wedding day. She jumped back to reality as the last of the toast popped up from the toaster.

The kitchen was alive with the wonderful smells of a big breakfast. Garret scooped up Corby from his blanket and placed him in a baby seat near the table so that he could be near everyone while they ate breakfast. Garret appreciated a big breakfast. There was little time for lunch once he turned his attention to the horses for the day. Cara was not a big breakfast eater unless it was closer to brunch but nonetheless, she tried to eat something for she knew there would be no time to stop until much later.

Anyone who knew the McCormack's would say that they lived a terrific life. Cara had changed so much from the hurt child, abandoned by her father. She made a real life for herself that she was proud of. It was a life she treasured beyond anything.

Cara and Mary cleaned up after breakfast while Garret went outside to continue the day's work with the horses. When the dishes were cleaned up, Cara got her warmer clothes on again to go back outside. Mary would watch Corby until the morning training was complete and then in the afternoon Garret's brother would be over to help with some of the driving so Cara could spend the rest of the day with Corby. This would be the routine for most of the spring. The days were very full and tiring sometimes.

Cara was enjoying her afternoon playtime with Corby right up until four o'clock when there was a knock at the door. As the door opened, a familiar voice called hello. It was Shana, Garret's brother Robert's wife.

"Hi Shana, what a nice surprise this is," said Cara. Although they lived only twelve miles apart, they did not see each other often as work kept them all occupied. Shana stood in the doorway. She had a larger, muscular build and short smooth dirty blond hair that was brushed back in a simple fashion. She wore black track pants and a green sweatshirt. It was her usual style of dress when she was coming from their cattle ranch as most of her clothes needed to fit under her coveralls. She was a hard worker and most of her build consisted of the muscle she developed over years of calving cows and other strenuous work that comes with running a cattle ranch.

"I've come to send you out to the barn again," said Shana. "Garret called and said he needed you so I will watch Corby while you are out there."

"Okay," answered Cara hesitantly. It seemed a bit strange that Garret had not mentioned anything to her. She welcomed Shana into the house where Corby was happily cooing and playing in the living room. Shana scooped her nephew up immediately to cuddle and talk to him.

"There's fresh coffee on," said Cara. "Help yourself to anything you need and thank you so much for offering to watch Corby."

"No problem," replied Shana. "Who wouldn't want to watch this little guy?"

Cara grabbed her coat and headed back outside wondering what was up with Garret. She could not figure out why he would not have just said something was going on prior to making all of the arrangements for someone to watch Corby.

"Hey guys," Cara chimed as she approached Garret and Robert. Robert was Garret's oldest brother and he had been helping Garret for most of the afternoon. Robert was older than Garret by a few years but their features and blond hair were very similar.

"What's up?" asked Cara.

"You are," said Robert. "I'll see you two later. I'm going to the house to spend some time with my little nephew."

Cara turned to Garret with a puzzled look on her face however it did not last for long. As Garret opened the barn door she could see their two faithful saddle horses. They were saddled and ready to go.

"This is a great surprise." Cara smiled before leaning toward Garret for a kiss. Garret kissed Cara softly as he passed her the reins from her saddle horse and then reached for his own.

"I thought you could use a little bit of a break and a relaxing ride after all of the hell I've put you through working around here lately," said Garret. "I know the work you do here isn't quite the same as that cushy teaching job you're used to," he teased.

"Ha, ha," replied Cara. "I could just see you handling my cushy class," she teased back. "Really Garret, thank you, this is a wonderful treat."

Cara turned toward her palomino gelding Breeze. Placing her foot into the saddle's stirrup she mounted the horse with ease. Garret smiled at his wife. He knew that nothing made her happier than moments like this.

"I was thinking that maybe we should ride down to Two Mile Creek," said Garret. "It should be pretty high right now with the spring run-off and the pussy willows and all of those things you love to see," he said.

"That sounds great," replied Cara as she turned her horse in the direction of the creek.

The sun was still quite high in the west and the first warmth of spring was appreciated. Garret rode alongside of Cara on his black gelding Coke. The pussy willows were indeed coming out. Cara noticed them immediately when they crossed a ditch to ride through a pasture. The new spring grass was desperately trying to peek through the dead grass from the previous year. They rode on through a small grove of pine trees, breathing in the fresh scents of the season. After a peaceful thirty minute ride, they arrived at the creek where they always stopped for a break. Garret and Cara both dismounted their horses and tied them to nearby trees. Once she tied her horse, Cara turned back toward the creek. She smiled at Garret as he brought a bedroll from the back of his saddle. Garret spread the heavy grey wool blanket on the grass beside the creek. Wrapped within the bedroll Garret produced a bottle of wine, two plastic cups and some assorted types of cheese.

"My, my Mr. McCormack, don't you always think of everything," laughed Cara.

"Well my dear, if you had a wife as beautiful and charming as I do, you would try to think of everything too," Garret laughed as he made a grand gesture with his hand for Cara to be seated on the blanket.

Cara sat down on the thick blanket and gazed peacefully at the creek running high with spring runoff water. She leaned back and soaked in the warmth of the sun. Garret poured the wine and lay down near Cara, propping himself on one elbow as he passed her a plastic cup of the wine.

"Thank you," Cara said with sincerity in her voice. "I really needed this today."

"I know," replied Garret. "I saw the first team of horses step on you a couple of times and that second outfit shoved you pretty hard when you were trying to untie them. I know it was not an easy day and I just wanted to remind you that I appreciate everything you do around the place to help me get ready." He kissed her and she smiled up at him.

"You know I wouldn't have it any other way," Cara pointed out as she reached for Garret's shirt collar to pull him in for a long kiss.

With a new baby and all of the work with the horses, it had been a long time since they had been together in any sort of romantic way. They were obviously both thinking the same thing. Soon Cara felt Garret's body crushing against her. Cara felt her heart rate quicken as she kissed Garret hard on the mouth. He returned her kiss as his tongue explored her mouth, asking for more. Cara's passion was fuelled by the desire she always felt from Garret. They grasped at each other's clothes, pulling them off quickly. They were overwhelmed with a hunger for more.

As he pressed himself against her, Cara felt the warmth of Garret's familiarity along with an intense need for the man she so deeply loved. She gasped in approval as he lowered his lips to her waiting breasts and lingered there for a long while. He made love to her slowly at first until the urgency of their needs could no longer go unanswered. Her hands grasped his shoulders as they satisfied each other passionately. Cara felt her breath catch in her throat as Garret gently bit her neck. The two became one and they clung to each other for a long time. Afterward, they lingered in a lazy kiss before Garret reached for the blanket, pulling it over them as they began to notice the chill in the air.

"Whoa," said Garret with a smile. "Where did all of that come from?"

"I was wondering the same thing. It was like that one time after the races, well except you haven't had quite that much wine today." Cara laughed out loud as Garret tickled her ribs. She squirmed on the blanket, laughing hysterically.

"You needed to bring that up again," laughed Garret. "You know I will get you for that one day."

As the air chilled, Garret and Cara dressed before lingering some more to enjoy their wine and cheese. Their time at the creek was the last little bit of quality couple time they would enjoy for a while. Their time would soon be filled with the agenda of race preparations. Garret and Cara watched the creek rushing by, filled by the water of the spring run-off from the nearby mountains. They laughed, talked and enjoyed one another's company before deciding it was time to gather their things to ride back to the ranch. It was the perfect ending to a long day and a busy session of spring training. They were now ready to take on the new race season.

The rest of spring training passed quickly and in no time at all the end of May had arrived. A barn hand was hired to help with all of the work that would need to be done during the race season and he seemed to be working out well so far. Michael DeWalt was the nephew of chuckwagon racing legend Bill Turner. Bill had retired from racing a few years earlier and when his nephew expressed an interest in racing, he contacted Garret to see if he would mentor him. Garret immediately offered Michael a job working as a barn hand. It was a great place to start if he wanted to get completely involved in the sport. He knew Bill for many years and he was happy to offer the position to Michael. It certainly did not hurt that Michael was not a kid. Garret knew that they were about the same age. He was sure that work ethic would not be an issue.

Michael was thirty years old and worked as a contract oilfield consultant. He did not plan on getting a job working for Garret; he would have been happy just to have the opportunity to come along and learn from him. The surprise offer was great news for Michael and he quickly arranged his summer schedule to accommodate the new venture.

Michael was tall with a muscular build and dirty blond soft curly hair that floated at the back of his neck. He seemed to have a smile that never quit and a zest for life and for learning new things that was contagious. Garret had sensed his enthusiasm and ambition as soon as they had met and he was happy to give him the chance to prove himself.

Michael lived in Calgary, Alberta as the city offered the greatest amount of consulting work. His bigger dreams included moving out of Calgary to live on his own ranch and race his own chuckwagon horses. He spent many years around the racetrack with his Uncle Bill. When Bill retired from racing, Michael was not in a place in his life that he could take up the lines himself so he had to drop the dream for a while. Within a few years he felt ready to take on the challenge and was thrilled when everything could be arranged.

Michael learned a lot from his uncle but there was always more to learn. He eagerly drank in the new knowledge that he acquired each day. He grew up with horses but understanding the business side of keeping race horses healthy required a great deal of studying what the pros were doing.

Cara liked Michael. He had ambition and a great sense of humor which was the perfect combination in such a demanding, stressful environment. He was quickly becoming an integral part of their team. Race season was going to be underway soon and having a team of people that worked well together was half the battle.

Chapter Two

It was time to pack up to travel to the first race of the season in Grand Rapids, Alberta. It would take the McCormack's about six hours of travel time to reach the city from their ranch near Spruce View. Travel was a little slower with a trailer load of thoroughbreds than it is when simply travelling by car. Much care needed to be taken to ensure that the horses were kept comfortable and safe on the journey to the race venue. This was especially true going to the first race of the season with some horses being new to travel. Anything could happen and it was not the time to take safety for granted.

Once the horses were loaded comfortably into their individual travel stalls within the trailer, the long journey got underway. Cara followed Garret's horse trailer with their pickup truck and holiday trailer. They would need accommodations at the track while racing. Staying in a hotel was too risky as it meant leaving horses unattended which could lead to unfortunate mishaps. Also, the McCormack's were very hands-on in every aspect of their horses care and staying at a hotel was simply not practical.

Dan and Mary Hartman travelled in convoy with the McCormack's to the first race of the season. They packed their own holiday trailer and Dan came over to help load the horses with Garret. Dan was now sixty-seven years old but he was young at heart. Ranching all of his life kept him in shape and his 5'10" frame still possessed an athletic build. His silver hair and weathered skin gave away his years but nothing slowed him down.

They all departed together in good time that morning. When the McCormack's and company arrived in Grand Rapids that Saturday afternoon, they had four days before the races would begin. There was still a lot of work to do in order to be ready. It was a beautiful sunny afternoon. The grounds in Grand Rapids were covered in beautiful clean sand and a short walk would take one down to the river along a fantastic nature trail. The setting made for a relaxing atmosphere during any available down time.

It was a long drive for Corby and he was starting to fuss. Even the breaks along the way were not enough. The infant balled his tiny hands into tight fists as he began to wail.

"Hang on Corby," Cara turned from the driver's seat and spoke to him in the back seat of the pickup truck where his car seat held him snugly. "Mommy's trying to hurry". Cara smiled reassuringly at the restless baby as she reached her hand into his seat so he could grab onto her fingers. This seemed to keep him content just long enough for Cara to get the truck and trailer into a camping spot.

Garret and his new barn hand Michael were already busy unloading horses from the trailer. On any day it was important that the horses not stand restlessly in the trailer for too long but it was even more important on warmer days. Restless horses could easily injure themselves trying to get outside. Garret wanted the horses that were new to travel to have a positive experience so that they would continue to travel well throughout the season.

Cara found a spot to park the holiday trailer which was close to where the horses would be stabled. She parked against a nice area of thick pine trees where they would be protected from the wind should the weather turn bad.

A good camp setup is important. This would be their home for the next week. With a forty foot holiday trailer that included two bedrooms with extra sleeping accommodations for company should they need it, they had all of the comforts of home as they traveled the race circuit. A full kitchen and living room area also complemented the holiday trailer which meant that food could be prepared and friends entertained just as easily as they would be if they visited the McCormack's at their home.

Cara unbuckled Corby and scooped him from the car seat just as he was resuming his cries. Corby was dressed in a soft cotton sleeper to travel the long distance in comfort. She quickly wrapped a light blanket around her son and carried him to the trailer. He was hungry and he certainly needed some time to stretch and play after the long confinement of the car seat.

Dan Hartman parked his holiday trailer alongside the McCormack's trailer. He and Mary busily set up camp for themselves as a bustle of activity carried on all around them with other drivers, outriders, family, fans and friends moving into the area for the races.

Cara took one of Corby's milk bottles from the fridge and warmed it in a pan of water on the stove. She laid Corby on the change table and began to change his diaper while the milk warmed. All of this activity kept Corby content long enough to help him forget about his hunger until the bottle was ready. When his diaper was changed, Cara tested the temperature of Corby's milk and then settled into the armchair with her son for his feeding. The baby looked up at Cara contentedly with his large blue eyes. He was back to being the happy little guy he usually was.

With the horses fed, watered and settled into their stalls, Garret and Michael were free to wander over to the holiday trailer for a late lunch. Garret and Michael set up the outdoor table and chairs right on time as the trailer door opened revealing Cara and a tray of freshly made sandwiches. Garret retrieved the tray from Cara and placed it on the table. Cara turned back into the trailer for plates, napkins and other condiments and salads to complete their lunch.

When Cara returned to the table with the rest of the food, the activity that usually stirs around camp had started. Friends from other chuckwagon camps began arriving and sitting down in the available lawn chairs to visit and discuss their predictions and prospects for the season.

"Hello Cara," the voice of Karl Stern boomed toward her. Karl was a large man in his fifties with brush cut gray hair. He had been racing wagons for over thirty years. Karl was a strong competitor and the younger generation of drivers often looked to him for advice about their own outfits.

"Hello Karl," Cara replied with a smile. "Did you have a good winter?"

"Well, sweetheart," Karl replied. "I have never found anything really good about winter, but it was good enough. It certainly can't hold a candle to the summer time when I get to race wagons and see all of the pretty girls like you."

"Oh Karl, I see you haven't lost all of that charm," Cara teased.

Karl was always the charmer and he enjoyed teasing the children and flirting with the ladies almost as much as he enjoyed the racing itself. He was a true Alberta old time cowboy with many stories to tell. At this stage in his life, he liked to remain competitive but racing was mainly about the social aspects and enjoying himself. He uncovered the secret to staying competitive long ago. He no longer worried about every season the way the younger drivers did.

Cara finished setting out the lunch while people continued to gather for a quick visit. In a chuckwagon camp everyone is always welcome.

A few people helped themselves to a snack or two at Cara's offering before she retrieved a sandwich herself. She sat down on a chair next to her husband, balancing her lunch plate on her lap. Garret now had Corby in his arms and was proudly introducing him to the many people who had not yet met him because of the distance apart that most of them lived.

Some of the other wives and friends of the other drivers also gathered and all of the smaller children began to play in the sand while the adults caught up on the events of the winter months. Most of the chuckwagon families lived a great distance apart and although they kept in contact through the winter months, they often did not see each other until the first show of the year.

Babies were born, there were new pregnancies to announce, children were quickly growing or had moved out on their own, new sponsors were introduced and friends of chuckwagon drivers had passed on. The winter brought many changes which meant that there was always a great deal to discuss at the beginning of a new season.

Barbie Hopkins was in her eighth month of her fifth pregnancy. She looked uncomfortable in the unseasonable warmth but nonetheless, she had a smile on her face as she settled down in a patio chair where she could keep an eye on her young children. Her long brown hair was pulled up in a knot on top of her head and she wore a pink maternity t-shirt paired with maternity jeans. She relayed with laughter to the others how her husband Neil was not so sure what would happen if she went into labor during the *Calgary Stampede* which coincided with her due date. Barbie's four children, ranging in ages from ten to three, played excitedly in the sand with several other children. The children had not seen one another since the previous race season but they quickly renewed their friendships.

"So how are you feeling Barbie?" Mary Hartman enquired. She had been around the races long enough that she knew nearly everyone.

"I'm exhausted and waiting for the due date," replied Barbie in a rather exasperated voice.

"Well, don't fret sweetheart," said Mary, pushing away a wisp of her hair from her own face. "Before you know it, this little one will be in the world and playing in that sand over there with the others. Time just goes by so fast and you have to treasure the times like these." Mary was still talking to Barbie but she was affectionately gazing at all of the little ones at play.

"You're right Mary," said Barbie. "I love it when they are little, I just don't necessarily enjoy the whole part of waiting until they get here!" Barbie smiled to Mary as she rose from her chair to gather up her playing children.

"It was nice seeing all of you," Barbie waved to the group in general before adding "I'll catch up with you later in the week Cara".

"That sounds good," said Cara. "If you need a hand with anything please ask." Cara could see that Barbie definitely had her hands full.

After lunch the visitors began to disperse with plans to check on their horses or drive into Grand Rapids for items they forgot to pack. With the first trip of the year, something always got left miles away at home.

Garret approached Cara, affectionately placing his hand on her shoulder. "Thank you for the nice lunch," said Garret as he leaned in to peck Cara on the cheek. "I'm going to run into town to see if I can pick up a few things at the harness shop," he said as he passed Corby to Cara.

"You're welcome," replied Cara as she gathered Corby in her arms. "Don't be too long. I'd like to spend time together this afternoon before everything gets too busy."

"I'll be as quick as I can, I promise," said Garret as he stroked Corby's hair before turning on his heel to leave.

Cara smiled as Garret walked to the truck. Chuckwagon racing was an important part of their lives, but Garret and Cara always agreed that racing was not their whole life. Family life needed to be gently balanced with racing and the two in harmony could work very well together. Without that balance, the stress of competition and travel could take its toll.

Things were coming together for the McCormack chuckwagon team and Cara felt that this would be the season for many of Garret's racing dreams to be realized. Of course, thirty-five other teams thought the same thing. Only time would tell who would come out on top.

The first night of racing was quickly approaching and, after a spring season of preparation and training, the drivers eagerly practiced their teams each day to see which horses would hold the most promise to start the year off right. With thirty-six very competitive teams, often dividing the standings by hundredths of a second, consistency was just as important as speed. Penalties could instantly send a driver from the top to the bottom in only a single race.

The drivers and the outriders were all taking their respective training times on the track. They teased and cajoled one another during their practices, but in the back of their minds the serious business of racing always existed. The outriders practiced perspective horses just as much as the drivers worked with the horses on their wagon outfits. Outriders had to know before the race how the horses would work for them. Costing a driver a penalty could cost the outrider his spot on that driver's team, effectively removing him from that driver's payroll.

Chuckwagon drivers make their racing money by selling advertising sponsorship on their wagon canvases as well as through prize money. Outriders make their racing money strictly through the drivers who hire them to ride. The drivers try to hire the best outriders to ride for them and then pay them accordingly. It is a wild sport known as a "feast or famine" or "hero to zero" sport because anything might happen to anyone on any given race day.

The first night of racing was usually referred to as "organized chaos" by most of the drivers. As the season wears on, teams fall into the routine of what it takes to be prepared for the races. New barn help is learning the ropes, some new equipment is being tried and it always takes a few races to establish the best practices for race preparation.

On the final night before the race season officially started Garret kissed his wife hard on the mouth before they went to bed. "This is it," he said to Cara. "This is what we have worked for and this is going to be our year. I can just feel it."

Cara smiled at Garret with a bit of dampness in her eyes. The beginning of the year was always such an emotional time just wondering what was about to come. She looked at their son who was now sleeping peacefully in his crib. She knew that right at that moment her life was more perfect than she could have ever asked for. "Thank you God for my life and my family," she said before heading off to bed.

In the morning the McCormack's along with Michael, enjoyed a big breakfast once the morning chores were finished. A routine was gradually being established around the barns and Michael was quickly falling into stride with the way things were done. The day carried on in a regular fashion right up to the point of the late afternoon when the usual pre-race chaos started.

Barn help and drivers eagerly dashed around the barns in an effort to be ready for their respective race heat. The horses were all groomed with care. Some of the horses' legs were wrapped and bandaged to prevent old injuries from reoccurring or simply in an effort to prevent a possible new injury. Outriding horses were saddled, the wagon horses chosen to run on the chuckwagon for the night were harnessed and all of the equipment was thoroughly examined to ensure that it was all in excellent working condition.

Cara usually tried to help in the barns, but with a new baby she had a new role to play at the races. Being Corby's mother was a far more exciting role than cleaning barns or working with the horses. Cara chose jeans and a white t-shirt with a mint coloured sweater to wear to the races. As the evening was rather windy, she pulled her hair back with a clip. She smiled at Corby as she picked him up from the toys he batted at on the floor. She took great pleasure in dressing him for his first-ever chuckwagon race. Cara changed his diaper before putting on his little undershirt followed by a plaid cowboy shirt and the tiniest *Wrangler* blue jeans she had ever seen. Of course the outfit was not complete without the addition of his very first cowboy boots. They were very soft for his tiny baby feet.

Cara had Corby ready in his stroller to take up to the grandstand. Corby was about to attend his first chuckwagon race. Cara took the diaper bag and a jacket from the trailer before pushing the stroller toward the barn area.

"We're here to wish you luck Daddy," Cara smiled at Garret who was still hurrying around to insure everything was ready. Garret stopped what he was doing and walked over to Cara and Corby.

"This is a huge moment in my life," said Garret.

Cara saw emotion streak across Garret's face and she knew without question what he was referring to. Garret was about to run his first race with a son in the grandstand. Even though Corby was young and would never remember this day, Garret would forever remember the first race he ran as a father, a family man. This was a momentous day in his racing career as far as he was concerned and no award or championships could top it.

"Wow, look at you Corby," Garret took note of the tiny western outfit that adorned his infant son. "You sure are ready for your first race."

Corby cooed happily to his parents without a care in the world.

With tears in her eyes, Cara hugged Garret tightly and smiled up at him. Garret hugged her back tightly and then bent down to kiss his son before his family departed to get a good seat for the races. No other words were spoken. Both Garret and Cara knew how they were feeling inside.

Barn hands and drivers continued to hurry through the barn area with grooming equipment and tack. Orders were yelled back and forth throughout the area as the excitement continued to build. Garret resumed working with his horses. He felt good inside and he was ready to race.

The anticipation of the race built around the McCormack barn as the first three heats of wagons were announced. Their chuckwagon team was harnessed and ready to be hitched to the wagon as Garret would run in the fifth heat of the night. The time quickly came for Garret to leave the barn area with his chuckwagon outfit and make his way to the track.

Both Garret and Michael slipped into their red nylon racing coats. Each barrel position has a different coat color assigned to it. The driver, the driver's assistant and the outriders all wear the same coat colour for their respective team so each team can be easily identified. The red coat symbolizes barrel position number two, the barrel that Garret would run for the first night of the new race season.

Michael quickly finished the last minute adjustments with the horses. His nerves were running high. In the few years that he was away from the track, he had not spent any amount of time near the wagons much less assisting a driver in the wagon. He wanted to make sure he did everything exactly as Garret asked.

Some of the drivers from the earlier heats were returning to the barn area from their races. Some with smiles on their faces at having made it successfully through the first race of the season, others grimacing at the misfortune they had found on the first day.

As Grant Wagner drove past Garret's team Garret asked "How'd you do Grant?" Grant simply shook his head in a negative motion and continued on driving toward his own barn. One of the barn hands walking past Garret said that Grant had hit both of his barrels and may also have been penalized for interfering with another driver. It was a dismal start to the year for Grant. Garret shook the notion from his mind. He was concentrating on having a positive run and he now took some space to think about what he needed to do when he got out on the track.

Michael quickly circled around the now ready chuckwagon team.

"Everything looks good from down here," Michael said to Garret.

"Okay Michael, we're ready to go then," replied Garret as he viewed the equipment from his position in the driver's seat and set the reins properly in his hands for maximum control of the team. "You can let them go."

Michael unsnapped each lead shank from the eager team of thoroughbreds and quickly ran to the back of the chuckwagon to climb aboard as the team lurched forward. Michael rode in the wagon with Garret up to the track in case he needed an extra pair of hands to help with the hyper horses while they awaited entry to the track. He would also ride on the track with Garret for his practice barrel turn prior to the race.

Each driver is required to do a practice barrel turn and during this time each driver is also required to have a driver assistant with him should there be any problems prior to the race. Michael could feel his stomach churning a bit as he rode in the wagon. He wondered how Garret could seem so calm but he knew that this was not the time to ask nor was it a time for small talk. He was determined to at least have Garret think that his nerves were under control. The excitement was becoming overwhelming.

As they made their way down the road that led to the racetrack, other drivers and barn crew members hollered at Garret to hold up. Garret did not get the whole jest of what had happened, but he knew something happened on the track in a previous heat to delay the races. He swallowed hard trying not to stir his early season nerves. He only hoped that both humans and horses were okay.

Cara was seated in the grandstand with a few friends. Corby lay peacefully in her arms, wrapped up in his blanket. Cara clenched a corner of Corby's blanket tightly. She tried to remain calm after what she and hundreds of fans had just witnessed in the previous race. Even with a lifetime of experience around horses and the dangers of them, nothing ever prepared her for the emotions she felt when things went wrong on the track.

As the teams crossed the finish line, one of the outriding horses lost his footing on a soft area of the track causing the outrider to be catapulted over the horse's head. The wagon driver running in last place in the race witnessed what happened with the outrider but it did not give him enough time to avoid him. The young outrider was run over by the driver's horses and the wagon causing him to tumble helplessly under the outfit before landing to rest along the outside rail of the track.

As the outrider lay motionless on the track, the paramedics quickly entered from the medic station. Jaimie Feldstrom, the injured outrider, had not moved since the wagon passed over him and it was uncertain how serious his injuries were. Cara could feel the tears welling up in her eyes and the lump in her throat as she wrapped her arms around Corby. This was not a part of racing that anyone enjoyed. The grandstand was completely quiet as the outrider lay motionless for what seemed like hours.

A spine board was promptly retrieved from the waiting ambulance as a neck brace was placed on the still outrider. A few of the outriders and wagon drivers stood on the track, eager to help in any way possible but really helpless in the situation. As Jaimie was loaded into the waiting ambulance the crowd applauded to show support for the desperate situation the young man was in. It was over that fast. The races had to go on before nightfall and the next heat of wagons was called to the track as quickly as possible.

The incident left everyone shaken, but at the same time, there was a show that needed to continue. Both the drivers and outriders would try to push the accident from their minds in an effort to do the best job that they could for the remainder of the evening's performance. Once the performance was over, everyone would learn more about the status of their fellow competitor and friend.

Garret and the other drivers who were waiting to get onto the track for the next heat were now called in by the Arena Director. Garret cleared his throat as he gave a yell to motion his team forward. It was time for the business of racing and the best thing he could do right now was to concentrate on the race and not on what just happened.

Garret's whole outfit glistened in the evening sun. As he passed the waiting crowd to enter the barreling area for his practice turn, the crowd clapped their approval at the look of his outfit. The horses were groomed to perfection. The white harness that they wore along with their blue blinker hoods and matching blue wraps on their legs really made the team stand out. The wagon itself glistened with fresh white and blue paint in a diamond pattern that was the trade mark of the McCormack racing team. It was a pattern Garret dreamed he would one day see gracing the side of his own son's wagon.

Garret moved his horses swiftly through the barrel pattern. As he swung out past his bottom barrel, the driver competing on barrel one entered the barreling area to complete his practice turn. For each night of racing, the drivers would be rotated through the barrels so that each driver had a chance to compete from each barrel position. It was the best way to maintain an even playing field.

The drivers in the heat had each taken their practice turns through the barrels and were now entering into their barrel positions to await the starting horn. Darryl Baker, the outrider holding Garret's lead horses, expertly grabbed the reins in between the lead team and guided them into the starting position as Garret brought the outfit to a halt.

Garret yelled to Darryl to pull his lead team further to the left as he felt it would be a better starting position. In the short pause before the horn sounded, Darryl was able to answer the command and positioned the horses perfectly. When the horn sounded signaling the start of the race, Garret's eager team surged forward to their top barrel as the outrider at the back of the wagon skillfully tossed the small rubber barrel into the back of the wagon known as the stove rack.

Garret rounded his top barrel and headed toward his bottom barrel in the figure-eight pattern familiar to all chuckwagon racing fans. Garret's team raced out onto the track with the three other wagons. The track was a little soft on the rail position so Garret was happy to give it up to the driver who entered the track from barrel position one.

Garret could feel his horses running hard on the firmer ground offered away from the rail. He was slowly gaining on the driver running on the rail but he also had a driver keeping pace with him on his right side he wanted to keep an eye on. He kept his team in check coming down the backstretch by keeping a tighter hold on his driving lines. When he rounded the final turn for the homestretch, he could feel the team wanting to offer him more. He freed more line from his hands, allowing his horses to run harder. Garret hollered to his horses and the familiar sound of his voice spurred them on further. His team rushed ahead of the other teams, crossing the finish line in first place. The exciting race brought roars of approval from the fans.

A smile brighter than the sun that poured across the homestretch beamed across Garret's face. He quickly looked back over his shoulder to see that his outriders made the journey with him on time. They both gave him a nod of approval. Everyone on the team successfully completed his job. It was a great feeling to have the first race of the season out of the way, especially when it was a successful run.

The outriders turned around quickly after crossing the finish line. They rode their horses back into the infield to pick up new horses they would be riding in the next heat. The outriders are truly the unsung heroes of chuckwagon racing with a commitment to each and every driver they ride for each night.

Michael climbed back on the wagon as Garret turned the team around to pass by the grandstand, making his way back to the barns. The applause grew loud as they passed the waiting crowd. Garret smiled at the crowd and waved as he passed the reins to Michael. He was letting Michael drive the team whenever the opportunity presented itself. It was a great chance for Michael to practice his driving skills and it gave him a greater sense of pride in the team as a whole. Garret immediately spotted Cara, holding Corby, smiling and giving Garret a wave. He overflowed with pride.

Cara breathed a sigh of relief as she smiled and waved to Garret. She was so happy that his race was over and that everything was okay. She was having a difficult time enjoying the races after witnessing the accident. She often wondered how Garret always seemed to maintain his composure no matter what the circumstances or how much pressure was on.

The drive back to the barns was refreshing and Garret smiled all the way. There was a lot of work to be done with unhooking the horses, cooling them down and getting the barn area and feed ready so the horses could enjoy a proper rest for the night. With the race a success, the work sure seemed to be a lot easier.

A further four heats of races ran before the first night of racing was officially over. There were some penalties in the final races but no further injuries or accidents. The evening sky was clear and it looked like they were in for some great weather.

The stat sheets were posted at the race office with the day's results one hour after the races finished. Garret placed sixth for the day. It was a great position to be in on the first day of the season. Garret was right where he felt he needed to be in the standings.

Chapter Three

After the chores were completed, camp usually came to life for the evening as everyone gathered around to share stories of the day's events and what went right or wrong, but tonight was different. As soon as everyone was able to leave, they were off to find out about Jaimie Feldstrom, the young injured outrider. People were afraid for him but everyone was trying to be positive.

The staff at the hospital would be less than enthused about the entourage of people trying to visit Jaimie but that is the culture in chuckwagon families. Competition is always fierce but when one person was down or hurting, the group hurt as a whole. It is a unique group of people found in almost no other competitive sport in the world.

Darryl Baker, a fellow outrider and Jaimie's best friend, was the first to arrive at the nurse's station.

"Can you please tell me where I can find Jaimie Feldstrom," Darryl asked the older nurse seated behind the desk.

Darryl was still mostly covered in the dust and dirt from the night's races. His dark wavy hair still had bits of dirt and mud where his helmet had not covered it. There were dark circles of dust around his eyes where his racing goggles once sat. He was still wearing the last colour of racing jacket he wore for the final heat of races that night. The jacket was supposed to be white as he rode the final heat off of barrel position one but with the dirt and mud of the track, it was more grey than white. The top few snaps of the jacket were open, partially revealing the athletic frame of the six foot, one hundred seventy pound veteran outrider.

The older nurse looked up from the pile of charts she was reviewing to peer at him over her wire rim glasses. It was easy for her to figure out who he was looking for. The smaller city of sixty thousand people had only one hospital and most everyone in the community knew when the chuckwagons were in town. The hospital also provided its ambulance service on stand-by at the racetrack so the staff was certainly aware of the races.

"Jaimie Feldstrom, the outrider, is in room four fourteen. He is allowed two visitors at a time until the air ambulance arrives," said the nurse.

"Air ambulance?" Darryl questioned, sounding alarmed.

"Yes," replied the nurse. "Mr. Feldstrom has some broken bones that will require surgery and he is being flown to a larger hospital in Edmonton for that."

Upon seeing the fear in Darryl's eyes the nurse added, "Don't worry your friend is going to be fine, he just won't see a racetrack for a very long time. You can go up and see him now. His girlfriend is the only person up there so he can have one other person right now. Please keep your visit short." The old nurse smiled at Darryl with reassurance in her eyes.

Darryl followed the nurse's directions to the elevators and made his way to the forth floor. He walked down the hall past the nurse's station until he located his friend's room. He spotted Jaimie's girlfriend Jennifer and knew that he had located the right room.

Jaimie and Jennifer were having a quiet laugh over something when she looked up to see Darryl. She smiled at him and Jaimie turned his head toward the door. Through the minor cuts and scrapes on his face he grinned at his friend.

"Hey, how'd you boys make out without me?" Jaimie tried to say with cheer in his voice that he didn't really feel.

"We got through it," Darryl replied, trying to sound upbeat. "When are we going to have you back out there? We need you."

Darryl and Jaimie tried to keep their talk to the business of racing. It was easier than talking about the inevitable situation at hand.

Tears began to well up in Jennifer's eyes and she said "Yeah, right. You'll be back out there all right! I'll give you guys some time to visit. I'm going to go find some coffee and then I'll be right back." She smiled at the two men through her tear stained cheeks.

The usually neatly groomed long blonde hair was tousled and wind blown from her time at the track and her frantic ride in the ambulance with Jaimie. The wreck had clearly shaken the young woman and she was trying to put on a brave front. She grabbed her purse from the side table near Jaimie's bed and headed toward the door. It was time for the two men to talk about the real issues.

Darryl started the conversation. "So what's the verdict?" he asked trying to sound casual.

"Well, I have a broken femur here in the top of my leg," Jaimie said pointing to the injured left leg. "They have to operate or the bone won't set right which would cause me to basically have one leg shorter than the other when it heals. They said there will be some pins and stuff to go in there. Also, as you can see, my right wrist isn't doing so well either and I guess I need some surgery on it but they have set it for now for the trip. Right now they just have me on some good drugs so I can sort of sit here and smile and pretend this is all good! The good news is when that wagon hit me in the head, my helmet saved me and other than the scrapes on my face from digging into the ground, I'm okay. It knocked me out for a while, I'm sure you knew that. I guess that was probably a good thing because I probably wouldn't have wanted to be awake when I was getting run over anyhow. They did a CT scan and my head is okay and there aren't any internal injuries or anything. Basically, I'm done for the year." Jaimie's last words broke off slightly.

It was distressing for Jaimie as he tried to get all of the words out but at least he was there to tell the story. His blue eyes were clouded over slightly and Darryl could not tell if he was thinking about what the future would hold or what he just survived. He noticed the bits of dry blood in his light red hair. It must have come from the cuts on his face. It gave Darryl an uneasy feeling knowing that what happened to Jaimie could happen to any one of them.

"Well I knew if you got hit in the head it wouldn't hurt a thing," Darryl tried to joke with his friend.

Jaimie laughed at the comment and enjoyed the cajoling. Darryl was a good friend and a great fellow-competitor.

"I'm just glad that you're okay. You scared the hell out of all of us. It won't be the same without you but you just concentrate on getting better and we'll make sure you get your rides back next year," Darryl assured him.

The two friends visited for a while but Darryl noticed that Jaimie was drifting off from the pain killers. When Jennifer returned to the room he gave his friend a light, friendly slap on the shoulder and wished him well. He gave Jennifer a reassuring hug before leaving the room. He would miss his friend at the races this year but he was relieved he was going to be okay. In the back of his mind remained the thought that it could have been so much worse.

As Darryl entered the main lobby area of the hospital he was met by other outriders and drivers all wanting to know if Jaimie was okay. He fielded all of their questions, much to the relief of the old nurse still seated behind the desk. A few of the outriders still wanted to say hello to Jaimie before he left for Edmonton, others were content with the news from Darryl and left the hospital so as not to have too many people visiting. Jaimie would be okay and that was all anyone really wanted to confirm.

Back at the racetrack, Michael was checking on the horses one last time for the evening. He flagged Darryl over when he saw his truck coming down the lane past the McCormack barn. Michael did not know Jaimie very well so he did not go to the hospital but just the same, he wanted to make sure that he was okay. Darryl pulled his truck up near Michael so that they could talk.

"How's Jaimie doing?" Michael enquired.

"He's going to be okay," said Darryl. "He's going to be flown to Edmonton tonight for surgery he needs on a broken bone in his leg and some bones in his wrist. He'll be out for the season but he will be ready for next year." Darryl went on to explain some of the details of the injuries and they discussed how lucky the outrider was.

"Well, I'm glad to hear that everything is going to be okay for him," Michael tapped the side of the truck box as Darryl was ready to drive away. "Thanks for stopping to let us know the news."

"No problem," replied Darryl. "That is some news I don't mind being able to give out." Darryl continued on down the lane. He would be stopped several times along the way to repeat this same news.

Michael knew he should walk over to the holiday trailer to let Garret and Cara hear the good news. He set the pitch fork down that he had been using and quickly made his way across the lane to the holiday trailer area.

Garret and Cara were outside when Michael arrived at their trailer. "I have good news," he called out as he approached. "Jaimie is going to be okay."

"Oh, that's fantastic news," cried Cara. "What did you hear?"

"He has to go to Edmonton tonight for surgery on some broken bones in his leg and wrist. He certainly won't be outriding again this season, but he should regain the full use of his leg and be as good as new for next year." Michael filled them in on the details he had heard from Darryl.

"Thank God," said Cara. She spoke for all of them when she made the statement. "It is a relief to hear that he is okay. It is too bad about the injuries but it certainly looked far worse than that when he was laying on the track."

Cara could still picture the immobile outrider lying on the track. For several moments she thought that he was dead. He would not have been the first wagon competitor to lose his life to wagon racing. Sometimes the reality of the dangers hit hard. She blinked the tears from her eyes and pushed back the growing lump in her throat as she turned away from Michael and Garret. Sometimes her emotions were strong but she learned to keep them to herself. It was a protective barrier she put up when her father left them and although she trusted in Garret's love, she never fully let go of this protective tool.

Cara stepped into the trailer to check on the now sleeping Corby while Garret returned to the barn with Michael to finish the chores. He was unaware of what just transpired with his wife. Cara gently stroked her son's hair as he lay in his crib. She pulled the covers up to his chin, smiling at him peacefully resting. She sat down on the sofa near his crib to watch him sleep. She was exhausted. She decided that a good hot shower and a sleep would put this day to rest for her at last. As Cara got up from the sofa to retrieve her nightgown and shower toiletries, she heard a light knock at the door.

"Who can that possibly be?" she wondered. She really wasn't in the mood for company at that point. She quickly went to the door so the knocking would not wake the baby.

"Hi sweetheart," Cara's mother whispered to her from the bottom of the trailer stairs. "I hope you don't mind. I just felt I should try to be here for the first race but my flight was delayed from all of the rain and fog in Vancouver."

Cara practically leapt into her mother's arms. She could not think of anyone she would rather see more right now.

"Mom I can't believe you're here," said Cara. "Of course I don't mind. Are you kidding? This is great. Get in here. I really can't believe it."

Karen Beaton was a busy lady who still operated a now thriving catering business in Vancouver, British Columbia. The horses were never her game but she always tried hard to support whatever her children were interested in. Karen entered the trailer and before she had closed the door behind her Cara had wrapped her arms around her in a huge hug. Cara had not seen her mother since Corby was born. At that time, Karen flew out to see her new grandson and to stay a while to help around the house. Cara was so exhausted after such a difficult birth. She remembered how grateful she felt when her mother came to help until she was able get back on her feet.

Karen was hardly a country person however she understood the atmosphere of the races and dressed down from her usual city clothes. Her outfit was a more relaxed look of well tailored khaki slacks paired with a light peach sweater and tan colored flats. Her jewelry was minimal consisting of a gold detailed ring on her right hand and small gold hoop earrings. Everyone knew the nights in Alberta at this time of the year were not yet very warm so she did her best to pack for Alberta from her Vancouver wardrobe. Karen's soft brown short hair was neatly styled and her blue eyes brimmed with tears of joy when she spotted Corby's crib. The baby lay on his back sleeping peacefully, his head tilted to one side and his little fists balled up near his cheeks.

"He has grown so much already," Karen spoke softly as she smiled lovingly down at her grandchild. "It seems like I just saw him the other day and he has already tripled his size. Sometimes I am just too far away."

"Well Mom, they are always looking for great caterers in Alberta too you know," said Cara. "Maybe it's time to move the business."

"I don't know about moving it," replied Karen. "You know how I am with a bunch of change, but there are days when I would simply like to retire from having to plan one more big wedding feast or someone else's celebration."

"If you ever actually decide to sell the business, and I'm not holding my breath for that one, you know you are always welcome at our place," said Cara. "We still have the other house on the property. I watched a lot of home improvement television when I was on bed rest before Corby was born. I'm sure we could have that place to your liking in no time at all," Cara joked.

A second house on the McCormack ranch was left from the days of the previous owners who were cattle ranchers. The house was used for their hired hands and was now used by Garret and Cara as a place for their barn hand to stay. It was actually a nice, comfortable little home. Other accommodation arrangements could always be made for a barn hand if Karen ever did decide to move to Alberta.

"That is a generous offer Cara and I know the offer has been a long-standing one. I'm just not sure if a city girl like me could handle life on an Alberta ranch," said Karen.

"Oh Mom, I think Corby could convince you that life in the country is pretty great," said Cara smiling.

"I think you are probably right about that," Karen agreed. "I will keep it in the back of my mind anyhow. Like I said, catering is not forever."

Karen pulled the blankets up a little higher on Corby before settling herself on the sofa.

"How about a nice cup of tea after so much travel," Cara asked.

"That is by far the best offer I have had all day," replied Karen.

Cara went over to the stove to put the kettle on. A cup of tea would be a relaxing way to end the day. So much had gone on with the nerves of the first day and the outrider's accident, she felt overwhelmed with emotion.

Just as the tea was ready, Garret came to the door. He lifted Karen's suitcase into the trailer before ascending the stairs himself.

"Good evening Ms. Beaton," Garret spoke to Karen with open arms.

Karen approached Garret and hugged him affectionately.

"Ah, Mr. McCormack," said Karen. "You are just always so polite and gentlemanlike."

The two were fond of each other and often teased one another affectionately. When Karen first met Garret she knew that this was going to be the man her daughter married. There had been other boyfriends over the years but there was just something different with this one. Although Karen did not like the idea of Cara leaving the Vancouver area, most-likely forever, she did like to see her daughter happy.

The distance did not allow for Karen to see Garret, Cara and Corby as much as she would have liked but she knew Garret well enough to know that he was a good man who knew the importance of family. That was really all Karen needed to see.

"You didn't need to bring my suitcase in," said Karen to Garret. "I fully intend to go to a hotel and be out of the way. I just wanted to stop by and see you guys and my grandson first."

"No way Karen, we wouldn't dream of you staying in a hotel," said Garret. "You are here to spend time with family and you can't do that from a hotel. Besides, we have plenty of room here in the trailer and the back bedroom is all yours."

"Thank you guys really, but I don't want to impose when you are already so busy," said Karen.

"Mom you are not imposing. Don't be silly, we want you to be here," said Cara.

"Well, then it is settled, but I'm going to be at least helping out with the cooking around here," said Karen.

"We wouldn't have it any other way," said Garret. "There is no prime rib in the country that can top yours."

"Thank you Garret," said Karen. "By the way that was very subtle." The three of them laughed.

Garret visited with the two women for a few minutes before gathering some fresh clothes and his shower items. The racetrack was equipped with locker room style shower facilities for the drivers, outriders and helpers. The track was either dusty or muddy so a hot shower following the evening chores was always appreciated. The holiday trailer was also equipped with a shower but it was not quite the same as the space and water pressure that came from a real shower hooked up to city water.

Garret would be gone for a while as the showers would be busy at this time of the night. All of the younger guys would be getting ready for a night on the town and they tended to fill up the locker rooms with their cologne and talk of their most often fictitious conquests. They were usually legends in their own minds if nothing else but their stories always brought humor to an otherwise dull locker room.

The steam of the showers, the odor of sweat and the smell of beer drifted through the room greeting Garret as he opened the door. It always reminded him of his days playing recreational hockey. He had enjoyed hockey as a boy and into the days of men's hockey, but had given it up a few years back when a broken arm threatened to end his racing career. He had decided that it was time to put racing first and put hockey on the shelf. His involvement in hockey these days consisted of coaching kids at the local rink.

The showers were abuzz with talk of the events of the evening. Everyone was laughing and joking with one another. Since it was now clear that their good friend Jaimie would be okay, they had no reason not to carry on as they normally would. The young outrider's injuries certainly gave everyone a scare so of course, mixed in amongst the fun and storytelling was talk of how the situation's outcome could have been far worse.

"Hey Garret," Garret's long time friend and fellow competitor Grant Wagner acknowledged him as he entered the shower room. "How's everything this evening? I saw your run. Looking impressive out there."

Grant sat down beside Garret, his towel and shampoo in hand. His face and hands were crusted with dirt from the evening of racing and chores. His jeans and torn navy sweatshirt had certainly seen better days. He hunched over placing his forearms on his legs for support. His silver blue eyes peaked out from under his well worn cowboy hat. His brown moustache with flecks of silver held tell-tale signs of his years of experience. His eyes had all the signs of a true story teller and his adventures over the years left him with no shortage of stories.

"Hi Grant," replied Garret. "Thanks. I was pretty pleased with how the team worked for their first time out this year. Sorry to hear you had some tough luck out there tonight."

"Yeah, that plan didn't quite go how I wanted it to," replied Grant referring to the penalties he incurred in his race. "After everything else that happened this evening though, I decided there are far worse things that can happen than getting a couple of penalties. I was just relieved to hear that Jaimie is going to be okay."

"For sure," said Garret. "As long as everyone comes out healthy that is always my first concern as well." A shower became available and Garret stood up to take his turn. "You take care and better luck tomorrow Grant."

"Thanks Garret," replied Grant. "You keep working like you did tonight and you are going to have one hell of a year!"

"Thank you. We are certainly going to try," replied an always modest Garret as he stepped toward the showers. His thoughts were still on the great run he had that night and the hope that more good fortune would come his way. Racing still relied heavily on luck and no one knew that better than an up-and-coming young driver like Garret.

By the time Garret finished his shower and returned to the trailer, all was quiet. His wife and mother-in-law had settled in for the night and he could hear the gentle breath of his son in the crib. He peered into the crib and made sure that Corby's blankets were tucked in before retiring to his own bed. Cara stirred as Garret got into bed but she did not awaken. It had been a very long first day and everyone was exhausted.

In the morning the usual routine was adhered to. Garret rose early to help Michael with the chores and Cara got up a short time later at the sound of Corby's soft whimper of hunger. As Cara's mother had the back bedroom of the trailer to herself, she had time to get ready at her leisure however she came out when she heard Cara and the baby. While Cara changed Corby's diaper Karen made coffee and retrieved items from the fridge to make breakfast.

"Hey Mom, you're supposed to be relaxing here," said Cara.

"I did not come here to relax Cara. I came here to give you guys a hand so don't you worry about what I'm doing," Karen smiled at her as she broke some eggs into a mixing bowl.

"Well thank you Mom," Cara smiled back. "It is just so nice to have you here. I don't want you to feel you need to work too."

"Cara, catering for a fifteen hundred dollar per plate gala for some political party's annual campaign fundraiser is work. Cooking breakfast for my family is a pleasure," said Karen matter-of-factly as she poured milk into the eggs and whisked the mixture for omelets.

As she fed Corby his bottle, Cara smiled at her mother. All of her life she had looked up to her mother. She was such a strong person. Her mother never let any kind of setbacks get in the way of her success. No matter how difficult things became at times, she just kept pushing forward and made the best life that she could for herself and her children. Cara was proud of the person her mother was. She only hoped to accomplish even half of what her mother had done with her life.

Soon Garret and Michael arrived at the trailer, fresh from finishing the chores. They washed quickly as the aroma of Karen's cooking filled the trailer, making their stomachs growl. Dan and Mary Hartman also arrived at the trailer just as breakfast was being placed on the table. They were early risers and had already eaten their breakfast but stopped by for coffee and a morning visit. They did not have a chance to visit with the McCormack's the night before as it was late when the races finished so they retired for the evening as soon as they got back to their own trailer.

The Hartman's greeted Karen with affectionate hugs. They knew her well from her visits to Garret and Cara's and they exchanged Christmas cards and emails over the last few years.

"We didn't realize that you were coming up to Grand Rapids," said Dan.

"Well, it was kind of a last minute plan but I really wanted to be here for the first race and to spend some time with my grandson," replied Karen as she placed the last of the breakfast condiments on the table. "He is growing so fast I'm afraid he'll be racing a wagon the next time I see him if I don't visit more often," she joked.

"Isn't that a fact," laughed Mary. "I don't know where the time goes between diapers and graduation."

"We heard that the young outrider is pretty banged up but he is going to be okay," Dan interjected the conversation.

"Yes, he is a very lucky guy," said Garret as he sat down to his breakfast after filling the Hartman's coffee cups.

The Hartman's were seated on the sofa across from the breakfast table. Corby was now fed and happily kicked on a blanket on the floor near the sofa. Mary cooed softly to the baby as Karen, Michael, Garret and Cara dug into the wonderful breakfast of omelets, bacon, toast and fresh fruit before them.

Most of the morning conversation focused on the accident and then later turned to the excellent race Garret ran the night before. Dan and Mary expressed their pleasure with his race and told him that they looked forward to another night of that. Garret assured them that he would be trying his best. The Hartman's finished their coffee, said their goodbyes and continued on their way to complete more morning visits with other friends. They promised to come by before the evening races so that they could get seats together with Cara, Corby and Karen.

The weather was once again beautiful for the second race day. Cara, Karen and the baby went into town after breakfast to do some shopping while Garret and Michael returned to working with the horses. The day passed quickly in the warm sunshine and soon it was time to get ready for the evening races once again. Garret would move to barrel position number three for the second evening and he and Michael retrieved their black jackets and placed them on the seat of the wagon before returning to the barn to finish harnessing the horses.

Soon Cara appeared at the barn along with her mother who was carrying Corby. They were ready to go up to the bleachers to find a good seat before the races started. The routine of wishing Garret good luck and the hugs and kisses were much the same as the night before however it felt like the pressure was off a bit after the success of the first night. Cara and Garret never discussed the races a great deal at this time. It was just known that her heart was out there for him and he would do the best he could do. Garret received a hug from his mother-in-law before the trio departed to join the Hartman's for the races.

As he drove his team to the track for his race, Garret was much more relaxed than he had been the first night. Michael fidgeted nervously with a strap on the backrest of the wagon seat. He had calmed down considerably from the first night but he was far from relaxed.

When Garret finally entered the track for his race and Cara saw him her heart skipped a few beats. No matter how many races she witnessed, Cara's nerves would always jump a little before the race was on. That feeling in the pit of her stomach would probably never change in fifty years of racing. That was just the way it was. She knew Garret was an excellent driver but the danger of the sport was never far from her mind.

Garret pulled into his barrel with ease and his horses stood patiently awaiting the sound of the horn. When the horn blew his team surged forward, expertly circling the barrels and entering the track. Garret won his heat and was well on his way to another high placing for the day. Garret waved enthusiastically to the cheering crowd as he drove past the grandstand following his race. It looked like this was shaping up to be the summer he hoped for, although he knew it was still a long journey ahead.

Chapter Four

After the second night of racing, the McCormack's sponsor hosted a barbeque for their staff and clients. A large tent was set up near the McCormack's barn and as soon as the races were over guests began to arrive at the tent. Garret was sponsored by Rock Creek Developments of Grand Rapids for this particular show. They were a new developer in the area and as such, were eager to advertise through a community event as big as chuckwagon racing.

The company knew that Garret was a younger driver on his way to the top. They felt that Garret's image mirrored that of their company quite nicely. The fact that the youthful driver placed fifth overall on this night, putting him into second place in the average, was a bonus that the company could not be more pleased with. As Garret entered the big tent with his family there were cheers from the crowd.

"Here's our guy," boomed the voice of Rick Nelson, the owner of Rock Creek Developments. Rick was a young businessman who showed a lot of enthusiasm for the sport of chuckwagon racing. Having a driver running amongst the top drivers of the show only spurred this enthusiasm.

"Congratulations Garret, you are certainly doing us proud," Rick gave Garret an energetic slap on the shoulder.

"Thank you very much," Garret focused his speech toward the large group. "I just wanted to thank you all for your support and all of the cheering in the stands. It means a lot to me and to my family to have this kind of support, both at the races and back here at the barns. I just hope I can do you proud throughout the show."

Garret's words were met with cheers and applause. The crowd went back to mingling and meeting with Garret personally to congratulate him on the success he had met with so far at the show. Cara mingled along with Garret as much as possible but it was difficult as she could tell that Corby was getting upset from the noise of the crowd and the late hour.

Grilled steak, shrimp and chicken breasts, all fresh from the grill filled several platters on a nearby table. Appetizers, salads and a variety of desserts lined another table along one wall of the tent near the grill. Ice filled coolers containing beer, wine coolers and a variety of other beverages overflowed. Cara and Karen prepared a plate of appetizers and found some available seats. The appetizers were wonderful and even Karen had to admit that she was impressed with the catering effort for an outdoor event such as this.

The two ate some of the appetizers and enjoyed some refreshments while visiting with some of the other people seated at their table. Corby was pleased now looking at all of the faces so he cooed happily on his mother's lap. Soon the ladies agreed that it was time to return to the trailer for the evening. Even though Rick begged them to help themselves to some steak or shrimp they politely refused his offer. It just seemed too late to eat such a heavy meal. The ladies said goodbye and thanked their hosts before gathering up Corby's things to return to the trailer. Cara waved goodnight across the tent to Garret who was engulfed in conversation with several of the sponsor's clients. He waved back, smiling to Cara.

For Garret, his night would not end for a few hours yet. It was important that he take the time to be there and visit with the sponsors and their clients. He wanted them to know how important their sponsorship was to him. It had been another long day and as grateful as Garret and Cara were for the enthusiasm and support of the sponsors, it all took its toll.

As the summer wore on there would be many more events such as this held by many other sponsors. For the sponsors, it was an evening or a weekend of enjoyment; for the drivers and their families, it was a way of life that was sometimes exhausting, no matter how appreciative they were. The race was never really over during the summer months.

It felt as though morning came much too soon. Cara had no idea what time Garret turned in for the night. She slept well until Corby woke up to be fed at five-thirty that morning. The baby was now sometimes sleeping through the night until about seven but the trailer was a different atmosphere than his own bed at home and he stirred a little more easily. As Cara climbed out of bed to tend to Corby she noticed that Garret was sleeping heavily. He did not usually rise for morning chores until 6:30 a.m.

"Hey sweetheart," Cara spoke softly to Corby as she lifted him from his bed. She pulled her terrycloth robe on over her pajamas as she cradled Corby in one arm. Even though the days were warm the mornings were still chilly. Cara turned up the thermostat as Corby's bottle warmed. She distracted Corby from his hunger by rocking him as she hummed a little tune.

Soon the bottle was warm and Corby satisfied his hunger. He drank the milk eagerly as he lay in his mother's arms. Although Cara was tired, she enjoyed this quiet time they had all to themselves. She knew that before long these times would be a thing of the past.

The sun rose early at this time of the year in Grand Rapids as the city is situated so far to the north. Cara watched the sun stream in the blinds and she knew that it was going to be another beautiful day. Soon Garret emerged from their bedroom in a pair of dark green sweat pants and his favorite, well worn *Edmonton Oilers* t-shirt. The *National Hockey League* team had been his favorite since he was a boy. He looked tired but he smiled at his wife as she sat on the sofa feeding their son.

"Good morning," Cara and Garret said in unison. They smiled at each other.

"What time did you manage to sneak away last night?" Cara asked.

"Oh, I think it was about one in the morning," answered Garret with a yawn. "They were still going pretty hard at that time but they did understand that I needed to get some sleep."

"Well, that's not so bad," said Cara. "I never heard you at all. I think I was asleep before my head hit the pillow. I know I only vaguely remember hearing the music coming from that tent."

Corby was finished his bottle so Cara slipped a change pad under him to change his diaper. He was drifting back to sleep so once he was dry she placed him back in his crib.

"That might buy me a little more sleep," said Cara smiling at Garret. She placed a good morning kiss on his neck as he wrapped his arms around her waist.

"If you have the opportunity to get some more sleep you should take it," said Garret. "I'm going to get dressed and get out to the barns to give Michael a hand. The track is open this morning and I want to hook an outfit. I promised Michael I'd let him work on his driving skills this morning."

"Okay," said Cara. "That should be a great time for him. You guys have fun out there. I'm going to go back to sleep until about seven if Corby will let me, and then I will get breakfast on."

"That sounds good honey," said Garret. "Thank you," he said as he kissed her on the cheek.

Garret returned to the bedroom area to get some jeans and a heavier sweatshirt on before going outside. Cara took off her robe and climbed back under the duvet on the bed. Before going back to sleep, she set her alarm to go off at seven. However, shortly before seven the little alarm known as Corbyn James McCormack was awake and ready to take on the day. Cara came to tend to Corby however Grandma Beaton was already on the scene. Karen had picked up Corby and was rocking him gently as he lay over her shoulder.

"Good morning Mom," said Cara. She pulled her hair back before starting the morning coffee.

"Good morning Cara. How did you sleep?" asked Karen.

"I slept well after all of the events of yesterday," replied Cara. "You?"

"I slept like a baby," answered Karen. "This place certainly keeps you busy."

The two women again prepared breakfast and visited while they awaited the arrival of Michael and Garret.

Michael was pleased with the opportunity to drive one of Garret's teams. He paid attention and took Garret's advice as they did a couple of practice turns through the barrels. Garret handled the lines differently than Michael's Uncle Bill had but he liked his style and mimicked it as best he could. Finally, Garret allowed Michael to take one last turn through the barrels before racing the team around the track. He stayed in the wagon to give Michael any assistance he may have needed. Michael was thrilled with the feeling it gave him and never admitted to Garret how tired his arms were by the time he had crossed the finish line.

When they returned to the barns, outriders Darryl Baker and Blain Cook were waiting to take Garret's outriding horses for a gallop around the track as promised. Within forty minutes each outrider had ridden three horses for Garret. Both reported to Garret that the horses seemed to be working well and that they were comfortable riding any of them during an actual race. Garret was pleased to hear that the extra spring training he completed with all of the horses was obviously benefitting them. It was one less thing he would have to worry about.

"Thanks for coming down this morning to ride guys," Garret said to the men.

"Anytime," said Darryl.

"Yeah, for sure," Blain agreed. "It is a pleasure to ride horses that are working that well. It made for some enjoyable riding out there."

"Well I'm glad to hear that," said Garret. "It's always nice to hear the outriding horses shouldn't be a concern. Well, I'll let you guys get back to it. I'm sure you have a busy morning ahead of you."

"Okay Garret," said Darryl. "We'll see you tonight off the four barrel."

Darryl and Blain continued on their way to the next barn to try out horses for another driver. The early shows of the season called for lots of morning rides for the majority of the outriders. Drivers were all trying new horses and since the outriders were responsible for the horses during the races, it was extremely important for them to know the horses they would be working with. Any outrider that was not up and working with the horses in the morning was usually setting himself up for problems during the races.

Garret and Michael finished a few more chores before going in for breakfast. After breakfast the men went back to work at the barns. Garret mentioned some harness that needed repairs and a few other chores. Karen and Cara took Corby for a walk in his stroller and spent some time visiting with some of the other drivers' wives.

Garret and Michael continued to work in the barns right up until lunch time. They stopped for a quick lunch back at the trailer with Cara, Karen and Corby before continuing on with other tasks that needed to be completed before the evening races. The day passed quickly and the weather became increasingly hot and dry which made it uncomfortable for everyone. Soon it was time to prepare for night three of the races where Garret would be racing off of the number four barrel.

Garret donned the yellow jacket identifying him as the barrel four driver in his heat. As his wagon rumbled into the infield for his practice turn, Garret could hear the rising cheers from the crowd. His team performed a nice practice turn and he proceeded down the track to turn around in preparation for his race. He slowly entered the barreling area as Darryl grabbed a hold of his lead team to get them into position. A hush fell over the crowd and the other teams pulled to a stop to await the sound of the horn. The only sound that could be heard was the banging of harness as the horses eagerly shuffled while awaiting the sound of the horn.

The blast of the horn pierced the still evening air. Garret's wagon surged forward as it had in the previous two nights. Garret felt the power of his horses as he began to make the right turn at his top barrel. Suddenly Garret's right lead horse stumbled as he turned the top barrel. The horse tried to recover but was forced to the ground by the push of the wheel team at his heels. Garret felt the driving lines rip from his hands and his feet lift from the corners of his wagon box. Before he could recover his balance he was tossed from the wagon box. Helplessly he flew through the air, the driving lines still in his hands. He struck the ground with a heavy thud before rolling in an attempt to get away from the impending wreck.

The lead team was forced to the ground by the momentum of the wheel team. In a matter of seconds, all four horses were on the ground, tangled helplessly in a dangerous web of harness and iron.

Garret's outriders as well as several race officials scrambled to the aid of both Garret and the horses. Cara, her mother, the Hartman's and the rest of the fans watched the event in horror. Tears welled up in Cara's eyes as she clasped a hand over her mouth.

"Mom, you need to watch Corby for me!" Cara shouted to the shocked woman over the noise of the crowd.

Karen quickly snapped back to reality as she took the baby from Cara. Her hands were shaking and she did not even have time to say anything to Cara before her daughter darted to the bottom of the bleachers, quickly crawling over the fence to run to the scene of the accident. She knew that she could be more help in the infield than she was sitting in the bleachers just watching. She knew the horses well and she was not afraid to dive in and help.

By this time, Garret regained his wind and was helping the others to free the horses from the entanglement of harness. Cara quickly stepped in and took direction to help out where she could. This was no time to lose her composure and she knew it. Throughout her many years at the racetrack she had witnessed many downed horses and she knew how to keep her cool under the strain of accidents.

Luckily Garret's team went down between his two barrels so the drivers coming down the home stretch would still have room to squeeze past the wreck. Race officials on horseback were quick to run to the third corner of the track. They waved to the drivers to move to the outside rail to avoid a collision with Garret's outfit. The three remaining wagons in the race crossed the finish line with little fanfare as the crowd focused its attention on the downed outfit.

Out of fear, Garret's horses thrashed violently but soon everyone involved had the team free of its harness and all four horses were standing on their own. It appeared that there were no serious injuries this time. The crowd rose to its feet and applauded the efforts of the group. The track crew quickly pulled the wagon from the track. Garret and Cara each took a horse as they made their way back to the barn area. Michael followed close behind, leading the two remaining horses. The outriding horses were not involved in the wreck and were returned to the infield to be retrieved at the end of the races.

During the walk, Garret's adrenalin had time to come down which gave him time to notice the severe pain in his ribs. Garret refocused his attention to the task at hand. He did not want to upset his wife any further and he wanted to make sure the horses were okay before he even considered getting himself checked out.

The horses were all examined and other than some minor cuts and scrapes, they miraculously seemed to be okay. After each horse was examined and washed Michael retrieved gauze, salve and wraps from the medicine box and began to treat the injuries on the horses. Some of the injuries were very minor in nature however they wanted to take every possible precaution to insure none of the injuries ballooned into anything more serious.

Cara helped examine and wash the horses alongside of Garret. She had no time to think of all that could have happened. When her mother returned to the barn with Corby, tears were shining in her eyes and reality began to set in for Cara. She hugged her mother and her son hard before turning to Garret and openly weeping. She had held it in long enough and now the dam of emotions broke through. She held on to Garret like she would never let go.

"Hey, hey," he spoke to her softly. "I'm okay Cara. It's over and everything is okay," Garret tried hard to reassure his wife as she continued to sob.

"I'll leave you two alone," said Karen cradling Corby in her arms. "I'm really glad everything's okay Garret." She squeezed Garret's arm lightly with her free hand and then walked away carrying Corby with her.

Cara reached up and held Garret's face gently in her hands. She touched his face to hers and closed her eyes as she felt his warm breath against her. The couple's breathing slowed until they breathed in one rhythm. They could always calm each other down. Tears slowly streamed down Cara's cheeks. They were tears of pure relief. As Cara relived the accident she could only imagine how she would manage if things turned out worse.

"I'm so relieved that you are okay," said Cara once they released from their long embrace. "You are okay aren't you?"

Garret smiled at her and replied "I'm fine Cara, but I think maybe I should have my ribs checked out just as a precaution."

He tried to make light of the pain he felt in his side when Cara suddenly gasped and pulled open his racing jacket. She lifted his t-shirt to reveal huge purple bruises down Garret's left side.

Many of the younger drivers and the majority of the outriders wore flak jackets to protect against such injuries however Garret rarely wore his as it was not a mandatory requirement. Upon examination of his beaten body, he thought to himself that he should reconsider his options.

"Oh Garret, this is not okay," gasped Cara. "We are going to the hospital right now. Why didn't you say something earlier?"

"Honestly Cara, I'm fine and the horses needed the attention before me," said Garret as casually as possible.

Cara went to the trailer to explain to her mother about the bruising on Garret and how they were going to make a trip to the hospital's emergency room. Karen offered to watch Corby and get him tucked into bed so that they would not have to worry about him. Karen was so relieved that, for the most part, everything was going to be okay. She was just happy to be able to help with something.

Cara grabbed her purse and the keys for the truck. Before she reached the truck, Dan and Mary Hartman stopped her in her tracks. Concern and fear poured across their faces.

"The horses are going to be fine and Garret is going to be fine," Cara spoke to the Hartman's before they had a word out. "We are going to the hospital just to get Garret checked over. He's got an awful amount of bruising on his left side."

"Oh Cara, we are so relieved to hear that," said Mary. "Garret gave us a heck of a scare. We won't keep you but if there is anything we can do please let us know."

"Thank you both so much," said Cara. "Your being here is always appreciated. I had better go get Garret so we can get to the hospital. I'll be in touch with you guys." Cara hugged them both and went to the barn to retrieve her ailing husband. By this time he looked ready to go to the truck.

Cara got into the driver's seat as Garret gingerly lifted himself into the passenger seat. A few of the other drivers looked at them as they drove out of camp but they chose not to stop to talk to anyone at this time and instead offered a wave as they drove on. Michael would finish the chores while they were at the hospital.

The old nurse was still working nights and she looked up from her paperwork as Cara escorted Garret into the hospital. Cara filled out the paperwork on Garret's behalf while he rested in a nearby chair. The nurse asked Garret a few questions about the nature of his injuries before escorting Garret and Cara to an examination room to await the doctor. The nurse shook her head in amazement as she returned to the nurse's station. It was hard for her to understand why these cowboys would want to be in a sport of such self-destruction. She wondered how many more competitors she would meet before the group left Grand Rapids for another year.

X-rays revealed that Garret had sustained three broken ribs in the accident. Not even the doctor could believe the pain tolerance the young man was showing. His adrenalin seemed to have taken over until Garret was able to finish with the horses. There was no internal bleeding or other injuries so Garret was free to leave the hospital. The biggest problem, as Garret saw it, was that he would have to get another driver to drive his wagon while he took some time off to heal. With broken ribs, there was simply no way he would have the strength to control his team.

The drive back from the hospital was quiet as Garret and Cara both had a lot on their minds. As they pulled back into the camping area near the racetrack questions flooded them from all directions. Garret explained the situation to several of the other drivers who were standing around their camp where Cara had parked the truck. Everyone was eager to know if Garret would be well enough to continue driving his own team. Garret explained that he would have to step down from the driver's seat for a few weeks. He spoke quietly as it was a difficult thing to have to announce to his fellow competitors.

Without hesitation, Grant Wagner stepped up and offered to drive Garret's team until he was well enough to drive again for himself. Garret heaved a gentle sigh of relief and a smile rose on his face when he heard his friend's offer. He was overjoyed to have the confident hands of Grant at the lines of his horses and he thanked the driver profusely.

"You have no idea how much I appreciate this," Garret thanked Grant as the two men shook hands.

"Hey, no worries," replied Grant. "I just want you to have the time to heal and I don't want you to worry about who you're going to find to drive every night. I'm not saying I can do the team the justice you have, but I will certainly try."

"Oh, I'm not worried about that," said Garret. "I have complete faith in your driving and this is your kind of outfit. They turn the barrels in the same style that you like and heck, my left leader used to be your horse."

"Yeah, thanks for reminding me that I let that good bay horse go to you," laughed Grant. "I can't say he worked that well for me, but he sure is working nice for you. I am at least pleased to see that. I've got some stuff around the barn to finish but I will catch up with you tomorrow to see what you want to hook for the race."

"Thanks again Grant. I'll see you later then," said Garret as he turned away from his team's new driver and back to the rest of the group, still standing around visiting. It had been another very long day and now, with injuries to heal, the days would be much harder for a while. Garret visited the few people left standing around before he said goodnight and went to the barns where Michael would still be hard at work.

Michael would be handling the majority of the chores and Cara would have to assist him until Garret was well again. The drivers that were standing around when they returned from the hospital teased Garret mercilessly about being relegated to diaper duty while Cara helped with the horses. He tried to laugh with the boys, but the pain in his ribs held him back. He felt lucky to have such a supportive, hard working family and such wonderful friends. Although it would be difficult getting through the next few weeks, he knew that they would be just fine.

As Garret approached the barn he could hear a lot of commotion. It sounded like something banging against the stall and instinct told him that something was wrong with one of the horses. He quickened his pace as much as he could and rounded the corner of the barn. One of his horses, Midnight Blast was down in the stall and thrashing his hooves against the wall. Michael was trying to ease his way past the horse to cut the rope in order to free him. There was little room for him to get past the horse without getting injured by the animal's flailing hooves.

Instinctively Garret ran toward the stall, grabbing the horse by the tail to slide his body around just enough that Michael could reach the rope with his pocket knife. As the rope came free the horse had room to bring his head down to the ground, gaining enough leverage to leap to his feet. Michael quickly grabbed the horse by his halter in order to prevent his escape from the barn area. As Michael checked the black gelding over for any injuries Garret slouched over, clutching his ailing ribs. It was not going to be easy trying to heal while trying to keep a bunch of wiry thoroughbreds healthy at the same time.

"Are you okay?" Michael stood in front of Garret who was still slouched over. "You've got to try and stay out of here man!"

"Yeah, I know," said Garret. "Sometimes that's easier said then done when you see a wreck in progress. Is Blast okay?"

"He's got a few rope burns from getting down in the stall and trying to claw his way up but other than that he looks fine. I'll get some salve on his rope burns right away," said Michael.

"Just what we need, another horse to doctor," said Garret in frustration. "I'm really hoping this isn't a sample of things to come for the season."

"I'm sure things will be fine Garret," replied Michael. "We're just off to a bit of a rough start. You worry about getting yourself healed and the rest will work itself out. I talked to a few of the guys while you were at the hospital and they are going to help me in the morning with the wagon and harness repairs we need to do. I had a feeling you might need to back off some of the chores."

Garret smiled at Michael in appreciation. With so much going on he did not even think about the repairs that would need to be done before the next race. Some of the harness was stressed beyond its limit and some pieces would need to be replaced. It did not seem like the wagon sustained a great deal of damage however it would need to be checked over to make sure.

"Thanks Michael," said Garret. "That's huge that you would go ahead and get that organized. You have no idea how much I appreciate that about you. You really are going to do well here. We couldn't be happier with your work."

"Thanks," said Michael. "I came here to learn and I feel like I am getting a whole lot of education in one big chunk. The bonus is that I am meeting a lot of great people along the way."

"Well, I think I'm going to go back to the trailer before something else happens that my ribs aren't going to like," Garret winced as he laughed a little. He walked down the long line of horses now quietly eating hay in their stalls. When he was satisfied that every animal looked comfortable, he waved goodnight to Michael, now at the other end of the barn applying salve to Midnight Blast. As he walked back to the trailer to try to get some sleep, he pondered what else could possibly be in store for him this summer.

When Garret entered the trailer he saw that his son was sleeping quietly in his crib. Cara and her mother were talking quietly and enjoying a cup of tea. Garret could tell that Cara had been crying but he did not say anything about it. He knew that it had been a stressful day and she just needed to get it out. Karen immediately rose from her chair and hugged Garret as she had not really seen him other than the brief moment at the barn after the accident.

"I won't hug you too tight," said Karen. "I'm just glad that you're okay."

"You and me both," said Garret. "The good thing is that I got that out of the way and now I won't have to try that again." Garret tried to make light of the situation and reassure both Karen and Cara, but neither woman was buying it.

"Yeah right, I don't think you should try that again," Cara said, her voice still choking a little.

Garret squeezed his wife's shoulder a little before turning to the stove to pour himself some tea. He was on a lot of painkillers, anything stronger than tea would not have been a good idea. He was well past his younger days of using whiskey for a painkiller. He sat and visited with the two women while he drank his tea. He decided that it would probably be best not to mention the incident that had occurred in the barn just before he came to the trailer. Cara would kill him if she knew he intervened to help Michael with the horse.

With each sip of his tea, Garret felt himself growing sleepy. He would have a sponge bath in the trailer tonight rather than take the long walk to the showers. The pain killers were kicking in and the stress of the day was taking its toll. Garret bid goodnight to Karen and kissed Cara on the forehead before ascending the stairs to the upper bedroom of the trailer. He entered the bathroom and removed his t-shirt and track pants which he had worn to the hospital. As he lifted the lid to the laundry hamper he saw the clothes he had been wearing during the races. His jeans were caked with the dirt of the track and his racing jacket had a tear in the left shoulder. It was a quick reminder of how lucky he really was.

Garret washed, brushed his teeth, put on some boxers and a t-shirt and then tried to inch his way into bed a little at a time. Cara came up to the bedroom to help Garret get into bed. It seemed there would be no easy task for him for a while. Finally Garret was into bed and Cara helped him with the blankets before kissing him goodnight and leaving him to rest. His broken ribs did not appreciate his efforts to get comfortable. Thankfully, painkillers allowed him to quickly drift off for some much needed rest.

That night Cara slept in the other bedroom with her mother. She did not want to disturb Garret or accidently roll into his ribs. She lay in bed for a long time, unable to fall asleep. Suddenly tears welled up in her eyes and she began to quietly weep. She turned away from her mother in an effort not to wake her with her sobs but mothers always seem to know. Cara could feel the assuring hand of her mother, rubbing her back just as she had when Cara was a child. She still found great comfort in her mother's touch and soon she drifted off to sleep.

Garret felt as though he had only been asleep a few hours and already the morning sun pierced through the blind slats of the windows, beckoning him to come outside and start the day. He began the task of simply trying to sit up in bed when the rigor of what his body had been through the night before quickly overwhelmed him. Garret lay down again, gasping at the pain. Cara heard his struggles and quickly rose from bed to investigate.

"Hey, I thought you would at least try to take it easy for a day," Cara scolded Garret quietly.

"I will, I mean I am," replied Garret as Cara held on to his forearm to lend some support as he tried to once again rise from the bed. "I just wanted to check things at the barns and see if there is anything Michael needs. If he can't handle it on his own I will have to find someone."

"I already told you I will help Michael until you are feeling better," said Cara. "End of discussion. I don't want you out there taking risks that are only going to set you back further. Mom is going to watch Corby this morning so you can come out and walk around, but that is all you will be doing."

"Yes, ma'am," replied Garret with a grin. He knew when Cara was determined and this was one of those times.

Cara helped Garret to get some clothes. She helped him with his t-shirt as he was not having an easy time trying to get his arms above his head. He opted for track pants as he could not imagine trying to get jeans on. His whole body ached and he preferred not to let Cara know the full extent of how he felt.

Once Garret was dressed and on his way outside Cara quickly brushed her hair, pulling it off of her face. She grabbed her favorite sweatshirt, a well worn shirt left over from her days at SFU. She pulled on a comfortable pair of faded blue jeans and her boots before heading toward the door of the trailer. She looked at Corby sleeping peacefully, smiling at him as she quietly closed the door behind her.

When Cara arrived at the barn Michael was already doing the chores. He turned out some of the horses into the exercise pens so they could walk around, stretch their muscles and roll in the sand. It gave Michael the opportunity to clean the feed buckets from the night before and refill them with fresh feed. Cara said a quick good morning to Michael before grabbing a pitch fork to clean out the stalls so she could put fresh straw down. She did not need a cue from Michael or Garret as to what needed to be done. She had been in this role many times while working at Hastings Park and later working alongside Garret before Corby was born.

Garret watched the morning routine as he walked along the exercise pens to look over his horses. He fought the urge to help out because he knew Cara would have sent him straight back to the trailer like a scolded child. He smiled as he thought about the authority she could take when she was worried about a member of her family.

As Michael and Cara were finishing the morning chores Karl Stern, Neil Hopkins and Grant Wagner appeared at their barn. The men first spoke with Garret to see how he was feeling and then moved on to the task at hand.

"We're here to see what repairs need to be done on the wagon and the harness," said Neil.

"Hey guys," said Michael as he pulled a bale of hay from a stack nearby. "Thanks for getting here so soon. I'm not the expert by any means, but I think some of this harness will need to go to Ed's repair shop." Michael picked up a few of the broken pieces of harness for emphasis as he spoke.

"Wow, that's definitely not going to be fixed with a few new buckles and some well placed duct tape," Grant joked as he held some of the broken pieces in his hands. "We'll get some of this harness laid out and see what needs to go to Ed's and then we'll come back to pick the stuff up after we have some breakfast."

Ed Desmond was a retired wagon driver who ran a small tack and harness repair shop on the edge of town. He would enjoy visiting with the boys as much as he would enjoy fixing the harness.

"Thanks guys," said Garret appreciatively. "Let's get it all out here and see what we've got to work with."

The men discussed the accident further which still sent a shiver down Cara's spine so, after thanking everyone for their help, she left for the trailer to get breakfast started. When she arrived she was not at all surprised to find her mother already happily preparing breakfast. Corby was content in his crib, kicking happily as he watched a mobile hanging overhead.

"Good morning sweetie," Karen said as Cara leaned down to squeeze Corby's tiny feet. "How is everything at the barns this morning?"

"Everything's great Mom," said Cara as she played with Corby. "The chores went fine and then Karl, Grant and Neil came over to offer a hand to take the harness for repairs and check the wagon over for any problems. It looks like everything will be back to normal before we know it."

"How are you doing today?" Karen asked with concern in her voice. "I know that wasn't an easy thing for you to go through to begin with and now with the extra workload you will be taking on and looking after the baby... well I can't say that I'm not worried."

"Mom, everything will be fine," Cara tried to reassure her. "Garret will be able to watch Corby most of the time and already we've been offered a lot of help." Cara wondered who she was really trying to convince as she thought of the long summer ahead of them.

"I know Garret can watch Corby in terms of supervising him, but he sure won't be able to pick him up or do much of anything for a while," Karen reminded her.

"I know Mom, but if Corby can't wait and needs to be picked up, I will only be a short distance from the trailer. Everything will be fine, you'll see," said Cara as she poured a cup of coffee.

"That's the thing," said Karen. "I wish I could see but I've got to return to Vancouver tomorrow and I know I should be here for you guys." Karen had tears in her eyes now as she looked at Cara and then over to her grandchild.

"Oh Mom no, don't think of it that way. Everything's going to be fine and we'll manage. I know you have other obligations and you can't worry about this. People will help us out, that's what we all do around here," Cara tried to sound positive. On that note, the two women embraced and dropped the subject. There was really nothing else to say. They both knew they just had to hope that everything would work itself out even though it would be difficult.

Soon Garret and Michael appeared for breakfast. The breakfast conversation was kept on a light note with Garret and Michael mainly discussing what repairs would need to be made to the harness. Karl, Neil and Grant had looked over the wagon before they left for breakfast. They determined that there was no serious damage to the wagon that would cause any safety problems. Most of the damage on the wagon consisted of scarred paint and a cracked wheel spoke, but nothing that would need urgent attention.

Michael and Garret ate quickly so they could return to help with the harness. All of the harness in need of repair was loaded into Neil's truck and the men departed for the repair shop. Ed assured Garret that the harness would be ready for the afternoon and after some small talk about the good old days of wagon racing, the men departed to leave Ed to his work. As soon as they returned to the grounds, Garret thanked them before going to the trailer to lie down for a while. He was exhausted just from trying to pack his ribs around that morning. Cara and Karen had taken Corby for his morning ride in the stroller so the trailer was quiet. Garret eased himself onto the sofa. He had a lot of things on his mind but he managed to drift off to sleep.

Chapter Five

Garret awoke with a start to the sound of knocking at the door. He had no idea how long he had been asleep but it felt like it was no more than a few minutes. Garret cradled his ribs as he went to answer the door. It was Darryl Baker, the outrider who rode most often for Garret and who had been holding his lead team the night before.

"Hey Darryl, come on in," said Garret. Garret returned to the sofa to sit down so they could visit. Darryl took a seat in the adjacent armchair.

"I just wanted to come by and see how you were feeling," said Darryl. "I heard that you won't be driving your outfit for a while. I also thought I should bring you a copy of the paper." Darryl handed the paper over to Garret.

Splashed across the daily edition of the Grand Rapids Observer was full coverage of the accident. The photographer captured the horror of the accident complete with Garret flying through the air and the horses tumbling to the ground. The ensuing article recaptured the incident and named Garret as the unfortunate driver.

The article went on to cover the many public comments from local residents debating the dangers of wagon races to both horses and humans. Some people commented that they loved the action and would not miss a race. Others were calling for a complete ban of what they considered to be a barbaric sport that was cruel to animals.

The controversy was the same from town to town each summer and was especially high if a horse was killed on the track. There was speculation that some of Garret's horses may have been put down after the accident. The article concluded with the mention of Jaimie Feldstrom's condition in the Edmonton hospital.

Garret was furious. Publicity for the sport was never a bad thing but the hint that his horses may have been put down was not acceptable. Garret searched the paper for a contact number before reaching for his cell phone and dialing. He spoke briefly with the receptionist before being directed to the reporter who wrote the article. After requesting an interview with the reporter he hung up his phone, satisfied that he would be able to clear the matter up with a further article.

"Sorry about that Darryl," said Garret. "I'm sure you didn't come here for all of that but I just wanted to clear this up before the protesters are standing on my doorstep."

"No problem," said Darryl. "I completely understand. Great picture though."

The two men laughed at the photo of Garret flying through the air. It was a pretty good picture and now that everything had turned out okay, it was safe to have a laugh about it. The laughter ended and a short lull ensued.

"Is there something on your mind Darryl?" asked Garret.

"I, I guess what I was really wondering is if I should have done something different with the way I set your horses coming into the barrels last night. Maybe they were set too narrow?" Darryl spilled the words out quickly as he rehashed the accident in his mind. He leaned forward in the chair, his elbows resting on his knees as he ran his hands through his waves of dark hair. "I'm just not sure if that could have changed something or not." The outrider's hazel eyes pierced Garret with concern as he waited for a reply. He felt bad about what happened.

"No, no way," Garret looked at Darryl in shock. "It had nothing to do with the way you set the team at the barrels. That was perfect. My right leader stumbled and he just couldn't recover in time. There's nothing you or I could do about that to change it. We've been running hard Darryl. Things have been going well.

I'm not going to blame one of my best outriders for something no one could have prevented."

"Well, I just wasn't sure," said Darryl looking somewhat relieved now. "I didn't really know what exactly happened and I just wanted to talk to you about it because I'm pretty sure neither one of us wants to go through that again."

"I'm pretty sure you're right about that," Garret held his ribs as the two men laughed.

"So I take it you're going to be out of the driver's seat for a while?" asked Darryl.

"Yeah, a few weeks probably, maybe less if I give myself a chance to heal," replied Garret. "Grant's going to be running the outfit for me."

"Oh, that's perfect," said Darryl. "He loves your outfit."

"Yeah, I was pretty pleased that he offered to drive because that is really his style of team to drive," said Garret. "I think everything's going to work out fine. We will just take it day by day."

"I'll get the outriding horses tonight and get them to the track for you," said Darryl. "At least I can help out that way".

"Thanks," said Garret. "That will help us out a lot."

"I realize you guys are going to have your hands full with you being on the mend," said Darryl. "Just let me know if there is anything you need and I'll try to help out where I can. Anyhow, I should be getting back to my trailer. I've got a few things I want to get finished before the races tonight."

"Yeah, I'm going to try and have a nap so I'm at my best for supervising everything tonight," Garret said with a smile. "Thanks for stopping by and for offering to help. I might have to take you up on that."

"For sure," said Darryl. "Make sure you do." Darryl rose from his chair and left the trailer, leaving the newspaper on the chair for Garret.

Garret tried to go back to sleep but so many things were running through his mind. He decided it would just be easier to get up, make himself a sandwich and carry on with his day. It was hard to sleep wondering how things would go with his fate now in someone else's hands. Just when he was off to the perfect start, this had to happen. He tried hard not to feel sorry for himself but it was not that easy.

Soon Cara, Karen and baby Corbyn returned to the trailer to make some lunch. Corby was napping peacefully in his stroller. A blanket had been placed over the top to protect the baby from the now very warm sun. Karen stayed outside with Corby while Cara went into the trailer to start lunch.

"Did you get a chance to rest?" asked Cara as she pecked Garret on the cheek.

"I had a little rest, then Darryl stopped by for a few minutes and I couldn't go back to sleep so I decided to make a sandwich instead," said Garret.

"Oh," said Cara. "What's Darryl up to today?"

"He had some concerns about the way he set my lead team last night. He thought that might have partially caused my accident," said Garret.

"Why would he think that?" asked Cara.

"I think it was just in the back of his mind and he just wanted to be sure that wasn't the case is all," said Garret. "I reassured him that was not the problem so he was on his way and everything's fine."

Just then Cara noticed the front page of the newspaper on the chair. She grabbed the paper and read through the article intently.

"They think you had to put horses down?" Cara felt her voice rise in anger.

"It's okay Cara," said Garret. "I already spoke with the reporter. He's coming down for a follow-up interview with me this afternoon and I will set the record straight."

"Well, I guess!" said Cara. "The media is just so frustrating sometimes."

Garret, Cara and Karen enjoyed some lunch outside while Corby continued to nap. Soon Michael appeared to announce that the harness was back from the shop and everything was ready to go. Michael ate some of the sandwiches that were prepared, made his comments on the news article and then returned to the barns to get ready for the evening's races. Garret took this as his cue to go to the barns as well but not before Cara reminded him that she would be helping with the horses and he would be taking it easy. There was little protest from Garret as he really did not feel well at all. He eased back into a lawn chair and watched his son sleep as Cara went off to the barns to help out.

Race preparations went off without any problems and when it was time for Grant to come get the team for their heat everything was ready. Grant had no problem driving the team and had the horses back to the barn in no time. Everything went according to plan and the last night of racing in Grand Rapids was completed. Getting everything packed up to move to the next show would be the latest challenge the team would need to deal with.

In the early morning Garret grabbed the first copy of the Grand Rapids Observer that he could get his hands on. The picture showed Garret proudly standing with all of the horses that had been in the accident. The article talked about the horses being in good health and Garret requiring some time off. Garret was pleased that the paper ran the article, even if it was printed on page eight.

By nine o'clock that morning Karen had her bags packed and she was ready to go to the airport. She did not want to leave when Garret and Cara had so much facing them but she had to return to her business. Summer was a busy time for her with so many weddings and other events along with employees wishing to take time off. It would be impossible for her to delay her time away any longer.

Cara looked at her mother standing in the trailer, her bags ready to go. She could tell that she looked worried. She tried her best to assure her that everything would be okay.

"Mom, please don't give me that look," said Cara.

"What look?" asked Karen. "I'm not giving you a look. I'm looking at my grandson and hoping you will all be just fine and I'm missing you all already."

The two women hugged for a long time. There was nothing Cara could say to make her mother worry less. That was the nature of being a mother and she had only just begun to understand what that was like.

"Okay, Mom," said Cara. "Let's get you to the airport before we stand here crying. Everyone will wonder what has happened now." Cara tried to laugh a little as she gave her mother one last tight hug.

Karen went to the barns to say goodbye to Garret as Cara loaded her things into the truck. Garret had to promise Karen that he would not over do it and that he would make sure Cara did not over do things either. Garret promised and Michael tried to reassure her as well.

"Thank you Michael," said Karen. "It has been wonderful getting to know you and I have faith that you will keep things running smoothly around here."

"Thanks Karen," replied Michael. "I will try my best. It was very nice to meet you. I sure hope you're able to come back later this summer."

"I'm going to try my best," said Karen. "I want to get back to see some races when Garret is back out there racing and I want to see more of my grandson so he doesn't forget who I am." She hugged Michael before walking to the truck.

The drive to the airport was a short one filled with small talk that had nothing to do with the situation at hand. Grand Rapids has a full service regional airport therefore Karen would have a direct flight back to Vancouver. She would be home in about an hour. Karen hugged and kissed Cara and Corby her last goodbyes before entering airport security. Cara cried most of the way back to the racetrack.

When Cara arrived back at the racetrack with Corby, she noticed that the place was alive with the activity of packing up to move to the next show. People were loading up their holiday trailers and horses and equipment moved in every direction as the barns were cleaned out.

The Hartman's were hard at work helping Michael to clean the barns and pack equipment away. Cara smiled at the effort that was being made to help out. Garret was moving some of the horses into a pen so that the stalls could be cleaned. He was able to lead the horses. At least that much he could help with.

Cara took Corby into the holiday trailer. She fed Corby a bottle so that he would be content while she packed up the trailer. It always seemed easier to unpack everything than it did to repack it all, nonetheless she worked quickly so that she would be finished in time to help load the horses.

As soon as the trailer was packed and ready for travel, Cara asked Mary if she would watch Corby while she hooked the truck onto the trailer. Of course Mary was happy to oblige and in short order the truck and trailer unit was ready for travel. Mary continued to watch Corby while Cara went to help finish up with the work at the barns. Cara did not want Mary doing the heavy work even though she knew the woman was more than capable.

As Cara and Michael loaded the horses into the trailer, Darryl stopped by. He had a sheet in his hand that contained the draw for the next show. Garret did not finish Grand Rapids too well as his accident caused him to receive a "no time" for the third night of racing. He quickly moved from forth in the average down to thirty-third. The bad news was that his team had some ground to make up in the next few shows; the good news was that Darryl had stopped by to tell him that he could still outride for him.

With the new draw came new drivers in each heat. Drivers would be shuffled according to their standings in the NCA with the top wagons running in the final heats and the wagons with less points running in the earlier heats. Garret's team would not be racing against the same outfits, therefore if he were hooked with someone that Darryl rode for more often, he would have to find a replacement. Luckily in this instance, Garret did not lose either of his outriders so that would be one less thing for him to worry about.

As Darryl and Garret conversed about the draw for the next show, a yell came from the trailer where Michael and Cara were loading horses. Darryl ran to look in the back of the trailer with Garret close behind.

The final horse to be loaded did not like the idea of standing near the back of the trailer. When the horse pulled back on his rope in protest, he knocked Cara to the floor of the trailer. Cara quickly scrambled out of the way as the horse pulled back once again, this time breaking his rope and falling backward down the ramp of the trailer.

Garret felt helpless as Cara and Michael scrambled after the now free horse who had quickly regained his composure. Michael grabbed what was left of the lead shank and he managed to calm the horse down while Cara retrieved a new rope. Before trying to reload the horse it was decided that the horse should be given a sedative, for his own safety, before reloading him into the trailer.

"Well, let's see if we can get out of this place without anything else happening," said Michael with a sigh as he latched the door of the trailer and began to winch the ramp into place for travel.

Cara had sustained nothing more than a small bump on the head from the incident and chose to keep this information to herself. She did not see the point of divulging this information when Garret already had enough to worry about. She was eager to leave Grand Rapids behind and get on to the next show. It felt as though it had been a very long week and she did not want to find out what else could possibly go wrong in this place. Moving on to a new show always felt like a new beginning.

Garret thanked Darryl for stopping by to let him know he could ride and for helping out with the horse. He was grateful that an extra pair of hands came along just when they were needed. Darryl penned Garret's name into his outriding sheet, bid farewell to the McCormack's and carried on to visit the next driver he hoped to ride for at the next show.

With everything loaded up and ready to go, Cara went back to the holiday trailer to tell Mary that they were ready to leave. Mary gave Corby one more hug before helping Cara get him into his car seat for the journey ahead. Michael would be driving the truck and trailer with the horses and Garret would accompany him. Cara would follow in the truck and holiday trailer and the Hartman's would follow her. The Hartman's would not be going on to the next show as they were going home to Spruce View to tend to things on their ranch. As much as they wanted to stay with the McCormack's to help out while Garret was injured, it was not possible with all of the work to do at home.

"You take care of yourself and don't get carried away and overdo it," said Mary as she hugged Cara.

"Don't worry, we'll be fine," said Cara. "Michael is working out great. He is a hard worker who obviously loves this sport. I really can't see us having any problems. The work load will be a little heavy while Garret is healing but we can handle it."

"Take care of yourself," said Dan as he gave Cara a big hug. "We'll be listening to the races on the internet so we'll keep track of everything that's going on until we can meet up with you guys later on. Don't worry about things at home. We will keep an eye on things there too."

"Thank you Dan," Cara said as she released from his hug. "We sure appreciate you guys being here this week. You were a great help."

"We had a great time," said Mary. "We can't wait to get back for another show. We need to get home and get the garden in and do a few other things and then we will be back for sure."

"You guys take care and thank you for everything," said Garret as he hugged Mary and shook Dan's hand.

Michael started the engine of the big Mac truck and everyone took that as a sign to get moving. They did not want the horses to get overly restless in the idle trailer. Garret gave Cara a hug, walked over to peek in the back seat of the pickup at his young son who was now sleeping and then walked over to his truck to begin the grueling process of getting into the seat with his broken ribs. It would be a tough journey.

"You have a safe drive," Cara called to Michael. "If you guys are stopping or you need anything just call me on my cell phone. I will be right behind you." Cara took off her jacket before climbing into the driver's seat of the pickup.

The three units began to move out of the Grand Rapids agriculture grounds. The Hartman's would follow the McCormack's for the first three hours before turning off in the direction of Spruce View. The McCormack's would travel all the way to Saskatchewan for the Saskatchewan Regional Fair. It would be a twelve hour trip before they reached the next race venue.

Before Cara turned onto the highway behind Garret and Michael, she turned her head to look back at her son. Corby was sleeping peacefully. She hoped that he would travel well as they had a long trip ahead of them. The few rest stops they would make might not appease the infant too much.

As Cara travelled down the highway she turned on some music and put the speakers to the front so it would not disturb Corby. She sang along to Taylor Swift, Keith Urban and Johnny Reid. They would be her travel companions for the next twelve hours. She was not a great singer but with no one listening, she sang her heart out. It felt good. With so many hours spent travelling down the road there were not many songs she did not know the words to. The travel really was the worst part of being in the NCA. Sometimes she forgot what her life was like before all of this although she knew she would not change it for the world. For one thing, she could not imagine what she would do with herself if she actually had a whole summer to spend away from horses and racing.

Two hours into the trip, Corby woke up crying. Cara called Garret using the two-way radio feature on her cell phone. Garret answered quickly.

"What's up?" asked Garret.

"We need to find a place to pull over," said Cara. "Your son is getting pretty upset."

"There is a rest stop up here in about three kilometers," Garret replied. "Will that work?"

"That will work," said Cara.

Corby continued to cry as Cara tried to comfort him for the next couple of minutes. She talked and sang to him as she held her right hand over the back seat, placing it on Corby's shoulder to comfort him. His cries softened but she was still relieved to see the sign for the rest stop exit. It was horrible to listen to a baby cry. They always seemed to have such a desperate, heart breaking tone.

Cara pulled to a stop in a parking space behind Garret and Michael. The Hartman's waved as they drove past the group. They decided to keep on driving as they knew there would be a lot of stops for the McCormack's with the baby. While Cara was taking off her seatbelt and retrieving the diaper bag, Corby got quite impatient again. Just as his little cries were turning into full blown wails, he was retrieved from his car seat by his dad.

"Hey little man, it's all right," Garret spoke softly as he rocked his son in his arms. "Your mommy's just getting you a fresh diaper and your milk and then you will be as good as new." Garret cradled his son in one arm and used his free hand to cradle his own ribs. It seemed to work well and he was not in a great deal of pain.

Cara searched through the bag to retrieve the items she needed. She held up the diaper and wipes to Garret and motioned towards the trailer. Garret followed with Corby in his arms. Once inside the trailer Cara took Corby from Garret, settled him on a change pad and changed his diaper while Garret got the baby formula ready.

Before long, Corby was settled in the comfort of his mother's arms, happily drinking his bottle. While Corby and Cara were occupied, Garret rummaged through the fridge looking for some good snacks to take in the truck for himself and Michael. Michael was outside having a short walk around the rest area to give his legs a break from the drive. Back inside the holiday trailer, Cara fed the baby while watching Garret put some snacks in a bag.

"How are your ribs doing?" Cara inquired.

"Actually not too bad," replied Garret. "Getting in and out of the truck is a bit of a challenge but other than that I feel pretty good. I should be ready to drive my wagon by the time we get to Saskatchewan," he joked.

"Yeah right," said Cara. "You'll be driving by Calgary if you're lucky."

"Don't worry Cara. I'll be back in there before Calgary. I don't want to be all rusty going into that show and besides, my horses need me driving them not someone else," said Garret.

"I know it's hard," said Cara. "I just don't want you pushing it too much and then having problems because of it."

"I won't," promised Garret. "I'm going to heal properly so I can get back out there and not have any problems."

"That's what I like to here," said Cara as she stood up from the sofa to plant a kiss on Garret. "I think we're ready to carry on."

Garret kissed Cara and then kissed Corby lightly on the forehead. With a full tummy of warm milk, he was now nodding off to sleep. Garret gathered the bag of snacks and the diaper bag from the counter.

Cara eased down the steps of the trailer with Corby in her arms. She carried him to the truck and placed him back into his car seat. Soon they were ready to continue down the highway again.

Half way through their journey they were able to stop at some vacant ranch land belonging to friends of theirs. It was a late summer cattle pasture so there were no animals on it at this time of the year. The horses were let out of the trailer into an empty pen for water and a chance to relax and roll. It gave both horses and humans some time to recuperate from the long journey. As the day was overcast and cool, Garret, Cara, Corby and Michael spent most of their free time relaxing in the holiday trailer. Corby had a chance to kick freely on the floor for a while. He was obviously pleased to be free of the constraints of the car seat. After an hour the horses were reloaded into the horse trailer without incident. They carried on with the final leg of their journey.

When the McCormack's arrived at Saskatchewan's Tri City Fair Grounds it was evening and the routine of feeding horses, setting up camp and fitting in some sort of a meal before falling into bed, began all over again. Cara and Michael worked with the horses while Garret watched over Corby and gingerly tended to his ribs. They would only have one day off before the races started at this venue and there was a great deal to do. Garret and Cara both went to sleep fast that night. They had so much on their minds but utter exhaustion conquered their thoughts, allowing them to sleep soundly.

In the morning relief came in the form of family. Garret was thrilled with the honking of a horn he heard just after breakfast. It was coming from the truck of Garret's brother and sister-in-law, Robert and Shana. They did not have any children so they did not have to worry about having kids in school. News of Garret's injuries had quickly travelled home. After making some arrangements with Garret and Robert's parents Edward and Sharon, it was decided that Robert and Shana would come help at the races while Edward and Sharon would keep everything running smoothly at home. They loaded up their holiday trailer with some essentials and headed east to Saskatchewan.

Garret's parents loved wagon racing but they were now in their seventies and Sharon had some health problems so they did not like to travel very far from home. Edward was still very agile and active so he would have no problem running any of the farm equipment that was needed. The cattle had been turned out to the pasture to eat the early summer grass so the work load was lightened considerably.

"Hey you guys," beamed Garret. "I can't believe you're here."

"Yeah well I didn't think we could leave you to your own devices anymore," said Shana as she and Garret hugged.

"Shana, you promised you wouldn't go there," said Robert referring to the accident. "You gave my wife quite a scare bro."

"I know," said Garret. "I gave my wife quite a scare too."

Just then Cara came running from the barn area as she recognized the truck and holiday trailer. There were hugs all around, some discussion of the accident and the grateful acceptance of Robert and Shana's help. During times like this, the value of family was immeasurable.

With the extra help at the barns and the help with Corby, it was easier for Garret to take the time he needed to heal. Grant was doing a great job of driving Garret's outfit and soon the team was climbing back into the top of the NCA standings.

The two families of McCormack's along with Michael travelled on to the other shows, all of which were back in Alberta. They spent three days racing at the Madison County Fair and four days at the Foothills Exhibition before arriving in late June at the Black Mountain Stampede.

The Black Mountain Stampede was the last big event before the *Calgary Stampede* began in early July. It was a really big event for Garret as he felt that he was ready to step back into the wagon and race his own horses once again. He had been driving the horses, along with a co-driver, for practice in the mornings. He felt that he was now ready to handle the team in an actual race.

There was some tension the first night out but Grant had truly done the team justice and kept them driving in the style that Garret drove them in himself. There were no problems at all and Garret felt like he had hardly missed a race. The Black Mountain Stampede lasted five days. Garret drove the team to perfection. He came away smiling with a second place finish overall. He felt ready for the *Calgary Stampede* and ready to prove that his horses were *Rangeland Derby* champions. The excitement he felt was surreal as he and his family made the journey to Calgary.

Chapter Six

The *Calgary Stampede* runs for ten days each July. Thousands of people come to witness what is known world wide as *The Greatest Outdoor Show on Earth.* Competing in Calgary is what every young cowboy or cowgirl dreams of. For Garret, his dream started the first time his dad took him to the famous stampede to watch the chuckwagon races. He was just eight years old at the time but he never forgot the excitement he felt.

After the races Garret's dad took him back to the barns to visit one of his old friends who happened to be a chuckwagon driver. Garret could still remember the chaos around him as outriders and barn hands brought the outriding horses back and chuckwagon horses were unhooked from the wagons. He watched eagerly as horses were walked to be cooled down and washed in the wash bays. Sponsors and fans filled every available space as they tried to celebrate with the drivers. The smell of horse sweat permeated the air and the atmosphere was electric. From that day forward, Garret longed for the chance to be a part of that action.

Garret came back to present day as he reached the Calgary city limits. He wound his way through the streets into downtown Calgary, making his way to the stampede grounds. Cara followed close behind with the truck and holiday trailer. Although Garret was feeling much better, Robert and Shana decided to stay and help until Calgary was over. Ten race days in Calgary took its toll on even the healthiest person so any extra helped was welcome.

When they arrived at the stampede grounds, Garret stopped at the office to be directed to his assigned barn. They would also tell him where their holiday trailer needed to be parked. Cara and Corby waited in the pickup and when Garret returned from the office he motioned for Cara to follow him. The holiday trailer was parked while Michael, Robert and Garret unloaded the horses, wagon and all of the supplies they would need as they would not be able to leave the truck and horse trailer at the grounds. Space was precious in the downtown core of Calgary and any equipment which was not necessary had to be removed. Everyone worked quickly to get everything set up in a manner that would allow for maximum use of the storage space they were allotted.

The races would start in one night. When the horses were fed and resting for the night, Garret, Cara, Michael, Robert and Shana had a chance to relax and have one last breath before all of the action got underway. The group sat down together in Garret and Cara's holiday trailer to have a relaxing dinner while Corby slept peacefully in his crib. All of the travel had made the little explorer quite exhausted.

Cara had prepared T-bone steak, roasted baby potatoes, tossed salad and mixed garden vegetables which she served with fresh dinner rolls. She chose a Shiraz to compliment the meal.

"This is wonderful Cara," Garret raved. "You're getting us off on the right foot here anyhow."

"Thank you" said Cara. "I just thought we could have a nice meal before all of the chaos starts tomorrow. You and I both know we literally won't see each other for most of the next ten days between barn cleaning and horse care."

"I know," replied Garret.

"I guess it has been awhile since I've actually worked at the *Calgary Stampede*," added Michael. "One always thinks he has the routine down until he comes here."

"Yes," Cara agreed. "It always amazes me how everyone competes so hard to get into ten days of hell."

"It's one of those 'no pain, no gain' type things," Shana laughed.

"Ah yes, well thanks for reminding me that it is just as much work or more than what I can remember," Michael laughed.

"Oh, it's nothing to worry about," said Garret. "Just chalk it up to more experience." Everyone laughed at the comments going around the table.

Calgary is different from every other venue for a lot of reasons. The drivers are competing for over one million dollars in prize money so the stakes are higher. The space is very limited which means there is nowhere to turn out horses that all need to be exercised twice daily. Horses are mainly hand-walked unless one is fortunate enough to have a quiet horse to ride so he or she can lead the race horses for their exercise.

Calgary is a six in the morning to midnight job for ten straight days but it is Calgary. It is the pot of gold at the end of the rainbow. It is the cream of the crop and every other cliché that describes fabulous. Although the stress runs high, you will never find a driver not wanting to be there or an outrider who is not willing to ride every race he can.

The laughter and discussion was broken up by Corby's little cries. Shana sat closest to his crib so she went to him first, picking him up to comfort him. She rocked him back and forth while Cara prepared a bottle for him. When the bottle was ready Cara handed it to Shana who happily sat down in the rocking chair to feed her nephew.

Cara began to clear the dishes from the table and put the food away with a little help from the guys before they made an exit back to the barns. Relaxation time was over.

"So are you ready for the next ten days?" Shana asked Cara.

"I hope so," said Cara. "I guess if I'm not, that's too bad because here they are!"

"I think Garret is going to have a great Calgary," said Shana. "It just feels that way."

"I hope you're right," Cara replied. "He has worked really hard for this. It would be wonderful to see it pay off for him."

Cara wiped off the last of the counters and then took a now content Corby from Shana's arms to get him ready for his bath. Shana helped out by getting the bath water ready while Cara undressed Corby and took off his diaper. When he was ready for the bath Shana kissed him goodnight.

"I should go to the barns and see if there is anything else they need and then I'm going to try to get a good sleep," said Shana.

"That sounds like a plan," said Cara. "It is going to get hectic tomorrow. Thank you so much for staying and helping us out."

"Anytime," replied Shana. "We are always happy to help out if we can. You make sure you get some rest tonight. It has been a long summer for you already and it is about to get whole lot longer. Goodnight."

"Goodnight Shana," said Cara as she gently set Corby into the bath water.

"Well little man, I guess it's just you and me," said Cara as she washed Corby. "This is going to be quite an adventure for you," Cara cooed. "You are making your own history right now just being here at your first Calgary Stampede. Don't worry if you miss some things this year. You will see a lot of these in your future." Corby was growing quickly over the summer and he was now more attentive than ever to his mother's voice. He had also started to push up on his hands in an effort to crawl.

Corby cooed happily as his mother talked to him. She finished his bath, lifted him from the tub and wrapped him in a soft towel. She continued her conversation with him while she put on his lotion, diaper and a soft pale blue sleeper. Cara cradled him in her arms as she sat down in the rocking chair to let him finish his bottle. Corby gently drifted off to sleep in her arms. She too drifted off into dreamland for a while. She dreamt of horse racing, of Garret's smiling face and the warmth of a quiet summer day. She was awakened a few moments later when Garret placed a gentle kiss on her forehead. Cara smiled up at Garret as he took a peacefully sleeping Corby from her arms and placed him in his crib.

"Hey sweetie," whispered Garret. "I think you need to find your bed."

"I think you're right," Cara replied as she rose from the chair. "Are you coming to bed?"

"Is that a question or an invitation?" Garret asked with a mischievous grin.

"That might be a little of both," Cara answered playfully as she leaned toward Garret and kissed him.

"That is what I was hoping you'd say," said Garret as he switched off the light near Corby's bed and followed his wife to their bedroom.

After they had washed and prepared for bed they quickly fell into each other's arms. Garret kissed Cara passionately, exploring her mouth with his tongue. She answered back with a quiet sigh before moving her kisses to his neck and then his chest.

"I love you so much," Cara whispered to Garret.

"I love you too Cara. God I love you," Garret said in a hoarse whisper.

They loved each other passionately. She loved it when he looked into her eyes with such intensity that she thought she would burst. They fell into each other's arms, exhausted. Garret cradled Cara in his arms as she rested her head on his chest. She leaned up to kiss him one last goodnight kiss before they both fell into a deep, contented sleep.

In the early morning the chores were finished before the McCormack's were required to attend a corporate sponsor's breakfast function. Several other drivers were also in attendance at the breakfast. Fans and sponsors enjoyed meeting the drivers in person and getting some autographs. After the breakfast it was back to the barns to check on the horses. When they arrived at the barns, Michael was just finishing washing the last of the horses and Garret helped him to return them to their stalls. Robert and Shana had gone for their own breakfast and were just returning from a quick shopping trip.

With everything in order at the barns, there was time to take a break and enjoy some of the exhibits at the stampede grounds. There was plenty to see and do. Much more than they could see in a couple of hours but they did the things they enjoyed best. They took in the western art exhibits, ate ice cream on the midway and watched part of the Alberta Young Talent contest. Soon it was time to return to the barns to get ready for the first race of the show.

Shana looked after Corby while Michael, Robert and Garret got the wagon horses harnessed and the outriding horses saddled. Once all of the horses were ready, Cara and Robert took the outriding horses out to the infield pens where they would be held until the outriders came for them. When Garret's heat finished, they would take the horses back to the barns to unsaddle them.

Garret would be running in heat five so Cara would get to watch the earlier heats from a spot along the infield fence. As the races were about to start, she saw Shana carrying Corby to the infield grandstand. They waved to each other before Shana disappeared into the crowd. The warm afternoon sun beat down on the full capacity crowd awaiting the start of the races. The excitement of the commencement of the races was building. For many fans, this would be their first live *Rangeland Derby*. Outriders occupied themselves with some warm-up stretches before putting on their protective flak jackets and coloured outriding jackets for the first heat of the night.

Cara was enjoying the races but as each heat finished, her nerves rose a little in anticipation of Garret's heat. Finally, the time came for his heat to run. Cara and Robert insured the horses were ready for the outriders to take them. Once the outriders had their horses, they quickly raced back to the fence to watch Garret's race.

As the horn sounded and the cheers rose in the grandstand, Cara and Robert jumped and yelled for Garret as his team lurched forward and successfully raced out of the barreling area. It was difficult to see the first corner of the track from Cara's vantage point. She looked up at the giant screen in the infield to watch the races instead. As she cheered for Garret, she caught Barbie Hopkins out of the corner of her eye. Barbie's husband Neil was also in this heat. Something seemed wrong and it was then that she realized that Barbie was not cheering like everyone else. She was now slouched alongside of the fence clutching her very pregnant abdomen.

A great number of people surrounded Barbie however, in the excitement of watching the races no one seemed to notice her distress. Cara squeezed past several spectators in an effort to get to Barbie. As she reached the spot where Barbie was crouched, she gently touched her shoulder.

"Are you okay?" Cara shouted above the noise of the crowd.

"My water just broke," said Barbie in a rather calm voice, the kind of calm that only comes from being in such a situation before. "I guess this is it!"

"Okay, I'll be right back," said Cara. "Stay right here. I'm going to get the paramedics to get you out of here."

"Oh, don't worry," replied Barbie. "I'm pretty sure I'm not going anywhere."

Cara once again pushed past the crowd which still seemed oblivious to Barbie's situation. The wagons crossed the finish line with Neil winning the race and Garret following in a very close second place.

As Cara summoned the nearby paramedics who are always on hand at the racetrack, Darryl brought Garret's outriding horses back towards Cara. Normally Cara would help gather their outriding horses and tie them up when the race ended but today would have to be different.

"Darryl there's been a change of plans," Cara yelled over the crowd. "Barbie's gone into labor and we will never get her out of here in a vehicle with this crowd and the way they stop all vehicle traffic while the races are going on. Can you help Robert with the outriding horses after the races? I'm helping Barbie get to the hospital."

Darryl was a bit taken aback by the whole conversation. He rubbed the dirt from his face on the sleeve of his red outriding jacket and looked at Cara in confusion. Suddenly everything clicked and he processed what she was trying to tell him.

"Of course I can," Darryl said with a grin. "I will also get word to Neil that his wife is in labor and you do what you need to do. Don't worry about things here and tell Barbie good luck or whatever you're supposed to say in these situations."

As the paramedics approached Cara to see what the problem was, she gestured rapidly for them to follow her. As they made their way back toward Barbie she explained that Barbie's water had broke and they needed to get to the hospital right away.

By the time the paramedics got Barbie through the crowd and into the waiting ambulance, she was looking rather relieved.

"Cara, will you come with me?" asked Barbie. "I don't think this is going to be a long labor and I have a feeling Neil won't make it there in time. I'd like to have a friend with me if I can."

"Of course I can," Cara answered as she climbed into the ambulance with her friend. She knew Shana would wonder what happened to her but she also knew that Robert and Darryl would make sure Shana knew what was going on.

By the time the ambulance departed the stampede grounds, the next heat of racing was underway. Darryl did not have time to tell Neil the news and get back for his next heat so he sent word with one of the barn hands. By the time Neil was able to get out of the barn area with a vehicle, Barbie and Cara had already welcomed Daniel Travis Hopkins, a seven pound four ounce baby boy, into the world. Little Daniel was in a bit of a hurry and arrived safely into the arms of the paramedic just as the ambulance pulled into Calgary's Grace Falls Hospital. Cara and Barbie hugged and cried as the medical staff took over in the emergency room to insure both mother and baby were healthy.

"Congratulations Barbie," Cara said through her tears. "Your son is beautiful."

"Thank you Cara," replied Barbie through her own tears. "And thank you for being here for us. If it weren't for you, he may have been born right at the racetrack."

"Wouldn't his Dad have loved that," Cara replied with a laugh.

"Oh can you imagine?" laughed Barbie.

Cara gave Barbie one final hug before retreating to the waiting room so that the medical staff could finish their examination. As Cara waited and mulled over the events that had just occurred, Neil came bursting through the hospital doors.

"Neil, over here," Cara waved to him as she rose from her chair. "Mom and baby are fine. Come this way and I will show you where your wife and new son are."

"I have a new son?" Neil asked excitedly. "At the ultrasound they told us it was going to be a girl."

"Well put away the pink paint Mr. Hopkins. It's definitely a boy. Congratulations," Cara smiled as she ushered Neil toward Barbie's room.

"Daniel Travis?" Neil asked.

"Yes, that's right," said Cara.

"Yeah, that was our name choice if we had another boy," he smiled as Cara showed him to the room.

Neil moved quickly to Barbie's side and embraced his wife. He held onto her and kissed his son who slept peacefully in her arms. Cara quietly closed the door as she backed out of the room to give them their family time. She walked outside the hospital in order to use her cell phone to call Garret and tell him the news. This was certainly a *Calgary Stampede* she would never forget no matter what events occurred throughout the rest of it.

"Hey Garret," Cara spoke into her cell phone as she covered her other ear to drown out the noise of the traffic. "The Hopkins family just welcomed a new baby boy into the world."

"That's great news Cara," answered Garret. "Tell them congratulations for me."

"I will," said Cara. "I'm going to go back inside to say a quick goodbye and then I'll be back to the track. How'd you make out tonight?"

"I'm sitting in second place right now and the brand new father is in first," replied Garret. "The sponsors are already at the barns celebrating."

"Oh Garret," said Cara. "That is great news. This has truly been an amazing day all around. I'm on my way as soon as I can get there."

"Okay sweetheart," said Garret. "Do you want me to send Michael to pick you up?"

Cara was so wrapped up in all of the news and excitement that she had completely forgotten her ride to the hospital had been in the ambulance.

"Oh yeah," she said with a laugh. "I kind of forgot about needing a ride. Please tell Michael I'll be waiting at the Emergency entrance of Grace Falls."

"I will tell him," replied Garret. "Shana is looking after Corby until you get back so I can spend the time with the sponsors."

"Sounds like you have everything organized," said Cara. "I'll see you soon."

Cara closed her cell phone and put it back into the pocket of her jeans. She walked back into the hospital and went up to the maternity ward to say goodbye to Neil and Barbie. Neil was sitting on the bed beside Barbie holding their new son in his arms. The three of them looked very content. Cara said a quick goodbye, hugging each of them before leaving to wait for Michael. It had been quite a first day at the stampede this year.

When Cara returned to the hospital entrance she recognized their pickup pulling up to the curb. Michael drove up near to where Cara was standing and stopped for her.

"Hey, stranger do you need a ride?" he quipped.

Cara laughed at his remark. "That would be great," she said as she opened the passenger door of the truck. "In all of the excitement I kind of forgot that I didn't have a vehicle here. Thanks for coming to get me."

"No problem," answered Michael. "We need your help back at the track too much to leave you here." He laughed as Cara gave him a friendly slap on the arm.

Michael was still wearing the jeans and navy t-shirt he had worn for the races. He was covered in the dirt and grime of the horses. He had perspiration and dirt marks on his face and his short curly blond hair that had only recently dried from the sweat of his hard work.

"It looks like you've been doing a little bit of work yourself," Cara said with a grin.

"It has been crazy busy for this show but at the same time I love all of the action," said Michael. "It has been a wild ride so far."

"I'm glad to hear that you are having some fun," said Cara. "That isn't always easy at the end of the work when pure exhaustion just wants to set in."

"With Garret sitting in second spot it makes the load seem a little lighter," said Michael enthusiastically.

"Yes, he told me the great news over the phone," said Cara. "I can hardly wait to see him in person. He sounded so happy."

They travelled the balance of the journey making small talk about the horses, the people of the NCA and the fans that surrounded the sport. Before long they were back at the barn area of the stampede grounds where the sponsor-hosted parties were in full swing.

Michael dropped Cara off near Robert and Shana's holiday trailer where she would find Shana with Corby. He parked the truck and returned to the barns to finish any remaining chores for the evening. Robert was still in the barn helping. The horses had all been walked and bathed after the races and were now happily eating their evening feed and relaxing in their stalls.

Michael gathered up any items that needed to be stored before he washed the alley between the stalls and cleaned up with a large push broom. Garret was busy with his sponsors and their clients. They were having a barbeque just outside of the barn entrance. At last the work was finished for the evening.

"Thanks for your help Robert," said Michael.

"No problem Michael," replied Robert. "Cara got back here after all of her excitement?"

"Yup," said Michael. "She's in your trailer with Shana and Corby. "I guess the Hopkins' have a new baby boy."

"That's what I heard," said Robert. "That's great news. I'm going to grab a bite to eat from the sponsor's barbeque. I'm starving. Are you coming?"

"Sounds good to me," said Michael as he stored the broom he was still holding. They quickly washed their faces and hands at the sink nearby before making their way to the sponsor area.

When the two men arrived, the barbeque event was packed with guests. Garret was busy visiting with the sponsors and fans. It seemed everyone was eager to speak with him. He carried on many friendly conversations as he mingled throughout the crowd. His face always displayed a smile but his eyes suggested exhaustion.

Garret waved to Robert and Michael as they approached him with their plates of food in hand. Garret introduced them to the sponsors he was speaking with before finally being able to graciously exit the crowd to turn in for the night. The evening fireworks were beginning and Garret estimated the time to be near midnight.

When Garret arrived at his holiday trailer, he noticed the lights were still on inside. He thought this was unusual as he knew that Cara was back from the hospital and had picked up Corby from Shana's trailer a couple of hours earlier.

Once inside the trailer, Garret could hear Corby's cries from the back bedroom. Concerned, he immediately went to investigate. Cara was sitting on the bed with Corby propped over her shoulder, patting his back and rocking him back and forth as he cried.

"What's going on? Garret asked with concern.

"Corby has a bit of a fever," said Cara as she continued to rock the baby. "I think he is teething. I gave him some fever medication and I'm just hoping it will settle him down enough to fall asleep. I thought I would just lay down with him back here."

"Is there anything I can do?" asked Garret.

"No," answered Cara. "He'll be fine. He isn't terribly warm, he is just really agitated. You get some sleep and we'll be fine."

"As long as you're sure," said Garret as he kissed Cara on the top of her head. He ran a finger along his ailing son's cheek. "His little cheeks are so red."

"I know," said Cara. "It is just one of those baby things."

"Goodnight Cara," said Garret. "If you need me at all, please wake me."

"I will if I need to. Don't worry about us," said Cara. "We'll be fine. Oh, and Garret congratulations once again on a great night. We're very proud of you."

"Thank you again," Garret answered. "Coming from you, that means the world to me."

Garret gently closed the bedroom door behind him and made his way to the upper bedroom. He was exhausted and he knew that Cara was too. He hoped that Corby would fall asleep soon so that his wife could rest. They still had a long week ahead of them.

Cara ended up rocking Corby until about one in the morning before he finally fell asleep. Fortunately he was able to sleep through the night. In the morning he seemed to be back to his cheery self again.

The next afternoon it was learned that a healthy Barbie Hopkins and the new baby had already been released from the hospital. Barbie, the new baby and the rest of the Hopkins children would be spending the rest of the *Calgary Stampede* in Edmonton with Barbie's parents. The stampede grounds were no place for a new baby and an exhausted new mother. Barbie was a little upset as she had never missed a stampede by Neil's side since the year they were married but if he made the Dash she knew her parents would make arrangements for her to return. Neil would have to carry on without his family but he knew their support was with him and that was all that mattered.

The ten days of the stampede were zooming by and the excitement was growing in the McCormack barn. Night seven arrived and Garret was sitting firmly in second spot. A lot of other drivers had taken penalties in the first six nights but Garret had managed to stay away from the penalties. Dave Southern was also running clean and just a little faster. He was hanging on to the top spot. Neil was running a pretty successful Calgary but he had taken a barrel penalty and a late outrider penalty which had knocked him into eighteenth position. He was now well out of the chance to make the final heat.

Garret finished harnessing his team for the race while Michael saddled the outriding horses. Cara appeared at Garret's side momentarily to give him a quick good luck kiss before departing for the race-track with the outriding horses. Corby was already on his way to the track with his Auntie Shana while Robert busily checked over the wagon to make sure that it was ready for the race. Everything seemed to be in order.

Garret made his way to the track for the ninth and final heat of the evening. He moved to the ninth heat on the sixth night of the races as he now held the second spot overall. The later the heat, the better the driver was in the standings. Garret could not be happier with the success he was having.

All of the drivers made their practice turns, and drove up to their barrel positions to wait for the sound of the horn. When the horn blew Garret completed a seventh night's perfect turn out of the barrels and headed down the racetrack, winning the heat over Dave Southern. Garret was all smiles as he crossed the finish line but when he looked over his shoulder he only counted three of his four outriders making the journey with him. Garret hoped that he was wrong about that. As he pulled up his team and turned around on the track, he clearly heard the announcer speaking about the late outrider he had. He swallowed his disappointment as he waved to the cheering crowd before exiting the track for the barns. The penalty would cost him.

When Cara returned to the barn with the outriding horses she could sense Garret's disappointment. He was upset about the penalty he had received although he chatted amicably with the people around the barns. Cara gave Garret a wink as she rode past him to unsaddle the horses. He winked back at her.

"Nice run Garret," said Cara. "We'll get it back tomorrow."

"Thanks," said Garret. "I'm not going to panic about it."

Cara stopped near the stalls where the outriding horses could be unsaddled. She dismounted her horse and she and Robert tied them up and began unsaddling them. Soon the horses were all unsaddled and they took them to the wash bays for a quick bath. Michael and Garret took care of the wagon horses which also all needed to be washed and walked. There was never a shortage of work to be done around the barns.

The one second late outrider penalty was a disappointment but it was not going to hold Garret back. The only thing he felt he needed to do was have a strong day eight and nine which is exactly what he did. At the end of night nine the four drivers who would be racing in the $100,000 dash were announced and Garret made it. His sponsors and friends celebrated wildly at his barn while he turned in early to prepare for the race he had been waiting his whole life for. The next day he would have the chance to become the new *Calgary Stampede* champion. He could hardly believe this was happening for him.

When Garret entered the holiday trailer Cara let out a whoop. She jumped up from the couch and wrapped her arms around him. He held her tight and then kissed her hard on the mouth. They held each other for a long time, drinking in the moment.

"Can you believe it?" Garret exclaimed as he released Cara from his arms.

"Of course I can!" Cara grinned as she squeezed him once more before they both tumbled onto the couch. "I'm so happy for you."

"I'm so happy for us," said Garret. "This is our team. You know that I wouldn't even be looking at that dash tomorrow if it weren't for my team."

"I love you," said Cara.

"I love you too," replied Garret. "Thank you for being my rock and helping us to get to this point."

"I wouldn't want to be anywhere else," said Cara as she kissed him again.

Corby slept peacefully in his crib while Garret and Cara talked excitedly about the big race as they got ready for bed. Neither would get much sleep but they would try. When Garret climbed into bed he wrapped his arms around his wife. She snuggled close to him as they drifted off to sleep. She cherished it when he fell asleep holding her this way.

It was Day Ten of the *Calgary Stampede*. The McCormack barn crew was up early. Exhaustion was not slowing them down at all. The excitement stimulated them throughout the day. When the time came to get ready for the final race of the stampede, everyone eagerly pitched in to insure that things ran smoothly.

Garret was picked up in a truck driven by *Calgary Stampede* officials shortly before the start of the evening's races. He was driven to the infield where he stood on the stage in front of the capacity crowd that packed the huge grandstand. He and the three other *Dash for Cash* drivers drew for their barrel positions. Dave Southern had been in this position many times before and he made easy conversation as the men stood on the stage. Dave drew out of the hat for his barrel position first as he was the aggregate winner of the stampede. He drew the number two barrel. Karl Stern finished the regular show in second place. He drew barrel number four. Garret still managed to hang on to third spot and it was now his turn to draw. The crowd cheered as Garret pulled the number one position from the hat. This would leave barrel three for Grant Wagner who made the final spot in the dash. The crowd cheered at a deafening level as the drivers got back into the truck to return to the barns in preparation for the big race.

Garret's personal cheering section was in place. Dan and Mary Hartman came to Calgary for the finals. Both Cara's mom and her brother came in on a flight from Vancouver as soon as they confirmed that Garret would be in the dash. Garret's entire family had joined Robert and Shana for the big race. Garret's parents, Edward and Sharon had their seats front and centre. Their tickets had them seated near the top of barrel position two in the infield grandstand. Garret's sister Suzanne, her husband Barry and their twelve and fourteen year old daughters Casey and Morgan were even there. They lived in Edmonton and did not share Garret's love of racing but they were as excited for him as anyone.

Garret was quiet during the short ride back to the barns. It seemed unreal to him to be hooked in this big race with the guys that had been his heroes for what seemed like his whole life. The four men wished each other luck as they were dropped off at the barns before going their separate ways.

Cara and Robert had already left for the racetrack with the outriding horses and Corby was in the grandstand with Grandma Beaton and his Uncle Jason. All that was left to do was harness the team and win the race. Garret, Michael, and Shana joked with each other as they prepared for the race. Shana had stayed back to make sure the guys had an extra pair of hands if needed. They talked about anything in an effort to relax and to keep their nerves down. When it was finally time to go Garret felt that he was as ready as he could possibly get.

From her perch on the fence, Cara could see Garret pull out onto the backstretch of the track. She clenched her hands nervously on the fence railing. Her heart swelled with pride as she watched him appear to effortlessly drive through his practice turn. It never ceased to amaze her how calm he always seemed to be, no matter the stress of a situation. The crowd cheered loudly and Cara joined in. If nothing else, it calmed her nerves.

As Garret pulled up to barrel position one, he heard nothing but the clink of the chains in his team's harness as the restless horses waited to run. His black cowboy hat was pulled down firmly on the crown of his head and he focused straight ahead. His driving lines were clenched tightly in his fists as he held his team steady. The still evening air was penetrated by the sound of the horn. Garret's hands rose high in the air as he commanded his eager team to start. The crowd hollered encouragement to their favorite drivers as each surged forward to his top barrel. Garret's team turned a perfect barrel and he easily took command of the lead as he snatched the rail position of the track. The other drivers were in hot pursuit of Garret but it was truly his night to shine. He held the lead from start to finish.

When the head judge's word became official, Garret cried tears of joy at the realization that he had just made the latest page of the *Calgary Stampede* history book. Cara still had tears of happiness streaming down her face as the outriders returned their horses to her and offered their congratulations. Michael ran to the infield to take the outriding horses from Cara so that she would not miss out on Garret's award presentation on stage. Cara was grateful for his thoughtfulness. Cara fought her way back through the crowds in an effort not to miss the presentation.

Garret had to return his team to the barn before once again being picked up at the barns by race officials. They drove Garret to the main stage in front of the large grandstand to accept chuckwagon racing's highest honor. He was named *Calgary Stampede* champion and presented with a cheque for $100,000 in front of thousands of screaming fans. Nothing compared to the way he felt at this moment. He could not describe it even when the media asked him to.

Shortly after the awards presentation, Cara managed to make her way onto the stage with Corby in her arms. Karen began to move toward the stage immediately following the race so that Garret could have his son on stage with him. She managed to catch up to Cara and pass Corby to her before she ascended the stairs leading to the stage. The crowd cheered as Garret, Cara and Corby embraced. They cheered even louder when Cara latched onto Garret's lips for a long passionate kiss. A dream was realized on this night. It was something few people could ever hope to achieve. The moment was Garret's to own. The celebration at the McCormack barn amongst family, friends and sponsors lasted long into the light of the next day.

There was no rest time, even for a champion. The *Calgary Stampede* was over and it was expected that all of the drivers would be out of the grounds by noon so that the huge clean-up could begin. This was no easy task as the morning skies brought rain which made packing everything that much more difficult. Luckily for the McCormack's there was a lot of help around with all of the family and friends coming to the final night. It did not take long to pack. By eleven o'clock in the morning the McCormack's were covered in mud but leaving Calgary as champions. They would go home to rest their horses for a few days until it was time to move on to the last leg of the race season.

It was a muggy July day in the rain after having so many hot days. Garret was happy to get out onto the open highway where the horses could catch a better breeze through the trailer. Cara and Corby followed Garret and Michael down the highway. Other family members had departed earlier. The whole crew was still smiling with the victory still fresh on their minds.

As Garret entered a northbound curve on the highway between Calgary and Red Deer, he suddenly realized that the traffic was not moving due to a serious collision. With the weight of a full load of horses behind him he had little time to make a decision. He tapped at his brakes in an effort to slow down without rolling his liner. With no chance to get his truck stopped, he veered toward the left ditch in an effort to avoid the smaller vehicles stopped on the highway. His passenger, Michael grabbed at the dashboard as they veered over the edge of the pavement.

The ditch proved too sharp for such a large load and the truck and trailer tumbled over. The truck broke free of the trailer, rolling several times before coming to rest in the field. The trailer lay on its side in the ditch. The horses violently thrashed inside trying to free themselves. A crumpled heap of metal was all that remained of Garret's truck.

Cara watched in horror at the scene ahead of her which had literally taken seconds to unfold. She had time to stop before she reached the traffic as she had observed Garret trying to brake. She quickly unlatched Corby from his car seat and ran toward the wreckage with the baby in her arms. Because the police were already at the scene of the previous collision, they quickly attended the wreck. Beating Cara to the wreckage, the police and firefighters held her back.

"Ma'am you need to stay back!" the policeman was forceful.

"That's my husband in there!" she screamed back at him. "There are two men in that truck," she spoke with desperation to the officers.

One of the firefighters took Corby from Cara's arms as she collapsed to the ground. As the paramedics and police took control of the second accident scene, Cara sat in the ditch with Corby and a firefighter. She shook uncontrollably with fear and the chill of the pouring rain. One of the firefighters covered her and Corby with a blanket to protect them from the elements. She could hear the horses banging in the trailer, desperately trying to break free. She cried at the sound of their banging and whinnying and she cried waiting for the rescuers to bring her news.

In what seemed like hours, Michael was suddenly pulled from the wreckage. He appeared to have little more than superficial wounds as he stood on wobbly legs while the paramedics checked his vital signs. Cara felt a surge of hope until Michael caught her eye. Pushing the paramedics aside, he slipped and stumbled in the mud as he ran toward Cara and Corby. Garret was gone. Michael did not need confirmation from the paramedics to know this. He wrapped his arms around Cara and Corby as she screamed toward the weeping heavens and pounded her fists on his chest.

Chapter Seven

The Tuesday following the end of the *Calgary Stampede* was the day that Cara began to make the funeral arrangements for her husband. The funeral would take place in their home town. This was the town that they had built their dreams around. This was a town that should have been celebrating their *Calgary Stampede* champion's homecoming, not asking what they could do to help prepare for his funeral.

Cara methodically made the arrangements that she felt would honor Garret's memory best. She spent a great deal of time thinking about what he would have wanted and then she went out and made it happen or found someone who could.

Cara felt that Garret would have wanted the day to be a tribute to his life. He would not have wanted people to mourn him. He would have wanted his racing friends to be there as they had always been there for him so Cara made sure that the funeral would take place before the NCA's regular season tour resumed. She spoke with the minister at their community church and he agreed that the funeral could take place as early as Friday.

Cara contacted the pallbearers immediately so they would know of the arrangements. She had asked Grant Wagner, Neil Hopkins, Karl Stern and Dave Southern to be pallbearers. She also asked two of Garret's long time friends from Spruce View that he had grown up with. She spoke with Dan Hartman and asked that he give the eulogy. She felt that Dan knew Garret well but he would still be able to handle the emotional task. Dan was honored by her request.

The ladies from the church sat with Cara to arrange what would be served for lunch following the funeral. A caterer was contacted to make the lunch as it was felt the crowd would be too large for the church ladies to handle. The church ladies would put out the food and organize the lunch as needed. It was expected that about eight hundred people would attend.

The final task for Cara was to meet with the funeral director to pick out Garret's casket and drop off his clothes. She picked out a simple oak casket with fine detailing before handing the funeral director Garret's clothes. Cara knew that Garret would not want to spend eternity in anything other than western attire.

She had chosen black *Wrangler* jeans, his western cut dress jacket, and a simple tan coloured western shirt with a black tie. She further explained that his favorite cowboy hat would also need to be placed in the casket. As Garret's second passion outside of horse racing was hockey, she had to chuckle a little through her tears as she explained to the funeral director that Garret would wear his beloved *Edmonton Oilers* t-shirt underneath his western outfit. The funeral director smiled at Cara and nodded his head knowingly. He too had a lump in his throat at the thought of burying a man he had known for most of his life.

With what seemed to be the last of the arrangements completed, Cara drove home and collapsed on her bed in a heap of exhaustion and sobs. Mary Hartman had been watching Corby for Cara and she came to the bedroom and sat on the edge of the bed.

"It's just not fair," Cara sobbed with her face buried in the pillow. "We had everything going for us and then it just gets ripped away. I can't believe this is even my life."

"I know," said Mary as she placed a hand on Cara's shoulder. "It isn't fair at all." She knew that there was little she could say to comfort Cara at that point so she just rubbed her back until her sobs stopped and the poor woman finally drifted off to sleep. Mary covered Cara with a blanket from the end of the bed and quietly closed the bedroom door as she left the room.

Mary was playing with Corby when a rental car pulled into the driveway of the ranch. She recognized the driver to be Karen Beaton. She was happy to see Cara's mother. If there was ever a time Cara needed her mother, it was now. Karen and Jason Beaton had returned to Vancouver the day after the Stampede had ended but they were now at the ranch to help Cara in any way they could. Mary picked up Corby from the floor and went to the door to greet Karen and Jason. The three stared into each other's faces. They were all filled with exhaustion and despair. Looking at each other, they broke down and cried. Karen took Corby from Mary's arms and held him tight. The baby was oblivious to what was going on around him and cooed happily in the familiarity of his grandmother's arms.

Cara did not sleep for long. She recognized the voice of her mother in the foyer so she rose quickly to go and greet her. Before she left her bedroom she pulled a sweater from the closet to put on over her pink t-shirt and blue jeans. She felt cold all of the time. The grief was really overwhelming her.

As she turned from the closet, she looked at the family picture on her nightstand. Tears welled up in her eyes as she looked at Garret's smiling face. In the picture he was holding Corby in one arm while his other arm was wrapped snugly around Cara's waist. She took the sweater off and tossed it to the floor before crawling under the covers on the bed. Her mother could wait. She simply could not face another person right now. She softly cried herself back to sleep with the covers pulled over her head.

Cara dreamed beautiful dreams. She dreamed she was riding her horse alongside of Garret in a soft grassy meadow. They stopped for a while and got off of their horses. Garret was teasing Cara and as he grabbed her hand to pull her in for a kiss she noticed that she could not see his face. It was just a blank canvass and Garret's bright smile and beautiful eyes were not there at all. She awoke with a start.

It was evening now and Cara could smell supper cooking in the kitchen. With a lump in her throat and a heavy heart unlike anything she had ever known, she got up and headed for the kitchen. Karen came toward Cara as she entered the kitchen and embraced her daughter for a long time in silence. Her heart ached so much for her daughter but she knew that there was nothing she could do to fix it. Cara had suffered so much loss when her father had walked out on them, it did not seem fair that she should have to ever suffer so much again in her lifetime.

Mrs. Hartman had gone home shortly after Karen's arrival. Karen had gone to work putting together a beautiful meal for the three of them and she had already fed Corby. She tried her best to handle the things that she could take care of for her daughter.

The phone rang constantly throughout the evening but Karen took care of it and spoke with anyone who called. She felt that Cara would have enough to deal with the next day at the funeral. Cara and Jason had lots of time to talk which comforted her a great deal. They had been close as children so having this time together brought that closeness back for both of them.

"Is there anything at all you need from me for tomorrow?" Jason asked Cara as they sat quietly in the living room.

With his short straight brown hair and blue eyes, Jason looked a great deal like their mother. He had an athletic six foot frame which he easily maintained in his career as a high school physical education teacher. He leaned ahead in the easy chair he was seated in and grasped Cara's hands in his own.

"No, there's nothing more to be done," Cara replied. "I appreciate you being here though. I don't know if I have what it will take to get through tomorrow."

"Of course you do," said Jason earnestly. "You're still the toughest chick I know." He smiled at her as she leaned forward from the sofa to give him a hug.

Karen smiled through her tears as she walked into the living room with a freshly bathed Corby in her arms. It made her feel a little better to see Cara drawing on her brother for some strength.

"Corby is ready for bed," said Karen.

"Thank you Mom," said Cara. "I'll take him to bed," she said as she rose from the sofa.

"I can do it if you'd like," said Karen.

"You've done so much already Mom," said Cara. "You relax with Jason for a minute while I tuck Corby in."

"I'll put on a pot of tea," said Karen.

"That would be wonderful."

Karen handed Corby to Cara. His arms were outstretched toward his mother. She carried him to his room and laid him in his crib. She started his music mobile and he settled easily as he always did. As Cara watched him drift off to sleep, she saw a little smile on his face. Her throat tightened a little as she wondered if his Daddy was talking to him in his dreams.

"Get it together," Cara told herself. "You have a son to raise and a long road ahead of you. He doesn't need you breaking down at every turn."

For the first time since Garret's death only a few days earlier, she scolded herself for crying, pulled things together, kissed Corby on his soft forehead and quietly left his bedroom. She was determined to get through this and be the person that her son needed her to be.

When Cara returned to the living room where Karen and Jason sat, she felt as though she had interrupted a private conversation. The two ended their conversation the minute they noticed her return. Whatever the conversation, Cara was not interested or annoyed by the sudden stop. She entered the room in a completely different frame of mind. She did not know where this new strength was coming from but she planned to hang on to it. The three visited together, mostly telling funny stories about when they were growing up. As Cara laughed out loud during one of Jason's stories, she suddenly felt a little guilt. She actually found herself wondering if it were okay to laugh now with Garret gone. She also wondered if she would every really laugh freely again. She excused herself to go to bed. Tomorrow would be a long day.

Just as Cara was turning off the lights in the foyer, a quiet knock was heard at the door. As the door opened slightly, Michael peered inside. He was still staying in the spare house on the ranch and taking care of the chores. Two of Garret's wagon horses and one of his outriding horses had died in the wreck but the rest were spared and had only minor injuries. Michael had not been seen around the house too much but Cara often saw him working out in the barnyard.

"Hey Cara," Michael whispered. He stood in the foyer in a plaid work shirt and blue jeans. He had obviously been working all day.

"Michael," Cara said with concern. "How are you? Is everything okay out there? I feel like I have been totally ignoring you. I'm sorry for that."

"Hey, you have enough to worry about," said Michael. "Everything is fine. I was just wondering, well I know you wanted some horses hooked for the funeral but I'm not totally sure what you wanted or who is driving them and..." his words broke off.

"I'm sorry" he said. "I didn't mean to bother you with this. I can figure things out."

"No, don't be silly," said Cara. "It's fine. I'm the one who's sorry for keeping you in the dark. I know this hasn't been easy for you either. Neil Hopkins is going to drive the wagon team to the cemetery after the funeral. He knows what he is hooking and he will be by first thing in the morning. Can you please just help him out?"

"Of course I can," Michael said. "Anything you need at all."

"Thank you Michael," said Cara. "I'm sorry. It just kind of left my mind and I forgot to tell you."

"It's okay Cara," Michael replied. "You look like you were just going to bed so I will say goodnight."

"Goodnight Michael," said Cara. "And thank you for all of your help through this."

"Of course Cara," he replied. "If there is anything else that you need in the morning, you know where to find me." Michael closed the door softly and returned to the spare house. He felt terrible for Cara and for Corby. They would have such a long road ahead of them without Garret. He too was grieving Garret's death but along with his grief he felt guilt. He felt that he should have been the one to die in the wreck. He had no responsibilities or a family to look after. He felt that it would have been different if he had been the one to die. With no one to leave behind it would have been easier for so many people. Garret had a family who loved him and a new child. It hardly seemed fair that his number was up. His parents often said that when it was your time, it was your time but this still did not make it right as far as Michael was concerned.

Before Cara turned out the lights she sat down on her bed with her laptop balanced on her knees. She reviewed some of her email before suddenly deciding to take one last look at the racing blog

Garret maintained. It was filled with hundreds of tributes from people who truly loved him. There were even messages from strangers who had only seen him from a distance, racing around the track. There was also an outpouring of support and condolences for the family he left behind. Cara barely read any of the messages when her eyes became too blurred with tears to read anymore. She turned off the computer and the bedside lamp and quietly sobbed herself to sleep.

Cara rose early in the morning. It looked as though it would be a beautiful summer day. She quickly showered and started breakfast even before Corby woke up. Both her mother and Jason joined her in the kitchen for coffee and they visited as though it were a day like any other. When Corby awakened she fed him and dressed him just shortly before Mrs. Hartman's granddaughter, Riley arrived. She would be watching Corby as Cara felt he was too young to attend the funeral. Riley was thirteen years old. She lived in Edmonton but she was staying with her grandparents for a few weeks of her summer vacation. She knew the McCormack's but not well enough to need to attend Garret's funeral so she offered to babysit while the funeral service was on.

"Have you had breakfast yet Riley?" Cara asked as the girl scooped up Corby to play with him. Her dark red hair glistened in the morning sun.

"Grandma had a big breakfast ready before I left," replied Riley. "You just let me know where everything is and that will free you up to do anything you need to do."

"Thank you Riley. I really appreciate your help."

"Of course," she said as she gave Cara a hug. "I'm very sorry for your loss."

"Thank you Riley," said Cara. "Corby has had his breakfast and he was just changed before you got here so he should be happy for a while."

Cara showed Riley where all of Corby's things were before leaving her to play with Corby while she got dressed in her bedroom. She moved somewhat mechanically throughout the morning but she managed to keep moving nonetheless. She was glad she had her family there for support. She did not even need them to say anything, she just needed their presence.

Cara looked through her closet aimlessly. She never thought the day would come that she would be picking out clothes for her husband's funeral, at least not at this stage of her life. She chose a simple black suit which consisted of a knee-length skirt and matching jacket with button detailing. She picked a deep purple blouse and low black heels to wear with it.

She would wear her diamond engagement ring along with her wedding ring and the pearl earrings that Garret had given her the day they were married. She had rarely worn her engagement ring for fear she would catch it on something while working with the horses. Looking at the diamond now, she fought back her tears.

Cara pulled her hair back from her face in a simple knot and clasped it with a barrette. Her makeup was kept minimal as it always was. She felt as though she were walking around in a dream, watching someone else. Nothing seemed real anymore.

Cara gave herself a moment to breathe as she looked at her reflection in the mirror. She was determined to get through this day. She grabbed some tissues from the bathroom and put them in her purse before leaving her bedroom. Jason and Karen were waiting for her in the kitchen.

"Are you ready to go sweetheart?" asked Karen.

"I'm ready Mom," she answered softly. She kissed Corby on the forehead as he bounced happily in Riley's arms. "See you soon my son." Cara turned away from Corby as one tiny tear escaped her.

As the trio left the house Michael met them in the driveway. He said a soft good morning before advising Cara that the horses were ready and he would wait for Neil to arrive to take the team to the funeral. Cara thanked him. It seemed that everything was arranged and she had nothing left to do but face the day.

Karen, Jason and Cara took the rental car to the church in time to meet with the minister before the funeral began. The family was asked to wait in a small waiting room at the back of the church while the guests arrived for the funeral. For Cara, the wait felt burdensome as she pondered how she would face those in attendance. Soon the minister came to the waiting room to tell the family that it was time to be seated.

Cara led the group with her mother and brother by her side while Garret's parents, brother and sister along with their families followed close behind. Schubert's *Ave Maria* sung by members of the church choir, ushered the family in. Cara's heart crumbled as she walked past their many friends on her way to the front of the church. Garret had been so loved.

The funeral service consisted of many beautiful tributes as well as several humorous stories about Garret's life. When Dan Hartman came to the front of the church to do his eulogy Cara felt her throat tighten a little as she noticed the tears gleaming in his eyes. He smiled at her reassuringly before he began.

Garret was a strong man who was loved by many and I was honored to be one of the people who could call him a friend. He was important to so many people. He was a husband, a father, a friend, a neighbor, a hockey coach and truly an angel who walked among us that God has called back home...

Cara could no longer hold back her tears as Dan continued the story of the man that she had loved.

Many of you knew Garret for his love of wagon racing but he was so much more than that man to many people. He and Cara built their lives in Spruce View and along with that they never hesitated to help build this community. As many of you know, Cara is a teacher here and Garret often volunteered with the kids at the school who perhaps didn't have the opportunities all kids should have. He helped to raise funds to get those less fortunate kids equipment for sports and many of those kids he took out to the McCormack ranch so that they could fulfill their dream of learning to ride a horse .He was a very active hockey coach who looked forward to coaching his own son one day.

When I look around this room at all of you here today, I think that it is truly a testament to this man that we all cared so much about. We love you and we will miss you my friend.

Dan choked out his final sentence before departing the podium. Cara rose from her seat and hugged him before he returned to his own seat. There was not a dry eye in the church.

After the service Neil Hopkins pulled up in front of the church with Garret's horses hitched to the wagon. Garret's casket was loaded into the back of the wagon by the pallbearers and driven the few blocks to the graveyard. Cara was not prepared for the emotions she felt as Garret's coffin was lowered into the ground. She was sure that she would wake up from this horrible nightmare at any moment. After a few moments she left the gravesite in silence, hanging on to her mother and brother for support.

Upon attending the hall for lunch, Cara spoke with as many people as she could. She was hardly in the mood for conversation but at the same time everyone that attended was important to her. She spoke with every wagon driver along with their wives. Every outrider approached her to offer their condolences as well. It almost angered her that they would all leave this hall with their families and their lives virtually untouched and she would still be left with this nightmare. Why her? Why Garret? These would be the questions that would pull at her heart for a long time to come.

When the lunch had finished and most of the crowd departed, Cara's mother told her that it would be okay for her to leave if she was ready go. She was more than ready to go. She just wanted to be anywhere else in the world right now. She just wanted her life back.

"I'm ready Mom," said Cara. Just give me one minute to speak with Garret's Mom and Dad." Cara walked over to Edward and Sharon and the three of them hugged tightly.

"Let us know if you need anything at all Cara," said Edward in a weak voice.

"You guys too," answered Cara. "Please come over when things have settled down a little. It would be good for Corby to see you."

"We will," said Sharon. "You take care of little Corby and if you need anything at all, you call us first."

"I will," said Cara. They hugged again before Cara walked to the car. She knew that the loss of their son was more than they could bear right now. They would all have to get through this together.

As Cara walked toward the exit she felt a light grasp at her forearm. She turned to see Darryl Baker looking at her with so much empathy in his eyes. He was dressed in western dress attire the same as many of the cowboys in attendance. Cowboys do not usually wear suits but they always dress in their finer clothes, their best jeans and their best cowboy hats for events that matter to them. This was one of those days.

For so long Darryl was one of Garret's best outriders. He was a part of their family. He hugged

Cara before he spoke a word. She squeezed her eyes tightly as she returned the hug. She did not want anymore tears to escape.

"I'm so sorry Cara," said Darryl. "If there is anything that you need..."

"There's nothing Darryl," Cara replied. "Thank you for being here. You meant a great deal to Garret, to all of us."

"He was a hell of a guy," Darryl spoke softly. "I really meant what I said about if you need anything. I know people always say that but I want to help if I can."

"Thank you Darryl," said Cara. "I appreciate your offer. Right now there isn't anything but I'll call you if something comes up. I want to get home to Corby now but thank you again for being here."

"I understand," said Darryl. "Just remember the offer is there, okay?"

"I will," said Cara squeezing his hand before walking out the door. She spotted the car and headed directly toward it, hoping that she would not have to have another conversation that afternoon.

Karen, Jason and Cara drove home in near silence. They were physically and emotionally exhausted from the day and the quiet was nice. With Jason driving the car and Karen in the front passenger seat, Cara stared out the window from the rear seat she occupied. She admired the beautiful summer day as she looked out over the miles of blooming mountain flowers that dotted the pastures. She thought about how this would have been the perfect day to go riding down to the creek with Garret. There was never time to ride their saddle horses during race season and now there would never be another chance, ever. Once again Cara found herself squeezing back the tears.

When the car pulled up in front of the house back at the ranch, Cara went in to see Corby and let Riley go home to enjoy the rest of the summer day. She walked around the house performing tasks methodically. Jason exchanged glances with his mother as they watched her. When she finally left Corby with Karen so that she could go change her clothes, Jason had the opportunity to speak with their mother in private.

"I think we need to finish the conversation we were having last night," said Jason to Karen.

"I don't know if this is the best time Jason," Karen replied. "She's just buried her husband. I think we at least need to give her some time to properly grieve."

"Well, you know what's best," said Jason. "I'm just really worried. I've never seen her like this. I know she has lost a lot but I don't want her to lose herself too."

Cara had been gone quite a long time by now and Karen thought she should go check on her. When Karen knocked on the bedroom door there was no answer so she let herself into the room. Cara was sound asleep on the bed, wrapped in one of Garret's old sweatshirts. Her hair was damp on the sides of her head from crying. Maybe Jason was right, perhaps it was time to discuss their plans with her.

Close to supper time, the ringing of the phone awakened Cara. She reached for the phone on the nightstand before anyone else in the house had a chance to answer it. Grant Wagner was on the other end of the line. Cara sat up in an effort to fully wake up.

"Hi Cara," said Grant. "I hope I'm not disturbing you?"

"No, no of course not," answered Cara trying to sound like she had not been asleep. "How are you?"

"I'm fine Cara. The service today was real nice," said Grant sincerely.

"Thank you," answered Cara.

"Look, I'm not calling to upset you. It's just that there isn't a great deal of time to make a decision," said Grant.

"What do you need Grant?" asked Cara.

"Well, to cut to the chase, I spoke with the officials from the NCA and they are willing to let me run another outfit to fill Garret's spot," explained Grant. "Now before you think I'm some disrespectful ass I want you to understand my reasoning."

"Really Grant, I would never think that," said Cara, a lump rising in her throat. "You have done far too much for our family for me to ever think that."

"Well Cara, then what I'm hoping for is that you will let me use Garret's horses," said Grant.

"What?" She was not sure if she had heard him right.

"I want to use Garret's horses not only in his memory but also to get you a fair price for them at the end of the season. I can't imagine you wanting all of those race horses kicking around your place anymore."

Cara felt the tears slip from her eyes at the thought of the horses. It had not occurred to her that the best thing for them would be to find them new homes where they could continue their racing careers.

"I, I hadn't really thought about any of this," said Cara in a trembling voice.

"I'm sorry Cara. I'm not trying to put this all on you now. It's just that I have to leave for the next show as early as tomorrow and if you want to do this then I need your answer pretty fast," Grant reasoned.

"No, of course," said Cara trying to think. "I understand and the answer is yes. There is no person that I would rather see race those horses than you. I really appreciate your offer."

Grant and Cara stayed on the phone for a few more minutes to discuss the arrangements. She agreed that Grant could have the use of any of Garret's equipment that he might need and if Michael agreed, she would pay him to travel with Grant to look after the horses.

Cara hung up the phone with new business to attend to. She quickly dressed in blue jeans and a t-shirt along with the sweatshirt of Garret's that she had been wrapped in. She needed to go discuss her plans with Michael right away.

Karen and Jason were speculating about the phone call when they saw Cara zip past the kitchen and run outside. They watched her dart across the barnyard toward the barn and they wondered what on earth could be so urgent. They looked at each other with puzzled looks as Karen continued to prepare supper while Jason played with Corby.

"Michael, are you in here?" Cara called as she opened the barn door.

"I'm down here," his answer came from the far end of the barn.

Cara walked past all of the horses in their stalls to the far end of the barn where she spotted Michael pouring feed into the horse troughs. The hay had already been rationed out.

"You still have them on their regular feeding program?" said Cara.

"Yeah, I um, well I didn't know if I should change things or not," Michael tried to explain. "I thought that they should still be on all of their vitamins as well just to get over the, well the accident."

"No, this is perfect," explained Cara. "They are going to be leaving for the next show in the morning and you are going to be travelling with them if you are willing?"

"Whoa, back up a little", said Michael. "What do you mean?" He was afraid the emotions of recent events had made Cara lose her mind.

"Grant Wagner called," she said. "He is going to be running the team. I want you to travel with the horses, look after them, and help Grant. I can pay you from the sale of the horses."

Cara and Michael sat on some straw bales in the barn and discussed the situation for a long time.

Michael agreed that he would finish the season with Grant. When they finished their long discussion, Cara invited Michael to come to the house for supper so that he could help her explain everything to her family. They were going to think she had lost her mind. She knew they were discussing what they thought was best for her behind her back. She knew they would want her to sell the horses now and be done with it but she simply could not bring herself to do that.

Cara returned to the house with Michael. The smell of steaks grilling on the barbeque wafted through the air from the deck. As they entered the house Cara could hear the clinking of dishes as Karen and Jason finished preparing the meal.

"We're going to have one more guest," Cara called to them from the foyer.

Cara washed for supper in the bathroom just off the foyer as Michael went in to say hello. When Cara returned to the kitchen Michael took the opportunity to wash for dinner as well.

"Supper smells wonderful," said Cara. "I'm starving."

"Well that's nice to hear," said Karen as she finished tossing the salad. "It is nice to see you are getting your appetite back."

"Yeah, I'm feeling much better Mom and I sort of have some news," said Cara in a hesitant voice.

"What news?" Jason asked as he set the table.

By now Michael had returned to the kitchen so Cara felt she could tell Jason and Karen the plan.

"Well," Cara began. "You know I received a phone call before I went running outside?"

"Yes, continue," said Karen with anticipation.

"It was Grant Wagner. He made a bid with the NCA to fill the open spot on the tour. He wants to use Garret's horses so that I will be able to sell them for a good price. Drivers will pay more for horses they can see in action than ones that are just standing in the pasture and Calgary proved that Garret's horses have what it takes to be champions. Anyhow, to make a long story short, I agreed to his terms and Michael agreed to finish the tour and look after the horses," Cara rushed through the details as Michael nodded in agreement.

"Wow," said Karen hesitantly. "I guess that's good."

"Of course it's good Mom," said Cara feeling a little exasperated by both her mother and brother's lack of reaction.

"It would be pretty difficult for me to sell these horses on my own and God knows I can't keep them no matter how much it hurts to let them go," Cara tried to explain.

"No, I understand," said Jason. "This is a good thing. It will be much easier for you to sell this place if you don't have to worry about finding homes for all of the horses."

"Sell this place?" Cara stared at her family in disbelief. "That's what you think!"

"Cara, don't get all pissed off at me," Jason raised his voice slightly. "I'm not trying to be the bad guy here. I just don't see why you would stay out here and try to be this ranch girl or whatever when you could come home to Vancouver with Corby where you will have the support you need. I can get you a job teaching there and you can get on with your life."

"Well I'm so glad you've got things all figured out for me!" Cara's voice rose in anger. "Is that what the two of you have been scheming about every time I leave the room? I've got news for you, this is my home and this is Corby's home and this is where we will be!" Cara was crying now as she stormed out of the kitchen.

Steak, shrimp, baked potatoes and salad filled the supper table but suddenly no one was hungry. Michael made an excuse to leave the house and check something in the barn while Karen glared at Jason for bringing everything up the way he had. Cara took Corby to the bedroom with her when she left the kitchen. He was her family now and she would not take everything away from him. Running back to Vancouver is not what Garret would have wanted and it was not what she wanted either. After all of this time she thought her family knew her better than that.

Cara bathed Corby in the tub in the master bathroom. They played together on the bed for a while until it was Corby's bedtime. Cara only returned to the kitchen long enough to retrieve a bottle for Corby. Karen had cleaned up the kitchen and put the food away. She was now in the living room reading a magazine but she did not make any effort to speak to Cara when she saw her. She could tell when her daughter simply needed her space.

Jason had retreated to the family room to watch some television. He felt bad that he had angered his sister but he also felt that she was just being stubborn. As if she needed the hassle of running this ranch. He had no idea what exactly she felt she needed to prove at this point but he certainly was not going to cross her on the issue again. He would give her the night to cool off and he would speak to her in the morning before he and his mother left to catch their flight back to Vancouver.

Early in the morning Grant arrived as promised and Michael helped load the horses. Grant had an extra trailer which his hired hand would drive for him to get the horses to the next show. Grant and Michael loaded the supplies they would need and before long they were ready to leave. They stopped at the house to say goodbye. Cara answered the door when she saw them approaching.

"I see you're all set," said Cara trying not to get too emotional.

"Yup, we're ready to go," replied Grant. He hugged Cara as he tried to hold back his own emotions.

"Good luck," said Cara. "Thanks Michael. If you need anything call me and also give me a call once in a while just to let me know how things are going."

"We will for sure," answered Michael. He too hugged Cara before turning to go to the truck.

"We'll take good care of them, don't worry," said Grant before he turned to leave.

Cara watched as the trailer departed down the gravel road until she could no longer see the dust from the vehicle. The tears fell from her cheeks as her thoughts returned to Garret and how they should all be travelling down the road right now as a family.

Jason, Karen and Cara made amends before they departed for the airport. Each apologized for their own outbursts and doubts about how Cara would make it on her own.

"You've always been a strong woman Cara," said Karen. "I know that you will get through this on your own terms but if you need us don't be too proud. That's all I'm asking."

"Thank you Mom," said Cara as she hugged her mother. "We'll be fine."

"I'm sorry Cara," said Jason as he hugged his sister. "I'm just worried about you."

"I know," said Cara. "Just don't worry. We will be okay and if we're not you'll be the first to know."

"Okay," said Jason. "I'll hold you to that."

Jason and Karen hugged Corby and handed him back to Cara as they got into their rental car to return to the airport. She watched them leave and waved Corby's little arm goodbye to them. She rocked him in her arms and as she turned to go into the house, she suddenly realized that she had never felt so alone in her life.

"We're going to be just fine sweetheart," she said to Corby as she kissed him on his tiny head. She was trying hard to reassure herself but the pangs of loneliness were already attacking her and her tears began to fall. She had never simply been left. If the races were on, she was there. She had no idea how to deal with her feelings right now. She wondered what she was supposed to do while everyone else carried on with their lives.

As the summer wore on, Cara busied herself doing a lot of the things she never had the time for in the past with all of the race travel. She tended to both her vegetable garden and her flower garden which were usually quite badly neglected. This gave Corby lots of outdoor time in his playpen. With a little help from Mary, she learned how to can some preserves. She bought a carrier for Corby that she could strap on her back. With Corby safely attached to her, they spent many hours on her faithful horse exploring the countryside. She saw beauty in everyday things that she somehow never noticed before and more importantly, she let her heart begin to heal.

Sometimes Cara just sat back and thought how funny it was the way so many things had changed in her life and yet how they seemed to stay the same. She looked after her son, she tended to her yard, she still wondered what the future had in store for her and she still checked the daily race stats. It was different to be at home, listening to the races on the internet, but she still cared about those people and their lives. It was not just something she could let go of.

In between all of her activities she did to keep busy, she received many phone calls from Michael. They discussed the horses and how the races were going. Michael said that Grant already had buyers lined up for several of her horses. Everything seemed to be going well on the tour and somewhere along the line Michael and Cara began to really get to know each other in all of their conversations. They often found themselves having regular conversations about other things besides horses and Cara noticed that she was starting to look forward to Michael's calls. It was nice to have a friend, especially one that she seemed to have so much in common with.

Oftentimes, Darryl Baker would call to see how Cara was doing. He loved to talk about what was going on at the racetrack. She enjoyed hearing his stories about the races or the latest outrider antics. It was nice to have someone else call that was not afraid to tell her what was going on. It actually made her feel good to know that fun things in life were still happening. It seemed that the majority of the people from the NCA were avoiding her. Michael and Darryl were the only two people who still talked to her about racing and they made no apologies for it. She appreciated that as she struggled in this strange new world of hers.

Everyone who had been so supportive at the funeral really had no time for her now. They had all gone back to their lives. Most of the people whom she considered friends were on the tour, busy with their own families. At first some had called but it always seemed awkward. They did not seem to know what to say. It was like they were all afraid of bringing up Garret's name and hurting her. People were over protective of her feelings and in the end, they simply stopped calling. Cara and Corby spent the majority of their time at home, alone.

A few days before the NCA finals, which were to be held during the September long weekend, Michael called to say that he would be coming home for a while. He told Cara that things were going well but he just wanted to take a break for a few days to get organized for the work he had planned for the autumn season.

When Michael pulled into the driveway in a truck he borrowed from Grant, Cara and Corby went out to greet him. At first glance of the two of them standing on the sidewalk, Michael almost felt nervous. Cara looked beautiful in a pale blue cotton sundress, her long auburn hair tumbling over her tanned shoulders. Corby seemed to have grown a foot since Michael had seen them last.

"Get serious," Michael told himself as he parked the truck. "This woman lost her husband six weeks ago, she is your boss in all reality and she hardly needs some guy in her life right now. As if I could ever fit into that picture anyhow. Just get out of the truck, put your head on straight and tell her what you're really here for." Michael waved back as the pair waved to him.

"Hey Cara," Michael said as he approached them.

"It's good to see you," she said as she leaned over to give him what seemed a rather awkward hug. "Do you have time for some iced tea or something?"

"That sounds good," replied Michael.

"Why don't you take Corby around to the deck and I'll go in the house and get the tea and glasses," said Cara as she handed Corby to Michael.

"Um, okay," he said as he took Corby from her arms. "How are you doing little man? It's been a while." Corby happily kicked his feet and cooed as he looked up at Michael with his big blue eyes.

Cara went into the house to retrieve the iced tea. As she took the cool drink from the refrigerator and placed the pitcher on a tray with some glasses, she thought to herself that Michael seemed a bit awkward. She concluded that they had not really seen each other since the funeral so maybe it was just hard for him to be back here. She took the tray out to the deck and brushed the thought from her mind.

It was a beautiful day for late August. When Cara appeared on the deck she smiled at Corby who was happily chewing on his teething ring as he bounced on Michael's knee.

"Here we are," said Cara setting the tray down. She took Corby from Michael and placed him in his playpen nearby so that they could drink their tea.

"So you're back to get things in order before you go back to the oil patch?" asked Cara as she leaned back in a deck chair sipping her tea.

"Well, yes and no," answered Michael as he swirled the ice cubes in his glass.

"That's a pretty definitive answer," she laughed. "You're starting to sound like a wagon driver," she teased.

He smiled at her thinking how relaxed she seemed and how maybe this was the right time to bring up his business idea.

"Cara, I don't know if you're going to think I'm crazy or not but I figured the worst thing that can come out of this is you saying no," Michael tripped over his words.

"You've definitely got my attention," Cara said sitting up in her chair. "What's going on?"

"Well, I've been doing a lot of work with the horses and Grant and Karl Stern have been giving me lots of opportunities to drive the wagons, the same way my Uncle Bill always did. The same way that Garret did," his words broke off slightly. He did not want to upset Cara by mentioning Garret but he did want her to know how much Garret's help had meant to him. "Look, I know they're your horses but I'd like to make you a deal before you decide to sell to other people," Michael spoke slowly in an effort to fully articulate what he was trying to say to her.

"Okay, I'm not sure if I'm totally following you yet," Cara said still smiling.

"I want to make a deal with you to buy the horses," he finally said.

"What? Why? Are you planning to race them?" asked Cara in disbelief.

"Well, I know that probably sounds crazy because when I came here a few months ago I was just interested in getting started a few years down the road but now I think I've got the itch," he tried to explain. Grant thinks I should try for a spot on the tour for next year but I won't do it without your blessing and I can't do it without your help," Michael finished.

"I have to say, I'm more than a little shocked Michael," said Cara. "That's a huge step. I mean I knew that was your ultimate plan, I just didn't think that was your plan so soon? Running with the NCA is no small thing. I'm not trying to be your mother or anything but there is a lot more to consider than just getting in. It's expensive, it's a lot of thankless work day after day for maybe a little payoff now and then, and it's a huge commitment. Regardless, you hardly need my blessing if this is what you want to do. Our deal was simply to get Garret's horses through the season. You don't owe me anything," she took a breath as she finished speaking her mind.

"The thing is, I really can't go it alone," said Michael. "I need your horses and I want your expertise. I can't afford to just start up on my own for one thing. I know that it is a big commitment and I also know that you know that as well as anyone. I was hoping we could have a business partnership in this until I can pay you back and keep things afloat on my own. I was also hoping you would help me out with all of the work."

"I, I don't know Michael," Cara hesitated. "You're asking a lot. It's not that I don't want to help you out but I don't know that I can afford to keep the horses and look after things all winter. I'm going back to work in the fall while you go back to work somewhere in the patch. It's just more responsibility than

I can handle. I'm sorry. I know what it's like to love these animals and live for that dream."

"Please just hear me out before you say no for sure," he said. "I will pay for their winter feed and I will look after them. I can get an oilfield operator's contract right in this area. In fact, I've already checked and I've got a guy calling me back this afternoon with an offer. If you let me rent the spare house, I will make sure the horses are looked after and all of the chores are done. You can carry on with your job and whatever else it is that you and Corby plan to do."

Michael held Cara's attention as he continued to tell her of his plans. "Grant has already put the price on the horses for sale so that any interested buyers know. I will pay that price so you know the price is fair. I will pay you back for the horses and I will pay the fees to get into the NCA. I'm not just messing around Cara. I've done my research. So what do you say?" his eyes were almost pleading with her.

"Well, Mr. DeWalt," Cara answered with a smile. "I'd say you are obviously crazy enough to be a wagon driver and other than working out a few details, I think you've got yourself a deal." Cara extended her hand to Michael but he jumped out of his chair and gave her a huge hug instead.

"Thank you so much Cara!" he exclaimed. "You have no idea what this means to me!"

"Oh, I think I have a rough idea," she laughed. "You just get back to that track and get yourself qualified first of all."

"I will," he said. "I won't let you down."

"I'm not worried," said Cara as she finished her iced tea.

"Thanks for the iced tea," said Michael. "I really have to be going. I do have a lot to do before I get back to the track."

"I believe it," said Cara waving him off as he jumped from the top step of the deck.

Cara gathered the empty glasses on the tray and took them into the house before returning to pick Corby up from his playpen. She could not believe Michael was considering this and she could not believe she agreed to this partnership. She hoped she would not regret her decision. She was not sure she wanted to remain around such a strong memory of Garret. It would not be easy for her. She really hoped that keeping the horses would not mean keeping her wounds open as well.

Chapter Eight

In order to qualify to become a driver with the National Chuckwagon Association, any interested driver must have at least four drivers from the NCA vouch for his driving ability in a signed letter presented to the NCA Board of Directors. Once the signed letter is received, the driver is given dates and times to race on the track in three exhibition races against three current NCA drivers. These races are observed by a panel of seven NCA driver/directors. These are the drivers who hold the top seven places in the NCA standings at the end of the Tour season.

If the panel is satisfied with the driver's abilities in the exhibition races, the driver is invited to race in a competition where the top five drivers will qualify for a spot on the NCA Tour. If the driver accepts the invitation to join the Tour he must write a membership cheque to the NCA for $25,000. Drivers from the current year's tour who find themselves in the bottom five spots must re-qualify for one of the five spots.

Competition is fierce for any open spots on the Tour as the NCA is the top-paying, most recognized association in the profession which means that their prize money and sponsorship is always the highest.

Cara had not heard anything from Michael on the days she knew he was competing but she did not want to call him. She remembered Garret earning his stripes to get in and she also remembered the pressure being enormous. She had checked the internet for news of the driver standings but found no information.

The day the qualifications ended, Cara eagerly awaited the news from Michael. Finally, toward evening Grant's pickup rumbled up the driveway pulling the loaded horse trailer. Cara watched out the window as they drove past the house to unload the horses at the barn. She desperately wanted to run to the barn to get all of the details but she decided against it. If things did not go well it would be easier for Michael to tell her on his own terms.

After what seemed like an eternity, Michael came walking up to the house as Grant drove back down the driveway. Cara was trying to read his body language but she really could not tell if he seemed pleased or not. She opened the door of the house before Michael had a chance to knock. He looked surprised to see her standing there waiting for him.

"Well?" was all Cara said as Michael stood looking at her from the porch.

Michael smiled at Cara who stood in the doorway with her hands on her hips, a million questions in her eyes. It was a sparkle of anticipation that he had not seen on her face since before the accident and he thought the look suited her. She looked beautiful in her blue jeans and a simple fitted white polo shirt. Her hair was pulled back and held in a hair clip. He felt pretty grungy standing there in his dirty jeans, t-shirt and worn out ball cap but he knew that she understood the work and the dirt that came with it.

"Well Cara, I have to admit there was a lot more to it than I thought there would be," he said with a grim look on his face.

"Yeah, it's not easy to get in that's for sure," Cara answered cautiously. "It's not the end of the world if you didn't make it Michael. Some things just aren't meant to be."

"I know, I was thinking that exact same thing," he said. "I just wanted it so bad and lucky for me, it was apparently meant to be!" He burst out laughing as he shared his good news.

"Oh, ha, that's really funny," she shook her head. "You got me! Now I don't know if I should congratulate you or not." She laughed as she stepped aside to invite Michael into the house.

"Come on Cara, I couldn't just tell you. That wouldn't have been any fun at all," he said still laughing.

"I'm glad to see you have a sense of humor anyhow Michael. You will need it to get through the days ahead. You may as well come in and sit down and we can start making some sort of a training plan for you," she smiled at him as he took off his shoes and followed her toward the kitchen table.

Cara stopped at the phone desk along the wall to get a pen and paper. After setting the items on the table she went to the refrigerator to get them something cool to drink. She spotted some beer on the bottom shelf and held one up to offer it to Michael.

"That would probably taste pretty good right now," he said. "Thank you."

Cara poured the beer into a frosty mug before setting it on the table in front of Michael. She then turned back to the kitchen to retrieve a bottle of wine from the wine cooler and a wine glass from a cabinet. She opened a bottle of chardonnay at the counter and poured herself a glass before sitting down on a chair adjacent to Michael.

"Where do you want to start with this?" Cara asked, pen poised and ready.

"What do you mean? I actually have no idea what we are supposed to be planning," Michael looked confused.

Cara laughed. "Well, what Garret and I used to do after the race season was write down a list of what we had for horses, what positions on the team needed improvement, what we needed to buy for additional horsepower, that sort of thing."

"Oh, I'm not sure. I just don't even know where to start," said Michael looking uncertain.

"Okay, I think maybe I have a better idea," said Cara getting up from the table. "Come on," she said gesturing for him to follow her.

They went into the family room where Cara turned on the TV and the DVD player. She began to rummage through her collection of DVD's, picking out a few and setting them aside.

"These were Garret's DVD's from the last two seasons," she said. "He used to pay Grant's wife Nicole to film his races so that he could see how his horses were performing. Obviously some of the horses are no longer on the team but for the most part it shows what we have to work with. It should give you a pretty good idea of who drives best where and what their quirks are, that sort of thing."

"That's perfect," said Michael. "I mean, I have a pretty good idea of where the strength in the team is but it would help to watch a few races too. Let's see what we've got." He settled into an easy chair, his beer in hand, ready to watch the racing footage.

Cara slid the first DVD into the player and sat down on the sofa with the remote in one hand and her glass of wine in the other. She felt her breath catch in her throat as the DVD began to play and Garret talked to the camera. Nicole had filmed him hooking up the team at the barn in Grand Rapids. He was telling jokes to the camera as he talked race strategy. Cara felt the tears sting her eyes when Nicole's camera caught Garret kissing her and Corby goodbye as they went to find a seat for Corby's first ever race.

Michael leaned forward in his chair and placed his hand on Cara's knee. "Hey, we don't have to do this now," he said in a soft voice. "There's plenty of time for this and besides, it's getting late. I'm pretty tired from everything anyhow."

"Maybe you're right," said Cara looking at him with tears in her eyes. "We'll do this some other night."

Michael rose from his chair and returned his beer mug to the kitchen. He turned to Cara who stood a short distance behind him.

"It's going to get better you know," he looked at her with concern.

"I know, it's just hard sometimes," said Cara. "I don't mean to start crying every time anything reminds me of him. It just doesn't seem to want to go away."

"It doesn't have to go away Cara," Michael took her by the hand now and pulled her toward him. "It's okay to miss him."

He held Cara for a few minutes while she cried softly. It was the first time in a few weeks that she had let her emotions show but somehow she felt safe doing it now. After a couple of minutes she released herself from Michael's arms.

"Thank you," she said to him as she wiped her damp eyes. "We'll catch up to those videos a little later okay?"

"No problem Cara. Thank you. I owe you a lot just for this opportunity."

Cara showed him to the door and said goodnight before closing the door behind him. She returned to the kitchen to refill her wine glass before returning to the family room. She finished the bottle of wine as she watched chuckwagon races and happier times.

"Damn you Garret!" Cara began to cry uncontrollably. "You promised you'd never leave me. We had everything going for us and now Corby and I have to make it on our own. I can't do this, I just can't!" Cara cried herself to sleep on the sofa. When she awoke a few hours later her face felt dry and tight from the tears she had cried. She switched off the TV and the lights, checked on Corby and then headed for bed. She awoke early in the morning to the sound of Corby's cries and a headache that lingered from the wine.

"Good morning sweetheart," she said as she lifted Corby from his crib. She carried him over to the change table in his bedroom where she changed his diaper before taking him to the kitchen for his breakfast.

Her head still throbbing, she thought back to the hours of racing footage she had watched. She thought about how kind Michael had been when she lost it the night before. He really was a good friend. Most of her friends would have run for the door at the first sign of her tears. She would go talk to him this morning once she and Corby were finished breakfast and she had a chance to clean herself up.

After breakfast Cara gave both Corby and herself a sponge bath before they got ready to go outside. The sun was still low in the sky as autumn was approaching and the daylight hours were getting shorter. She placed Corby in his little green plastic wagon and pulled him out to the barnyard where she knew she would find Michael. When she slid open the big barn door she saw him throwing hay into the mangers to feed the horses.

Michael turned when he heard the door slide open. "Good morning," Michael gave Cara a wave from the far end of the barn. "How are you guys this morning?"

"We're just fine," said Cara as she picked up Corby from his wagon. The baby's face lit up as he eyed the horses that were walking into the barn and going into their stalls. Cara held Corby and watched the horses until Michael had snapped a shank to each horse so that they would remain in their stalls. When the last horse was tied up he joined Cara and Corby.

"What are you guys up to today?" he asked as he squeezed Corby's little foot.

"We were just, um." Cara tried to think about what she was trying to say. "I'm sorry about my little breakdown last night."

"It's fine Cara," said Michael softly. "Hey, no one expects you just to be over everything and getting on with your life. What you did was perfectly normal."

"Thank you," said Cara. "I just didn't think seeing those videos would have that great of an effect on me. I thought I was stronger than that. Anyhow, I stayed up and watched everything last night and I've dealt with what I needed to. You are welcome to come over this afternoon and watch the races if you'd like. I promise I'll be fine."

"Are you sure?" asked Michael. "There's no rush."

"I'm sure," said Cara with a smile.

"Okay then, I'll see you this afternoon," he said. "I have to go into town to pick up some supplies for the barn and get a few groceries so maybe we could watch the videos after that?"

"That sounds fine," said Cara. "Actually, why don't you come for supper and we can watch the videos afterwards?"

"Sure," said Michael. "That sounds far better than whatever I was going to throw in the microwave."

"I'm not sure if you're complimenting my cooking or not." said Cara with a laugh.

"Trust me, I am," he grinned. "I remember all of the wonderful meals you used to make when we were racing and I'm looking forward to it. Can I bring the wine?"

"Oh, um, sure," she said. "That would be nice." She didn't want to tell him that she had a headache from her self destruction the night before. "We'll see you later on then."

"See ya'," said Michael as the three of them left the horses to eat in the barn. He walked back to his house to have some breakfast while Cara pulled Corby over to the garden in his wagon. She was going to dig some potatoes and carrots.

Cara and Corby spent the majority of the day outside so that Cara could do some yard work. Some of the annual flowers were already beginning to wilt and the vegetable garden would need to be completely taken off soon. She enjoyed hard work. She had always busied herself when she was feeling stressed. She found that it helped her feel better.

She moved Corby from place to place as she worked in the yard, taking him out of his wagon at each stop so that he could crawl around on the grass. He was turning into quite the little explorer. He rarely fussed, especially when he was so busy. It was a beautiful day and Cara took a break to take Corby over to the old rope swing in the trees near the house. She sat on the swing with him on her lap and gently swung back and forth. She knew the value of each day and losing Garret only made her place that much more emphasis on it. She drew in a deep breath as she soaked in the warmth of the sun and the peace of the day. She still had so many fears about what the future would hold for her and Corby but they would just take it day by day.

The quiet was interrupted by the rumble of a pickup truck coming up the gravel lane toward them. Cara recognized the truck. It was Garret's parents. She had not seen Edward and Sharon much since the day of the funeral. They were good people but they did not often leave home and Cara could not seem to find it in her to go to their home. There just seemed to be too much of Garret there and she struggled enough to face that everyday at home.

Cara rose from the swing and carried Corby on her hip as she walked toward the driveway where Edward had parked the truck. She swallowed hard as Garret's parents got out of the truck. Edward and Garret had shared so many of the same features it was difficult to look at him without seeing her late husband.

"Hey guys," said Sharon as she walked over to give Cara a hug. "How's my grandson today?" she asked with arms outstretched toward Corby. Cara placed Corby into Sharon's waiting arms and then turned to give Edward a hug.

"How are you guys doing?" asked Cara casually.

"We've been pretty busy with the farm," offered Edward as somewhat of an explanation for why they had not been around.

"Well Corby and I have been busy taking off some of the garden," said Cara as she reached toward Corby and tickled at his little foot.

"Yes, I can see that," said Sharon as she eyed the garden.

"I heard you're busy with the horses again," said Edward getting more to the reason for their visit.

"Um, well yeah, not me so much as Michael," Cara felt the nerves rising in the pit of her stomach. "He has been offered a spot in the NCA so we've come up with a partnership to um, to get him started."

"I guess that's good," said Sharon. "The horses are no good to anyone just standing in the pasture. It seems the two of you get along so you may as well try to work together."

An awkward silence seemed to pass between the three of them before Cara had a chance to break it and invite them in for coffee.

"We actually can't stay," said Edward. "We just heard about Michael getting into the NCA and we were a little surprised we hadn't heard it from you."

"I'm sorry," said Cara sincerely. "I guess I have been so caught up in everything and well really, I didn't know if you wanted to hear these things or not."

"It's okay Cara," said Sharon softly. "We just want you and Corby to be happy and if this is what is going to keep you going then it is what you need to do. Really, we just wanted to tell you not to be a stranger. We aren't far away and you will always be a part of our family."

"Thank you," said Cara with tears in her eyes. "I guess we have just been trying to keep busy and sometimes I forget that you have lost a son."

"It's okay dear" said Sharon as she wrapped her free arm around Cara's shoulder. "Everyone is still hurting, we know that. We just want you to know we are here if you need us. You have always been so fiercely independent that sometimes we forget you might need a hand."

"Thanks guys," said Cara. "Same goes for you. Also, Corby needs to see his grandparents more and I will make a greater effort to make sure that happens."

"That's all we wanted to hear," said Edward.

"Why don't you two come over for supper tomorrow night?" asked Sharon. "We'll barbeque and just have a relaxing evening for a change."

"That sounds perfect, thank you," said Cara.

"Well, we have to get going," said Edward. "We'll have a nice long visit tomorrow."

"Sounds great," said Cara as Sharon passed Corby back to her.

Edward and Sharon climbed back into their truck and drove back down the driveway. Cara waved to them as they drove away. She thought that it was probably the most awkward conversation she ever had with Garret's parents. She made a mental note to make a greater effort to visit with them more. It was hard to see them but it was now time to get on with life and she knew that it was important for Corby to know his grandparents.

Cara took Corby into the house in order to feed him some lunch and lay him down for his nap. She brought the fresh vegetables with her and placed them in the sink to be washed. She decided to make her and Michael a pot roast with fresh potatoes and carrots. It seemed like an eternity since she had made dinner for company and she found herself enjoying the preparation of the meal.

She wondered what Edward and Sharon really thought about her new business venture. To Cara it really was a business deal but she knew how people liked to talk and it made her uncomfortable to think that anyone would think it was anything more. She tried to push the thought from her mind and simply concentrated on making a nice meal.

Michael came for dinner as planned and even helped clean up while Cara got Corby ready for bed. They watched the racing footage without any incidents this time. It was the most relaxing evening Cara could remember having since Garret's death.

Chapter Nine

As autumn quickly progressed toward winter there were many dinners with Michael. It gave Cara and Michael the chance to discuss horse care, feeding programs and what the training regime for spring would consist of. Cara, Michael and Corby were falling into a comfortable routine with each other and Corby was now very familiar with Michael's frequent visits. Corby was now pulling himself up on the furniture and he would laugh with delight at his new accomplishments.

Cara returned to teaching when school resumed in September. Both the staff and students welcomed her back with love and support. She could literally feel herself getting stronger through the love of her friends and family. Mary eagerly offered to watch Corby which put Cara's mind at ease a great deal.

Michael continued to run things on the farm along with his work as an oilfield operator.

One day, as the snow began to fall in late October and Cara and Corby watched the flakes through the kitchen window, the phone rang. It was Bob Vickers, Cara's old friend from Victoria, BC. He heard that she was staying in the business of racing horses and had a couple of horses he wanted to offer her the first opportunity to buy.

It was a generous offer. Cara knew the bloodlines of the Vickers horses well. She also knew that Bob had a talent for picking the right horses from other farms. During her time at *Hastings Park* she often went out to Vickers Farm to work with the horses they bred and trained. She quickly agreed to make the trip to the west coast the following weekend. She and Michael would travel to Victoria to see the horses. It would have to be a business decision they would make together because the horses would not come cheap.

Cara called her mother to make arrangements with her for Corby's care while she and Michael went to look at the horses. The three of them would fly to Vancouver where Corby would stay with Grandma while Michael and Cara took the ferry over to the island to see the horses. Karen was elated to hear that her grandson would be coming and immediately cleared her schedule for his visit.

The next weekend, as planned the trio headed to the Calgary International airport for the quick one hour flight that would take them to Vancouver. As they awaited their flight, Cara thought back to the last time she had been at the airport. She and Garret were flying to Cuba for a tropical holiday while Cara's students were on Spring break. They only recently learned that Cara was pregnant and they were elated. Garrett had been so protective of Cara on that vacation. Cara smiled as she remembered the way he would fall asleep each night, his hand placed protectively across the new life that grew inside of her.

"Are you okay?" Michael interrupted her far away thoughts.

"I'm fine," she said with a smile. "I'm just going to go freshen up before it's time to get on the plane. Could you watch Corby for a minute?"

"Of course," answered Michael as he took Corby from her arms and placed him on his lap. Corby continued to happily chew on the teething ring he had been holding.

Cara walked through the terminal in search of the washrooms. Her breath caught in her throat when she noticed the huge glass case which held all kinds of *Calgary Stampede* memorabilia. A special memorial occupied the centre of the case. It was a tribute to Garret and the *Calgary Stampede* championship he claimed so recently before his death.

Cara walked up to the case and stared at the photo of Garret holding the over-sized one hundred thousand dollar winner's cheque high above his head. His white teeth gleamed with the smile on his face. She ran her fingers lightly over the engraved plaque at the bottom of the case. It contained his name, date of birth and date of death. She felt a tear slip from her eye which she quickly wiped away. Sometimes life seemed to carry on like this tragedy never happened to her and sometimes it just reached out and grabbed hold of her like it would never let go.

"Not today," Cara said under her breath. "I can't do this today." She walked away from the display case, composing herself long enough to slip into the ladies washroom. Once inside a bathroom stall, she allowed herself to cry quietly. She spent a few minutes trying to convince herself that she would not have a complete meltdown but it was not working. She crumpled into a corner of the stall, hanging on to the wall for support before she wept. The noise of the washroom hid her cries until she was able to once again pull things together and return to Michael and Corby.

The plane left Calgary on time, bound for Vancouver where Karen met them at the airport. Karen spotted them as they came through the secure area into arrivals. She ran toward them with outstretched arms. She threw her arms around Cara who had Corby in her arms.

"Oh Mom," said Cara hugging her back. "We've missed you!"

"I can't believe how my grandson has grown. It nearly breaks my heart," said Karen with tears in her eyes.

Corby looked intently toward his grandmother. He was not sure who this lady was but he seemed to sense that she was okay and he did not make shy with her.

"Hello Mrs. Beaton," Michael offered a handshake.

"Well, what is this Mrs. Beaton stuff?" Karen said with a laugh. "Get over here and give me a hug. How are you?"

"I'm just fine," Michael answered with a smile as he gave Karen a hug. "It is nice to see you again." Michael felt comfortable with Karen since the first time he met her in Grand Rapids.

The group walked toward the baggage carousel to await the arrival of the luggage. Karen held out her arms to Corby and he decided that it was okay to go to her which pleased her a great deal. She talked and played with Corby while Cara and Michael identified their bags. When the luggage was gathered they walked to Karen's car. They would spend the first night at Karen's house and leave for the island in the morning.

"I can't wait to show you my new place," said Karen with enthusiasm of a kid at Christmas.

"I can't wait to see it Mom," said Cara. "It sounds like everything you've ever wanted in a home." The two women discussed the details of Karen's home as they searched for the car in the large parking lot. When the car was spotted, they quickly loaded their luggage, attached the car seat to the back seat and departed for Karen's place.

A light rain was falling as Karen maneuvered her black *GMC Acadia* out of airport parking. It was strange to Cara how everything seemed different. Vancouver was now so unfamiliar to her. It truly was not home for her anymore. Michael stared out the window for most of the drive, commenting on the scenery as they went. He was a small town Alberta boy who had never been to Vancouver. He did not enjoy city life all that much and, other than work-related trips to Texas, he spent little time outside of Alberta. An oilfield consultant in Alberta does not have to travel far for work if he does not want to.

Karen and Cara did some catching up during the drive while Corby drifted off to sleep in his car seat. Driving to the airport, waiting for the flight and flying to Vancouver had made the little one exhausted.

As Karen turned up the driveway of the gated community she lived in, Cara looked out the car window, admiring the beautifully landscaped grounds. It was a far cry from the tiny apartment she had shared with her mother and brother when they were growing up. Flowers lined the window boxes of each residence. The white stucco buildings that dotted the community's private street stood out against the dark sky. Karen turned into the driveway at the third building on the street and clicked the remote mounted on her sun visor, opening the door to underground parking. Cara smiled to herself as she watched her confident mother. She was so happy for her and for everything she had accomplished over the years.

"The landscaping here is gorgeous Mom," said Cara as they entered the parking garage.

"Thank you Cara," answered Karen. "You know, I didn't have an easy time deciding where I'd like to live. You would have thought I would be so happy to get out of that cramped apartment but there were just so many good memories there." Karen smiled as she squeezed Cara's knee. "I looked at a lot of places and something just made me fall for this one."

"Well, let's get the luggage out so we can have a look," said Cara.

Michael was already out of the car gathering luggage from the back while Cara retrieved Corby from his car seat. He awakened when the car engine was shut off. When everything was gathered, they walked across the parking garage a short distance to the elevator where Karen pushed the button to the third floor.

Upon entering the luxury condo, the smell of fresh cinnamon buns greeted them at the door.

"Wow Karen, this place seems great already," Michael smiled to her as he eyed the fresh baking cooling on racks atop the granite counters. The brushed stainless steel appliances gleamed in the open kitchen. At first glance, one could tell that the home was the perfect retreat for a chef.

"This is wonderful Mom!" exclaimed Cara as she set down Corby to crawl across the living room's plush moss green carpet. The modern home was decorated like a cottage retreat. Plush pillows covered the large print floral furniture. A baby grand piano sat in the corner of the living room near a large window that looked out onto the terrace.

"You got the baby grand!" Cara squealed with delight.

"It took everything for me not to tell you over the phone," Karen gushed as she sat down to the piano. "After all of those years of taking my frustrations out on that old piano with the three broken keys, I could finally afford one of the ones we passed by so many times in the window of Francine's Music Shop, so I went for it!"

"Play us something," Cara pleaded as Corby pulled himself up against his mother's leg.

Cara stood to the side of the piano with Corby in her arms while Karen played Beethoven's *Minuet in G*. The piano had a rich tone and Cara enjoyed the music to the very last note.

When the music stopped, she and Michael applauded.

"That was amazing," said Michael. "I didn't know you played."

"I learned to play as a child and I always found that when my troubles seemed to be getting the better of me, I could turn to the music to drift away for a while or to take my frustrations out on those keys," said Karen smiling. "I often tried to get Cara or Jason to take up the piano but Jason was into sports and I couldn't keep Cara away from the racetrack so it just never happened."

"I wish now that I had learned to play," said Cara with a laugh. "It sounds so beautiful. I should have learned how to do that."

"Well Cara, just as you would tell your students, it is never too late to learn," said Karen with a laugh.

"I guess you're right about that," said Cara. "This is a wonderful home you have here Mom."

"It's amazing!" added Michael.

"Thank you," said Karen. "I'm certainly enjoying it. Now let's get into the kitchen and see how those cinnamon buns turned out in my new oven." Karen rose from her spot at the piano to lead the group to the kitchen area.

"I'm just going to take Corby into the bathroom to change him first," said Cara.

"Of course," said Karen. "Just down the hall. It's the first door on your left."

Cara took Corby to change him while Karen placed a rack of the cinnamon buns on the cutting board. Michael looked out the French doors that led to the terrace and tried to think of some small talk.

"Does it rain here all the time like everyone says?" he asked. "What a dumb question," he thought. He could not believe he went straight to talking about the weather.

"Um, quite a bit I guess but we don't get the cold you get in Alberta," Karen answered while she cut up the cinnamon buns. "Why don't you sit down at the table? What can I get you to drink?" Karen smiled at Michael.

He took a seat at the table near the French doors where he had been standing. Karen was such a kind person. He had no idea why he felt so uncomfortable. He cared about Cara but it was not like there was anything going on between the two of them. It was just business. Thoughts dashed through Michael's head as he tried to just relax and fit in.

"Just a glass of water would be fine, thank you," said Michael.

Karen brought Michael the glass of water along with a plate for the cinnamon buns.

"Please have some," she offered as she pushed the buns toward him.

Michael took a bun and placed it on his plate. He reached for the butter and slathered some onto the bun which was still warm.

"So I hear you guys have quite the schedule while you're here," said Karen as she sat down at the table.

"Um, yeah, we have the horses to go see tomorrow and then I think Cara's going to take me to *Hastings Park* as I've never seen it," Michael spoke enthusiastically. He had a great deal to say when it came to talking about horses and racing which immediately put him at ease.

"It all sounds good Michael," said Karen with a smile. "The whole thing sounds good; the partnership, everything. Cara looks happy and that is wonderful to see. It will do her a lot of good just to get out there and work with the horses and I have you to thank for that."

"Well, don't thank me," said Michael. "I'm the one who's grateful. She has a lot of knowledge and she really cares about those horses. I'm lucky to have her on my team."

Karen smiled at him. He seemed to be a very genuine young man and she was happy that Cara had a companion. She did have the feeling though that not even Cara and Michael knew what they might be getting themselves into. When it came right down to it, the heart would take what it wanted. Karen was okay with that. Cara was a young woman. She needed to heal her aching heart but that did not mean she could not ever open her heart up again. It was remarkable how love seemed to be the only thing that could leave people with such deep wounds they were afraid to ever love again but at the same time, it was also the only thing that could heal them as well.

Cara and Corby returned to the kitchen. She had changed Corby into his pajamas so he was all ready for bed.

"Did I miss anything exciting?" Cara asked.

"You're missing your Mom's fabulous cinnamon buns," said Michael.

"Here Cara," said Karen. "You have a seat here and have a cinnamon bun and I'll feed Corby his bottle."

"Thanks Mom," said Cara as she passed Corby to her mother.

Corby drank his bottle and quickly drifted off to sleep while Michael, Cara and Karen visited around the table.

"I've set up the playpen for Corby in my room," said Karen. "You can sleep with me in there and Michael can have the guest room."

"Thanks Mom," said Cara as she stood up from her chair. Karen gently lifted Corby into Cara's arms so she could carry him to bed.

Cara spotted the master bedroom when she had taken Corby to change him. It too had a cottage feel to it. The large canopy bed was decorated with a rose and moss coloured quilt. A large antique dresser sat along one wall and a pretty floral print wingback chair and ottoman sat in another corner beside a reading lamp. The playpen was set up at the foot of the bed for Corby so Cara gently laid him down. He hardly stirred as she pulled up the covers and placed a kiss on his warm cheek.

Cara breathed in deeply. Her mother's home was both relaxing and welcoming and she felt completely at ease here. She had no plans to stay up too late as it would be a long day tomorrow when she and Michael traveled over to the island to look at the horses. Cara returned to the kitchen to finish her cinnamon bun and continue in the conversation with Michael and her mother. Soon it was time to turn in so that they could get an early start in the morning. Taking the ferry across to the island and then driving to Vickers Farm would take a few hours.

Karen showed Michael to his room so that he could get ready for bed while she and Cara tidied up the kitchen. When Michael came to say goodnight Cara took that as her cue to use the washroom while her mother used the one off of the master bedroom.

When Cara came to bed her mother was already settled. She looked at Corby sleeping peacefully before she climbed under the covers of the large bed beside her Mom.

"It's not often I get to sleep with my Mommy," Cara said with a laugh.

"That's for sure," said Karen. "You know, you are still my baby girl."

"Oh, I know Mom," Cara smiled at her mother and kissed her on the cheek. "Goodnight Mom."

"Goodnight," said Karen. "Sleep well. You are looking well Cara. I'm happy for you."

"Thanks Mom. We're doing alright."

Cara rolled over and closed her eyes. She smiled a little when she felt her mother pat her back as she drifted off to sleep.

Cara rose quietly in the morning before the alarm had a chance to go off. It was six o'clock and Corby was sleeping peacefully. She grabbed a few toiletries from her suitcase and headed to the master bathroom. She could already hear Michael getting ready in the main bathroom. She took a quick shower before dressing in jeans and a pink cashmere sweater. She dried her hair and ran her fingers through its soft waves, choosing to leave it down. She searched for a few items in her suitcase she would need for the day, including the small umbrella she always packed for trips to the coast. She went to her mother's side of the bed to whisper a quick goodbye before leaving the bedroom. There was no reason for her mother or Corby to be up this early.

When Cara closed the bedroom door behind her she saw that Michael was already waiting in the foyer.

"Good morning," she whispered.

"Good morning."

They gathered their coats, put on their shoes and quietly left the condo. When they entered the elevator Michael smiled at Cara.

"What?" she asked.

"Not a thing. I was just admiring your "city girl" look," he said with an even bigger smile. "Is that not cashmere?"

"Well, it's chilly this morning and this happens to be my favorite sweater which my Vancouverite mother gave me for Christmas last year," she answered him with a grin.

"It's beautiful. I think pink is your colour. You wear a lot of black and beige for a young woman," Michael said.

"Well I had no idea you were such a fashionista," Cara said with a laugh and a friendly punch to Michael's shoulder.

"Seriously, you look nice," he said in a more serious tone. "And here I am in just my jeans and western shirt."

"I think you look just fine," said Cara. "You know, normally when I see you, you are covered in dirt and grime from working with the horses so actually I think you clean up pretty well," she laughed.

"Gee, thanks," Michael said with a grin.

A moment passed between them where neither was sure what to say. They were both a little relieved when the elevator arrived at the parking garage and they exited to load their belongings into Karen's car.

Cara was doing the driving because she knew where she was going. Michael sat back in the passenger seat and stared in awe at the scenery. It was beautiful here. Not the kind of beauty one could appreciate in the country but rather beauty from a whole new perspective. The mountains were a sharp backdrop against the city skyline. The calm ocean water looked so peaceful and welcoming.

"No rain this morning," said Cara trying to make conversation. "That's a good start to our day."

"Yeah," answered Michael. "It really is quite beautiful here."

"It's not weekday, rush hour traffic. That's half the beauty right there," said Cara. "That is one of the things about living here that I do not miss."

"Anything else you miss?"

Cara thought for a moment before answering. What she really missed was being closer to her family but she knew her life was in Alberta now.

"I miss the ocean sometimes," she said. "That's one thing you can't get in Alberta." They laughed and carried on with their small talk until Cara reached the pier where they would wait to board the ferry.

The ferry was just arriving when they pulled up to get in line. Cara paid the fee and then drove onto the craft. With the car parked they were free to roam around and enjoy the journey to the island.

"Let's go get some breakfast," said Cara. "I'm starving."

"Breakfast?" Michael asked. "You can get breakfast on here?"

"Yeah, silly," she laughed. "You're in the big city lights now. C'mon."

Cara led the way to the cafeteria area where she and Michael ordered toast and coffee with some fresh fruit cups. They took their breakfast to a window seat where they could watch the sights as the ferry departed the harbor. Michael was fascinated. He had really never experienced anything like this.

He smiled at Cara. She seemed so relaxed these days. He thought that it was nice to see her getting back to being the lady he had met when he first came to work for the McCormack's. She was so full of energy and a love of life. After Garret had died he was afraid that she had lost that part of herself forever.

Before long, it was time to get back to the car. The ferry would be docking soon and they would be on the island. Cara and Michael departed the ferry and continued on with the two hour drive it would take to get to the Vickers Farm. Their conversation seemed to come more easily now and both relaxed and enjoyed the rest of the trip.

Before long Cara was turning off of the highway up a side road to Vickers Farm. It was everything she remembered and more. Automatic gates led up the tree-lined black top to the main house. The property consisted of two hundred fenced acres of beautiful, mature landscaped grounds that included ponds, waterfalls and brick paths which led to the 40 stall barn, pool with pool house or the tennis court.

Bob and Marjorie Vickers owned the most luxurious estate-style property on the island. The main residence was at least seventeen thousand square feet and included a gourmet kitchen, spa, wine cellar, library, home theatre, gym and an office wing where Mr. and Mrs. Vickers and their staff conducted their Thoroughbred breeding and training business.

Cara had spent a great deal of her time here, working with the race horses. The Vickers family always treated her well. She came out to the farm whenever she was given the opportunity. She looked across the grounds as she drove up the lane, taking herself back in time.

Michael let out a low whistle of appreciation as he admired the property. He had never seen anything like it in his life.

"Wow, this is unreal!" he exclaimed. "You didn't exactly tell me this is what I could expect."

"This little place?" she teased. "Bob and Marjorie are wonderful people so don't let the scenery scare you. They are as down to earth as anyone comes."

As Cara parked the car to the side of the drive that circled in front of the house, she immediately spotted Bob coming out of the house toward the car.

"Cara!" Bob said with a look of delight as he opened her car door. "You look wonderful. It has been too long my dear."

Cara stepped out of the car and into Bob's waiting arms. He hugged her warmly and kissed her lightly on each cheek. Cara could rarely remember a time when he did not have a warm smile on his face. He was a tall slender gentleman, now in his late sixties. He had a full head of neatly styled silver hair. He was dressed in a navy polo shirt and tan dress pants. He was still obviously very much in shape for an older gentleman and judging by the amount of staff moving about the grounds, business was still in full swing.

"It's wonderful to see you Bob," said Cara. "Bob, this is my friend Michael DeWalt. The business partner I was telling you about."

Michael was now on Cara's side of the car. He stretched out his hand to greet Bob with a handshake.

"It's a pleasure to meet you Mr. Vickers," said Michael.

"Likewise," answered Bob with a smile. "Please, call me Bob. Cara is like a daughter to me so I think we can save the formalities. Now before we go out to see the horses I'd like you to come in for a minute. Marjorie was so pleased when she heard that you were coming but she can't come out as she had a bit of an accident and twisted her ankle."

"Oh my goodness, what happened?" asked Cara.

"She actually twisted it on the tennis court," answered Bob. "We still aren't able to slow her down much. She just carries on like a twenty year old." Bob chuckled but one could see the pride in his eyes when he spoke of his wife.

"Well, I'm glad it isn't anything too serious," said Cara as they walked toward the mansion.

"We were so sorry to hear about Garrett," Bob spoke quickly and then turned to hug Cara again. "We should have been there for you but we were in Kentucky when it happened and didn't get the news until a few days after the funeral."

Cara could feel the tears stinging her eyes but she looked skyward and held them at bay. "Thank you. I know you guys would have been there if you could have."

"When I heard you were staying in the business and I knew I wouldn't be able to talk you into coming back to help me out here, I at least wanted to make you a good offer on a couple of my prized possessions," Bob smiled and squeezed Cara's hand gently before guiding her and Michael inside the mansion.

"Thank you Bob, it means a lot to me that you would still keep me in mind after all of these years."

"You always had a gift with horses Cara," said Bob matter-of-factly. "I would never forget something like that."

As they entered the main foyer of the mansion, Cara immediately spotted Marjorie on the leather sofa in the front sitting room, her foot propped up on a pillow. She looked very small in the grand, dark oak paneled room. Practically everything in the Vickers' home either related to horse racing or was antique. Although their collection of awards had grown over the years, the home remained virtually as Cara remembered it.

"Marjorie!" Cara exclaimed as she walked toward the sofa to bend down for a hug. "How are you doing?"

"Oh, I'm alright," she said in a voice eager to push any concerns aside. "I guess old ladies are not supposed to play tennis," she said with a smile.

"I heard you are still out there giving it your all," said Cara. "This one just caught you for once." The two women laughed.

Bob had made arrangements with the house staff to bring in some tea while the group sat down for a visit.

"Marjorie, this is Michael," said Cara gesturing toward Michael who stood a short distance behind her.

"Hello Michael. Welcome to our home," said Marjorie with a smile. "Cara told me that you are the young man she is in the chuckwagon racing business with."

"I am," said Michael. "It is pleasure to meet you Mrs. Vickers," said Michael extending a hand to the woman.

"Please forgive me for not getting up to greet you properly," said Marjorie as she shook Michael's hand from her spot on the sofa. "I'm supposed to ice this ankle for a few more minutes. I don't want you thinking I'm on my high horse here. By the way, Mrs. Vickers was my mother-in-law. Please, call me Marjorie," she said with a laugh.

"Well, Marjorie, I hope you are back on the court soon" Michael said with a smile.

"Thank you Michael. Perhaps after some tea Cara can take you for a little walk around the grounds. She knows her way around here very well. That's usually what I like to do but not today I'm afraid."

"That would be nice," said Michael. "You have a beautiful home here."

"After we look at the horses of course," said Bob with a laugh. "I know that Cara won't let me keep her away from that for too long."

"No I won't," Cara said with a laugh. "I've been looking forward to this ever since I received your phone call."

An easy conversation ensued amongst the group while they enjoyed the tea and biscuits which had been served by the staff. When they were finished, Cara and Michael said goodbye to Marjorie before going to the horse barn with Bob.

Once outside the mansion, Bob offered the pair a ride to the barn on a golf cart he kept parked near the driveway. They climbed aboard the four seat cart and Bob drove down the paved path toward the barn which was located a few hundred yards from the mansion.

Four cupolas ran along the peak of the forty stall, stone barn. The hand-carved stone gave the structure a presence all its own. Bob pulled the golf cart up in front of the wooden double doors at the front of the barn and shut it off. When the trio entered the barn they were greeted by a bustle of activity. Horses were being moved from various box stalls, fresh bedding was being put down and the staff was obviously hard at work.

The cement floor that ran down the centre of the barn's alley gleamed and the scent of disinfectant lingered in the air. The interior walls were lined with tongue and groove knotty pine. Each custom box stall had a sliding pine door with metal bars on the top half which allowed the horses to look into the alley. The metal bars could be raised or lowered to view horses more fully or simply to allow the animal to poke his head out of the stall.

Bob spoke to one of the staff nearest to where they had entered the barn, asking him to bring the horses out for viewing. The young man nodded to Bob and quickly went to retrieve the first horse Bob wanted Cara to look at.

The first thoroughbred the worker retrieved from a stall near the far end of the barn was a four year old bay gelding with a white star on his forehead and four white socks. He was a stunning animal that Cara estimated to be nearly seventeen hands high. His hair glistened in the sun which beamed in through the large double doors. His gentle eyes gazed at the onlookers.

"I have his *Jockey Club* papers in the office," said Bob as Cara and Michael looked the horse over. "I claimed him in a race at the *Columbus* track in Nebraska as a three year old. He won seventy thousand dollars as a two year old. They put him in a claiming race because he was sore in his hind quarters but it wasn't anything that couldn't be fixed. I've enjoyed some wins with him but I have a lot of young prospects that I need to look after and I just don't want to see his talent go to waste."

"He's a big, powerful looking horse," commented Michael as he ran his hand along the smooth back of the horse.

"He is that," agreed Bob. "You aren't going to have any problems getting him to pull a chuckwagon, that's for sure."

After a long look and some discussion over the first horse, Bob again spoke to one of the workers in the barn and asked him to bring the papers for both of the horses Cara and Michael would be looking at.

The bay gelding was returned to his stall and the same worker retrieved a flashy black thoroughbred gelding from an adjacent stall. This horse was six years old and had competed in several stakes races the previous year. According to Bob, the horse had placed and shown in several races and won two races in the previous three years.

Both Cara and Michael were impressed with the *Jockey Club* records of the horses and they were in awe over the conformation each possessed. Neither horse had sustained any serious injury over his racing career. Both were sound and ready to go into training. Cara envisioned wanting one of the horses before they had actually looked at them but now she was thinking that both were exceptional.

After coming to an agreement on the price of the horses, Michael and Cara were now the proud owners of two new thoroughbreds. Bob shook both of their hands when the deal was signed and arrangements were made to have the horses shipped back to Alberta. "Thank you so much for everything," said Cara to Bob. "I thought we might take one of the horses but you made us such a generous deal."

"You're very welcome my dear," said Bob. "I really wanted you to have both of them."

Once the paperwork was drawn up and signed, Bob invited Cara and Michael to join him and Marjorie for a celebratory drink and a late lunch before their departure. A light lunch of assorted sandwiches along with fruit and cheese trays was prepared by the staff and brought into the breakfast room which Marjorie insisted would be more comfortable for their guests than the living room she had been resting in. Both Bob and Cara helped Marjorie with her crutches so that she could join them. Each enjoyed a glass of wine bottled by *Victoria Estate Winery* especially for Vickers Farm to commemorate their fortieth anniversary.

When the small celebration was over, Michael and Cara prepared to return to the mainland. Cara promised the Vickers that her next visit would be much sooner. It was late afternoon when Michael and Cara arrived at the ferry dock. It had been an enjoyable, successful day. Neither Cara nor Michael could believe they would be adding both of the horses to their team.

When the ferry arrived Cara drove into the parking area down below as directed and Michael and Cara left the car to enjoy the view from the top deck.

As Cara leaned on the railing looking down at the water she took in a deep breath of the saltwater air and smiled at Michael.

"Well?" she said.

"Well?" he laughed. "You're a different person when you're out here Cara. Not that you aren't a great person at home, this is just a different side of you I'm seeing."

"I guess that's what happens when you go back to where you grew up," Cara smiled. "I had a pretty good childhood out here. I have some great memories of these places."

"It looks good on you," Michael turned to face her, pushing a wisp of wind-whipped hair from Cara's face. Before he had time to have any second thoughts, he leaned toward her to kiss her.

Cara quickly turned away from him, placing her hand on his chest and taking a step back. Her face was instantly flushed and she continued to walk away.

"I, I'll be in the car," stammered Cara, leaving him alone on the deck.

He did not try to follow her. He knew that he should not have tried to kiss her and now he felt like a fool. He rode the ferry from the same spot on the deck until it was time to return to the car. He did not know what to say to Cara so he waited for the last possible moment before getting back in the passenger seat.

They drove in silence as Cara wound her way through the streets back to her mother's place. She could feel her heart pounding in her chest so she turned up the music to drown out the feeling. She did not understand why Michael would do that after such a perfect day and she really had nothing to say to him.

By the time Cara parked the car in the underground parking, Michael had worked up the courage to speak first.

"Cara, I'm sorry," he said. "I guess I just got caught up in the moment. I didn't mean to actually ruin the whole day. Can you forgive me and we'll just forget that ever happened? Please?"

Cara looked over to Michael and smiled. "I forgive you. You are a good friend and a great business partner. Let's just stick to that okay."

"Deal," he answered.

By the time the two entered Karen's apartment the incident had been all but forgotten.

Before the weekend ended, they spent time with Karen and Corby, enjoying a few sights in Vancouver. Karen had arranged for Jason to meet them for dinner at one of Cara's old favorite Thai restaurants. Jason brought a young woman named Julia with him to dinner. Cara felt that she must be special as Jason never brought any of his girlfriends to meet his family. She thought it was nice to see him looking so happy.

It was difficult when Sunday night arrived and it was time to return to Alberta. With promises from Karen and Jason to come to Alberta for Christmas, Cara, Michael and Corby departed.

Chapter Ten

A few weeks after their return from Vancouver, the new horses arrived from Vickers Farm on a horse van destined for Toronto. Michael busied himself with the autumn training of the new horses while Cara comfortably adjusted to the routine of teaching school and spending her evenings with Corby. Cara often invited Michael to supper to discuss the day's events or his progress with horses. The trio seemed to have a routine that worked well for all of them.

One Saturday morning early in December, Cara took the Christmas decorations down from the attic. She decided that Corby might enjoy all of the sparkle and lights and she wanted the house decorated when her mother and brother arrived. Christmas had always been her favorite time of the year but as she began to decorate it became painfully obvious that this year would not be an easy one.

Box after box was filled with the memories of Christmases past and of the memories of Garret. It took Cara a long time to wade through the decorations. She stopped often to admire some little thing that reminded her of the happy times with her husband. When the house was finally decorated and the boxes were put away, Cara sat down with Corby to admire her handy work. Tears began to flow down her cheeks as she looked around the room. It did not feel like Christmas at all. She rocked Corby quietly as he giggled and pointed at the sparkling lights. She was desperately trying to find some inner happiness somewhere for the season that was now upon them.

As Cara rocked with Corby and drifted back to happier times, she was suddenly jolted by the sound of the doorbell. It was five o'clock in the afternoon by now and already dark outside. She did not see anyone drive up so she thought it must be Michael but normally he just opened the door and yelled a big "hello" before coming in. Cara walked to the door with Corby perched on her hip. She opened the door to see a well-bundled Mary Hartman.

"Hello, Mary," said Cara. "I never heard you drive up. Come in, it's freezing out there."

"I walked here," said Mary as she stepped inside the house, closing the door behind her. She pulled off her hat and mittens before unwinding the scarf from her neck. "I saw your Christmas tree lit up in the living room window when I came back from town so I thought I'd stop by and have a look. I hope you don't mind."

"Of course not," said Cara. "You know you are welcome here anytime. Come on in and I'll put some coffee on."

"Oh, don't worry about that Cara. I've got to get back home to make supper. Just wanted to see the decorating you've done. It looks beautiful," exclaimed Mary as she entered the living room.

"Thank you," said Cara. "It's just the same old artificial tree but I still like it."

"So how are you holding up after the decorating?" Mary wasted no time getting to the point.

"I'm okay," Cara smiled at Mary. "It was a tough stroll down memory lane going through all of that stuff but I had my time to deal and I think I'm going to get through this holiday."

"I'm glad to hear that," said Mary. "I was so happy when you told me your mother and brother will be here."

"Me too," said Cara. "I can't believe they will be here in two weeks."

"Meanwhile, we need to do some shopping," said Mary.

"Yeah, I know," said Cara. "I have no idea what Santa should bring Corby this year."

"Well, that too," said Mary. "I was actually thinking about a little earlier than Christmas. I was thinking about picking out gowns for the NCA's Winter Ball next Saturday in Calgary. I mean, we've always shopped together for that so I thought you'd want to do that again this year."

"I, I don't know," Cara hesitated. "That used to be my big event to help organize every year. This year no one even called me about it. I'm sure no one expects that I would want to go."

"Well of course you should go," exclaimed Mary. "You need to get out and do the things that have always been a part of your life. Take Michael with you. He needs to interact more with those people too. Who knows, it could land him some good contacts for a sponsor in the coming year."

"It seems like you've given this some thought," said Cara with a laugh.

"A little," Mary chuckled. "So what do you say?"

"I say we go shopping Tuesday. It is an early day at the school. I can be home by two and we can do it then."

"Perfect," said Mary. "I'll see you then. Meanwhile, I'd better get home to make some supper." Mary gave Cara a quick hug and kissed Corby's cheek before heading back to the entry way to bundle up and head back out into the cold. "See you Tuesday."

"See you Tuesday," said Cara.

"What's going on Tuesday?" asked Michael as he approached the door, waving to Mary who was already hurrying down the drive.

"Oh, hi Michael," said Cara as she took a step back to let him inside the house. "Mary and I are going shopping on Tuesday. Dress shopping in fact. How do you feel about going with me to the NCA Winter

Ball?" She didn't see the point in beating around the bush about the plans with the Hartman's.

"Yeah, I read about that on their website," said Michael as he took off his jacket and gloves. "If you'd like to go, I'd love to go with you."

"Well, it's all set then," said Cara. "Now let's get some supper. I imagine you're frozen."

"To the bone!"

That Tuesday, when school finished, Cara hurried home to pick up Mary and Corby. When she drove up to the Hartman's, Mary came out the door right away. She had Corby bundled up and ready to go. Cara got out of her burnt orange *Saturn* SUV and took Corby from Mary. She kissed him on the forehead before placing him in his car seat. Mary got into the passenger seat across from Cara and they were off. Cara drove the thirty minutes to the nearest larger city where they could shop at their favorite boutiques.

The first shop they entered was Celebrations Couture. It was located in the historic downtown district of the city. The shop was known for its large assortment of dresses and gowns for every occasion. Cara and Mary began to fan through the racks of gowns while Corby bounced happily on Cara's hip.

A perky blond sales associate immediately came over to offer the ladies some assistance. Cara explained what the gown was for and the associate immediately brought out several stunning styles she felt would suit the occasion. The first gowns she provided were for Cara to try on.

Cara tried on several gowns while Mary tended to Corby. The gown that caught her attention the most was a rich red evening gown. The satin fabric felt luxurious; the halter neck dazzled with rows of sparkle. The backside of the floor-length gown revealed crossed straps that elegantly placed one's back on display. The gown only added to Cara's amazing figure.

"Wow, Cara. I think that's the one!" Mary exclaimed as she smiled appreciatively.

"I think so too," said Cara with a grin. "What do you think little man? Will this work for your Mom?"

Corby laughed and clapped as Cara tickled his little knees before returning to the change room to remove the gown.

"This is the one," she told the sales associate.

With Cara's choice out of the way, she took Corby back from Mary while the sales associate began to bring out gowns for her to try on. It did not take Mary nearly as long to decide as it had taken Cara. She was pleased with the second gown she tried on. She chose a deep blue satin floor length gown that had a modest V-neckline and flutter sleeves that covered her shoulders. The finely pleated fabric crossed at the bust, creating a wrap effect. The waist was accented with a silk ribbon that tied off to one side with a rhinestone clasp. It was very stylish.

With their purchases completed much sooner than they had anticipated, the ladies had time to go for a nice dinner before returning home. By the time

Cara pulled into Mary's driveway Corby was sound asleep in his car seat.

"Thank you for a wonderful afternoon," she whispered. "We'll see you tomorrow."

"Thanks Cara," said Mary as she took her parcel from the back seat of the vehicle. She blew a kiss to sleeping Corby and waved goodbye to Cara as she gently closed the car door and walked up the sidewalk to her home.

When Cara crossed the road and drove up her own driveway, she noticed that there were no lights on at Michael's house. The cold weather was causing problems with oilfield equipment and he was working many late nights. She lifted Corby from the back seat, car seat and all, and carried him into the house before returning for the rest of the items.

When Cara returned to the house, Corby was just beginning to stir. She lifted him from his car seat on the floor so that she could remove his snowsuit. Once he was free of his warm clothes, Cara took him into the living room where he could crawl around and she could relax. She plopped down on the sofa and watched her son exploring the toys in the corner of the room. He was always such a happy baby.

As Corby continued to play, Cara saw the lights shining up the driveway. Michael was home from another long day. She watched as he drove past her house and up to his own. She always felt that she should invite him over as he was right there but tonight she just felt like spending the time alone with Corby. Without an invitation, Michael never intruded. Their relationship was very respectful of each other's space.

Much to Corby's delight, Cara walked over and turned on the Christmas tree lights. It never seemed to be a problem to keep him from pulling on the tree. He seemed most content to just watch the lights and ornaments. After Corby enjoyed some play time, Cara took him for his bath and then got him tucked into bed. She sat for a while longer in the living room, enjoying a cup of tea and watching the Christmas tree before going to bed. As she turned out the lights in the house she noticed that Michael's lights were out. She imagined he was pretty exhausted from the long hours of work in the cold.

The rest of the week seemed to drag and Cara realized that it must be because she was eager to go to the winter ball. She told herself that getting to wear the dress is what made her want to go but in reality, it was probably more because she had had so little social interaction with anyone from the NCA since Garret's death. She missed her friends but at the same time she understood; everyone had lives of their own.

Finally, Saturday morning arrived. Cara made arrangements to bring a sitter to Calgary to watch Corby at the hotel while she and Michael attended the ball along with Dan and Mary. Melissa Spade was in grade nine at the school where Cara taught. The Spade family had been friends with the McCormack's for many years and Melissa was happy to come along to help. Melissa arrived early to help Cara pack her sport utility vehicle for the trip to Calgary. Just as they were loading the last of the luggage, Michael drove up the driveway from the barn.

"Hello ladies," he said cheerily as he got out of his truck.

"Hi Michael," said Cara. "This is Melissa. She's the girl I was telling you would be watching Corby while we're at the ball."

"Hello Melissa," said Michael. "It's nice to meet you."

"You too," answered Melissa with a smile.

"Well, the chores are all done," said Michael. "Everything has extra hay and things should be good until we return tomorrow."

Michael walked back to his truck to grab his suitcase. The snow crunched under his feet as he carried his suitcase back to Cara's SUV to pack it with the other items. With everything ready to go, Cara placed Corby in his car seat while Michael and Melissa got settled in the vehicle. Michael sat up front with Cara while Melissa sat in the back with Corby. Cara got in the driver's seat, latched her seatbelt and drove toward to the Hartman's to see if they were ready. Dan and Mary were already at the end of their driveway, waiting in their pickup truck. They waved to Cara and motioned her to take the lead in her vehicle. They would be in Calgary at their hotel within a couple of hours.

From the moment she entered the lobby of the Beau Royal Garden hotel in downtown Calgary, Cara was inundated with hugs from old friends of the NCA. She was not sure how it would feel to be around everyone again but immediately she felt at ease. Cara checked into her room where she, Corby and Melissa would be staying while Michael checked into his own room on another floor. The Hartman's were busy visiting with everyone as well but Dan eventually made it to the check-in desk and completed their registration. Everyone agreed to meet in the main ballroom for cocktails before dinner.

The hotel porter assisted Cara with getting her luggage to the room. They were taken to the tenth floor where she carried Corby into the room and set him down to crawl around. She tipped the porter before he departed and then turned to admire the room. It was perfect. It consisted of a sitting room with two additional bedrooms; one with a king size bed and the other with a queen bed. Each bed was covered in a luxurious down comforter. The furniture throughout was contemporary and seemed to welcome its guests. Cara set up the playpen for Corby in the king room and Melissa was given the queen room. They had a little time before Cara would have to get ready for the ball so they relaxed in the sitting room with some television while Corby played with his toys. Before Cara ran her bath, she ordered room service for Melissa and retrieved Corby's baby food from his bag. Melissa would be able to warm his food in the microwave when it was time for him to eat.

"Why don't you start getting ready?" said Melissa. "We've got things covered here."

"Thank you Melissa. I think I'm going to start with a nice hot bath," she said as she retrieved her things from her room.

Cara ran the bath in the large marble Jacuzzi tub. She added some lilac scented bath salts before gently sliding into the soothing water. It was certainly relaxing but her nerves began to rise as the bath gave her time to think. She was nervous about seeing everyone at the ball. Even though people had welcomed her in the hotel lobby, it would be different seeing everyone at the ball. It seemed so strange to even be here at all without Garret by her side. She remembered the weekend being such a big deal for both of them every year. It was something they always looked forward to. She tried to push the apprehension from her mind, finished her bath and began to work on her hair and makeup.

Many of the ladies went to have their hair styled but Cara did not really feel up to that and instead did her own elegant French twist. Once she had finished putting her makeup on she donned her favorite faux ruby and diamond necklace and teardrop earrings to match the gown. With her slip on, she went to the bedroom to get into the gown. She pulled the gown from the garment bag, admiring it for a moment before slipping it on. It instantly boosted her confidence. Melissa smiled at her when she entered the sitting room.

"That gown is amazing Mrs. McCormack," she said.

"Thanks Melissa. You know you can call me Cara when we're not in school," she said with a smile.

"Oh, I know," said Melissa. "It's just habit. I think you and that dress are going to have an incredible night."

"I hope you're right."

Melissa answered the quiet knock at the door. It was Michael. He too, was ready to go in a sharp tuxedo jacket with western tie, black western jeans and his best cowboy hat. Cara had never seen him dressed up before.

"You look very handsome Mr. DeWalt," she said with a grin.

"Thank you Cara. You look stunning," he held nothing back.

"Thank you" she answered quietly as her skin flushed a little.

"You guys have a wonderful time," Melissa interrupted. "We've got everything under control here." She scooped Corby from the floor and Cara kissed him gently before picking up her evening bag and wrap.

"Thank you Melissa," said Cara. "If you need anything, I have my cell with me or the front desk will send someone to the ballroom. Goodnight Corby." She kissed him again before following Michael to the door he held open for her.

As they walked down the hall toward the elevators, Cara could feel her long gown swish along the carpet. She felt confident and elegant as she and Michael chatted amicably about anything and everything. They had now known each other for about eight months and being on the ranch alone, they had come to know each other well. They no longer had to think about things to talk about, the conversation simply carried itself. It was a nice feeling for both of them.

When Cara and Michael entered the ballroom several eyes seemed to be on them. Cara smiled confidently as she led Michael to the table where Dan and Mary were already seated. A waiter came by shortly to take their drink order. Cara ordered a glass of champagne while Michael opted for a *Budweiser*; a tuxedo, even one that was westernized, was not going to change his choice of beverage.

The chandelier in the centre of the room had been dimmed to set a quiet mood for the cocktail hour. Soft country music played in the background which was easily being drowned out by the ever-growing crowd of cowboys. The NCA Winter Ball was a charity ball that the association hosted each year to raise money for the charity of their choice and to get together to celebrate during the long Canadian winter. The ball often made upwards of fifty thousand dollars therefore, several charities were usually chosen as recipients for the money.

When Cara spotted Barbie Hopkins she excused herself from the table to say hello. She crossed the dance floor to a spot near the bar where Neil and Barbie were visiting with Grant and Nicole Wagner. Barbie spotted Cara in her stunning gown immediately.

"Cara!" she exclaimed as she wrapped her arms around her. "How are you? It's so good to see you here."

The rest of the group took turns hugging Cara and saying hello.

"You look amazing!" said Nicole. "I've been meaning to call you."

"Thank you, so do you guys. It's okay," said Cara. "I know you all have lives too."

"You came with the Hartman's?" asked Barbie.

"Yes. I came with the Hartman's and, um, with Michael DeWalt." Cara looked to the floor, feeling her confidence fail a little however she quickly regained her composure. "I thought it would be a good time for him to get to know everyone better and make some good contacts."

"Of course," said Nicole. "That's a good idea."

"Yes, that's a great idea," said Grant. "It will be an exciting year for him, it being his rookie season and all. Well, I think they're about to serve dinner so we should find our seats. We'll talk to you later Cara, it's great to see you."

"Sure, I'll see you all later."

The group moved to their table and Cara returned across the dance floor to hers, a sinking feeling in her stomach. They did not seem like the same people that she and Garret had always been so fond of.

"Hey Cara," said Mary. "How are those folks?"

"They, um, they're fine. Just sitting down for dinner like everyone else I guess."

Michael looked at Cara with concern but said nothing. He figured that this night might be difficult for her and his heart went out to her. People could not possibly understand what she was going through, nor could they expect her to be the same person she was before the accident. Michael smiled at Cara reassuringly as the waiters began to serve the first course. The dinner was lovely with a main course choice of prime rib or chicken along with roasted baby potatoes and asparagus tips in a white wine sauce.

When dinner finished, the Master of Ceremonies, John Long, the NCA's race announcer, announced that sixty-six thousand dollars had been raised for charity this year. He further announced that the money raised this year would be donated to the Corbyn James McCormack trust fund. His announcement was met with great applause as Cara looked up at him in stunned silence. She quickly regained her composure, and rose from her seat to walk to the podium. There were tears in her eyes and her voice shook with emotion as she attempted to thank the association for its donation.

"I, I'm not really sure where to begin," she said as she looked out at the large crowd. "I would of course like to thank you all for such a generous donation towards Corby's future. Racing with the NCA meant a great deal to Garret, to our family. It means so much to me that you would take this active role to insure that Corby has a successful future. Thank you." Tears streamed down Cara's face as she departed the podium. Her speech was met with great applause and she accepted many hugs as she returned to her seat.

John Long kept the rest of his announcements brief, limiting them to thanking the many sponsors and volunteers. He finished by announcing that the dance would soon be underway.

Michael, Dan and Mary were stunned by the news of the donation. They hugged Cara when she returned to the table. It was wonderful news that the NCA chose to donate to Corby's future like that. Cara had no idea that this was happening when she had agreed to go the ball.

With the announcements finished, Dan and Mary walked up to the bar to order some drinks. The DJ was already set up and the music began to play.

"Would you like to dance?" Michael asked Cara.

"Um, I," she looked at the nearly empty dance floor as she hesitated with her answer.

"It would be a shame for you to come here and not show off that beautiful dress," Michael reasoned.

"You're absolutely right," Cara said with a smile. She took his hand as he led her to the dance floor *All I Want To Do* by Sugarland was playing. Cara was happy to be dancing to an upbeat song. It felt good to be out on the dance floor and Michael was a great dancer. They laughed, talked and enjoyed the dance right to the last note. When the music stopped Cara excused herself to use the ladies room. As she exited the ballroom, she ran into Darryl Baker who was just returning to the party.

"Hello Cara," he said with a smile. They embraced in a warm hug before he stepped back to admire her. "You look fantastic!"

"Thank you Darryl, you look great too. I'm not used to seeing you guys all dressed up like this."

"I know. I'm not used to it either but at least I've got my cowboy hat so I still feel like myself," he laughed. Most of the men in the room were wearing their cowboy hats. It was the one piece of them they had to hang on to, even at a black tie event.

"It's been a while since I've heard from you," said Cara.

"It has. I'm sorry about that. I've been meaning to call and see how you're doing. I did hear that you went into a partnership with that DeWalt guy once he made the NCA."

"Michael," said Cara. "Yes, I did. He's actually here with me tonight."

"Oh, that's um, great," Darryl stumbled over his words.

"I thought it would be a nice opportunity for him to be around the contacts he needs to get to know," said Cara hoping to put an abrupt end to any rumors that were being started around the room.

"That's great," said Darryl. "You're right. This is a great chance for him to meet all kinds of people. Well I guess I should get back to my date. I left her with Jake and Mark over by the bar. You know how those guys can be."

"Yeah, sure," Cara tried to laugh. "You had better go and rescue her."

He and Cara both found it a little easier to exit the conversation with the excuse that Darryl should not leave his girlfriend with two of the wildest outriders on the circuit. Cara continued down the hall toward the ladies room. It felt as though she had been dealing with everyone else's feelings all evening. She sighed as she pushed the door open to the ladies room. It was at least quiet in there. She slipped into a stall and breathed a sigh of relief.

A moment later, Cara heard laughter and talking as some other ladies entered. She recognized the voices as those of Barbie Hopkins and Nicole Wagner. She was about to leave the stall to say hello when she suddenly realized that the conversation was all about her.

"Well, she seems to be getting on with life," said Barbie.

"Yeah, I'd say so," said Nicole. "I can honestly say I didn't except to see her here in a sexy red dress and with a date, no less."

"Maybe she's just comfortable with him because it means she's still around wagon racing," said Barbie as she stared into the mirror to apply more lipstick.

"Well, one thing is certain, after tonight's little fundraiser she won't need to find someone to look after her son's future," mused Nicole.

Cara could take no more of the conversation and stepped from the washroom stall.

"Hello ladies."

The two women stared at her in disbelief. They thought they had the room all to themselves.

"Nice to see you are enjoying yourselves this evening, even if it is at my expense." Cara spoke in an even, icy tone unlike anything they had ever heard from her before. "I'm glad you feel you've got my life all figured out. One thing is for certain, if I had any doubts about the people that are my real friends, you two are certainly making it easier for me to figure out."

Cara washed her hands at the sink slowly and methodically, trying not to cry. She accepted a towel from the ladies room attendant who kept her eyes to the floor.

Barbie spoke first. "Cara, we didn't mean anything by what you overheard."

"Honestly Cara, we didn't," added Nicole. "We only wish you the best."

"Thank you so much ladies. I only wish you the best too." Cara spoke in a tone that could have melted steel. She tossed her hand towel into the towel bin and grabbed her evening bag from the counter. She exited the room with grace and poise, leaving the two women dumbfounded.

Had Michael not exited the ballroom for the men's room, he would not have noticed Cara's hasty retreat toward the elevators. The red satin of her gown swooshed along the floor with every step as her pace quickened. He quickly darted after her, arriving at the elevators as the doors opened. Cara did not notice him step inside the elevator behind her and it surprised her somewhat.

"Michael, you startled me."

"Sorry. I was just trying to get in the elevator before the doors closed and you disappeared. Is everything okay?" He could see the tears welling up in her eyes but she seemed to will them to stay down. When she tried to answer his question she suddenly burst into tears.

"Hey, hey," he said as he offered her a tissue from his breast pocket. "What happened?"

"I'm sorry," she said. "I didn't mean to cry." She wiped away the tears with the tissue. "I don't even know where to start."

"Come on," said Michael. "We can talk in my room." He pushed the proper elevator button. "I don't want you to have to go back to Melissa like this."

When the elevator doors opened at his floor, they walked down the hall toward his room. He retrieved his room card from his pocket and opened the door for Cara. She stepped into the room feeling almost instant relief at being away from the party. She immediately sat down on the sofa in the sitting room while Michael walked over to the mini-bar.

"Can I make you a drink?" he offered.

"Do you have any white wine?" she asked.

"I imagine," he said as he looked through the contents of the mini-bar. "How does *Tinhorn Creek Chardonnay* sound to you?"

"That sounds just fine Michael. Thank you."

He took a wine glass from the shelf, opened the wine and poured her a glass. He retrieved a beer from the fridge for himself, poured it into a glass and then carried the drinks over to where Cara was seated.

"Thank you Michael."

"You're welcome," he said. "So are you going to tell me what's got you all upset?"

She was no longer crying but her eyes were still red and puffy. She drank the wine and mostly looked at the floor but she did manage to tell Michael the whole story of what had occurred in the ladies room.

"Apparently I am not grieving properly," she said as the tears began to flow again. He moved toward her, wrapping his arms around her as she cried her heart out. When she seemed better she sat up and had another sip of her wine.

"To hell with them Cara," said Michael.

The statement shocked her a little. She never heard anything from his mouth but respect and kindness.

"There is no manual for how you are supposed to feel or when you are supposed to move forward with your life," he said. "No one knows that better than you so don't let them get to you. They don't deserve that kind of power over you after what you've been through."

"You're right," she said. "I mean, I thought these people were my friends but I have never felt so alone in my life."

"Well, you have real friends Cara and one of them is right here in this room. So you decide if you want to go back and enjoy your evening and forget about those people or if you want to just stay here. Either way, I'm here for you."

"Thank you Michael. That means a lot to me and you really are a good friend. Let's go do this thing," she said with determination. Cara finished her wine, touched up her makeup in the mirror and then headed out the door. Two people who obviously were not her friends did not have the right to ruin her whole evening.

When Cara and Michael returned to their table, she could feel the eyes of Nicole and Barbie on her. Their stares seemed to bore a hole through her and she felt her skin flush in discomfort.

Michael could see her discomfort as could Dan and Mary. Before the Hartman's could make any inquiries, Michael grabbed her hand, making a playful, sweeping gesture with his free hand to invite her onto the dance floor. Cara welcomed the invitation and followed his lead. *Hair In My Eyes Like A Highland Steer* by The Corb Lund Band blasted through the speakers putting everyone in high spirits. Cara laughed as Michael spun her around the dance floor for the lively two-step. As they danced, they seemed to draw more stares from the group.

"To hell with them," Cara thought as she tried to play-up the good time she was not really having. "Michael has stood by my side when all of these people just carried on with their lives. He's the one that I owe something to, not them."

Cara tried to enjoy the rest of the evening. She danced with Michael and even had a couple of waltzes with Dan. The Hartman's felt that something was wrong earlier in the evening but they did not ask later when it seemed like Cara was having such a wonderful time. They were just happy to see her enjoying herself for a change.

The outriders were all out on the dance floor. Most of them spent the earlier part of the evening circled around the bar sampling various shooters. They were now ready to party. Everyone clapped and cheered as they took turns trying to outdo one another on the dance floor, with or without a partner. Cara laughed and clapped along with the crowd but in her heart she ached. If Garret were here they would be dancing, mingling and enjoying their friends. Cara felt like a stranger in this crowd but she masked her hurt with her enthusiasm for the antics of the outriders. When she did not think she could dance another step, she and Michael returned to their table. Michael excused himself to go to the men's room.

"Hey, you," Darryl Baker sat down at her table in the seat Michael had left momentarily vacant.

"Hello Darryl. It looks like you guys are having a good time."

"It's not too bad," Darryl said with a grin. We didn't get much of a chance to visit before. I just wanted to see how you're doing?"

"I'm doing okay," said Cara sincerely. "Thank you for asking."

"I just wanted to wish you and the little guy a Merry Christmas. I've lost people in my life Cara and I know this isn't going to be an easy time for you."

"Thank you Darryl. I think we're going to be okay. My mom and my brother are coming for Christmas. That will help a lot."

"I'm glad to hear that," said Darryl. "You take care and please Cara, if there is anything you need, call me."

"Thank you. That means a lot to me."

Darryl got up from the table, kissing her cheek before walking back into the crowd of outriders who were still dancing and carrying on. Cara thought it was nice that at least someone in the NCA was making her feel like she still belonged.

When the evening came to a close, Michael asked Cara if he could walk her to her room. She declined insisting that she could make her way there with the Hartman's who were on the same floor. She wanted people to see her having a carefree time; she did not want them to have the evidence they were looking for to further condemn her.

When Cara stepped into her room and closed the door behind her she felt a great sense of relief. She checked on Corby who was sleeping peacefully in the playpen in her room. She then checked in on Melissa in the other room. The girl opened her eyes when Cara opened the door and Cara whispered goodnight.

Cara removed her evening gown and hung it in the closet. She admired it one last time before closing the closet door. It was a fabulous dress, meant for a much happier occasion than trying to defend oneself to old friends. As Cara stood in the bathroom in her slip she stared into the mirror for a long time before she began to weep. She wondered if the road would ever get easier or if people would ever give her a chance to live life again without analyzing her every move.

In the early morning Cara packed her things. When Corby and Melissa awoke she was ready to go. She did not wish to stay for the brunch that was hosted by the NCA's Board of Directors. She had telephoned Michael in his room and asked that they leave early and get breakfast on the way out of the city. He understood how she was feeling and did not question her. Cara, Michael, Melissa and Corby were checked out of the hotel and driving up Centre Street in Calgary by nine o'clock. They found a quiet restaurant to have breakfast in. Melissa had many questions about the ball and both Michael and Cara stuck to the positive aspects of the evening. The donation to Corby's trust fund was definitely the highlight. After breakfast they drove back to Spruce View. Back to their lives and away from people that Cara did not wish to see for a very long time.

Chapter Eleven

There was little time for Cara to dwell on the events of the charity ball or how Barbie and Nicole made her feel. Christmas was right around the corner and she had a great deal to keep her mind occupied. She had plenty of work to do with her students who were eagerly practicing their songs for the school Christmas concert. Her mother and Jason would be arriving from Vancouver soon, and there was still some last-minute shopping to be done. The list just seemed to go on and on.

Cara fit in a quick first birthday celebration for Corby. She invited Garret's parents and siblings along with their families and a few close friends. She bought Corby a sled for his birthday and he laughed with glee the first time she took him out to pull him around in the fresh snow. Cara loved to watch his delight but at the same time her heart still sank at the thought of all the events Garret would never see.

With the birthday party finished, Cara tried to get back into the Christmas spirit. She wanted to get at least a small amount of Christmas baking done, even though her mother would come loaded with as much baking as they would allow her to carry on the plane. Cara's thoughts swirled through her mental list. She loved Christmas more than any other holiday but it was a lot of work. This year seemed to be more work than ever as she summoned the strength to get through each pre-holiday event.

The last day of school prior to the Christmas break finally arrived. When the bell rang to signal the end of the day, the students gathered up the Christmas projects they were taking home to give as holiday gifts. Cara announced a quick reminder to the class about times to be at the school before the Christmas concert that night. The children dashed out of the room, the excitement of the concert and the holiday season filled their hearts. Cara smiled as she watched them race out of the school. This was really what the season was all about. She just had to keep reminding herself of that.

On the way home Cara picked up a pizza for supper. She knew there would be no time to cook before she had to be back at the school for the concert. Dan and Mary brought Corby home for her as they too would be coming to the Christmas concert. When she entered the house, Cara was overwhelmed by the smell of apple cider and fresh gingerbread cookies.

"My good heavens Mary!" said Cara as she scooped Corby from his toys on the floor to give him a hug. "It smells wonderful in here. Kind of makes my pizza look a little sad," she laughed.

Mary laughed. "I just wanted to bring over a little baking to get you in the festive spirit before the concert."

"Well thank you," said Cara. She took a cookie from the plate and savored the taste in her mouth. "These are wonderful."

"Thank you," said Mary. "I've packed some up for Michael to take over to his place as well."

"That's very kind you. I'm sure he will appreciate the baking on his trip home for the holidays."

After enjoying the pizza along with some cider and cookies for dessert, Cara quickly changed into a black skirt and red sweater for the concert. She pinned a gold holiday wreath broach to her sweater to give it a little holiday cheer. Corby was dressed in a brown sweater and matching corduroy pants. Cara thought he looked terribly cute and she smiled as she bundled him up for the drive to the concert with the Hartman's.

The snow began to fall across the windshield as Dan drove down the road to Spruce View. It was pretty and certainly put one in the Christmas spirit. Cara looked out the window at the flakes, wondering how she would make it through yet another tradition without Garret by her side. A lump formed in her throat but she swallowed hard and pushed it away. This was supposed to be a happy event and she intended to make it one.

The concert was held in the school's gymnasium which was lovingly decorated with different Christmas themed decorations made by each class. Chairs were placed facing the stage so the concert goers could enjoy the performance. The event was as beautiful and cheery as ever, putting the whole community in the Christmas spirit. The beautiful voices of the children filled the gymnasium with Christmas carols and a Christmas play. Tears of pride sprang from the eyes of many of the parents and grandparents as they enjoyed the children's performances. It was a magical experience as always. When the final note of *Joy To The World* ended the evening, the warmth of the season could be felt throughout the building.

"That was a wonderful concert Cara," said Mary as they walked out to the car. "Thank you so much for the invitation."

"You're very welcome. Thank you for looking after Corby while I was with my students."

"That was pretty easy," Dan said with a laugh as he opened the car door for Cara and Corby. "He slept through most of it."

"I guess he's not quite ready for all of the celebrating," laughed Cara as she placed Corby in his car seat.

The snow was falling harder now. By the time Dan turned into Cara's driveway, drifts were beginning to form across the road. Karen and Jason were expected on a flight from Vancouver in the morning. Cara hoped the developing storm did not delay their travels.

"Thank you for driving," said Cara as Dan parked the car in front of her house. She unbuckled Corby's car seat from the seatbelt and lifted him from the car.

"Anytime Cara," answered Dan.

"Thank you for the wonderful baking too," said Cara. "I've got a little gift for you guys. I'll stop by tomorrow if that's okay."

"That would be wonderful," said Mary. "We can get a quick visit in before both our homes are filled with family."

"Perfect. See you guys tomorrow then. Goodnight."

"Goodnight Cara." Dan and Mary waved goodbye as she carried Corby up to the house. She had covered him with a blanket as the wind and snow whipped through the yard.

Early in the morning Karen called to tell Cara that they were at the Vancouver airport but their flight had been delayed due to the storm in Calgary. She told Cara they had been advised by the airline that they would be leaving Vancouver by noon which would put them in Calgary at about two o'clock in the afternoon, Alberta time. With the roads being icy, the drive to Spruce View would take a little longer than planned but they hoped to be there in time for supper.

Just as Cara finished feeding Corby his breakfast, Michael arrived at the house. He knocked gently on the door before opening it and calling out a friendly "hello".

"Good morning Michael. We're in here," Cara called from the kitchen. She wiped the last of the egg from Corby's face as he finished his breakfast in his highchair.

"Good morning," he said as he walked into the kitchen. He still had his big winter coat on.

"Take off your coat and stay a while," she offered with a grin.

"I'd love to but I am on my way home for Christmas and I promised I would be there to help my brother and sister with Mom's tree this afternoon. I've got a little gift for Corby and something for you."

"That's very kind Michael," said Cara. "You didn't have to do that."

"I know," he said. "I wanted to."

Cara set Corby down on the floor so that he could tear at the wrapping paper on the gift Michael had set before him. She helped him with the paper a little and eventually he got to the box. It was a play center for the bath.

"Oh, thank you Michael," said Cara. "He will love this." Corby giggled and cooed as he zoned in on the shiny wrapping paper all around him.

"This is for you," said Michael as he pulled an envelope from his jacket.

Cara opened the envelope. The inside of a beautiful Christmas card revealed open-ended return tickets to Vancouver. Cara gasped. She could not believe Michael would give her such a generous gift.

"Thank you," she said, her hand clasped over her mouth in disbelief.

"You're welcome Cara. I didn't really know what to get you but I know how important your family is to you so I thought this might work for you."

"This is so generous and thoughtful. Thank you," she said as she wrapped her arms around his neck for a big hug.

"I have something for you too but it isn't quite like that," said Cara reaching for an envelope on the counter. Cara had gotten him a gift certificate to the local harness and tack shop. Michael smiled when he opened the envelope.

"Thank you Cara. It's perfect. This is definitely something I will use," he said with a grin. Well, I should be going. I want to get to Calgary in decent time and I've heard the roads aren't great."

"I've heard the same thing," said Cara. "Please drive safe."

"I will. Well, Merry Christmas to you guys." He leaned down to gently rub Corby's head.

"Merry Christmas Michael. Say hello to your family for me."

"I will."

They hugged again before Michael turned back toward the foyer. In a moment he had his boots on and was gone out the door towards the truck. Cara had agreed to watch the horses while he was gone for the holidays although there was not a great deal to do. The horses were in winter pasture, a few miles down the road. She would go out to check on them and bring them some oats each day to make sure they were all healthy and accounted for.

Cara looked out the window and waved to Michael as he drove away. The snow was still falling but the wind had calmed down. Suddenly the house seemed so quiet, even with Corby happily playing in the background. Cara planned to busy herself with some baking and supper preparations before her mother and Jason arrived.

After changing Corby's diaper she put him down on the floor to play while she assembled the ingredients she would need. Corby was pulling himself up on the furniture now and walking along its edges. She had to be much more mindful of his whereabouts. She started him out near the kitchen table so she could keep an eye on him while she baked.

Between giving Corby the attention he needed and turning out batches of Christmas cookies, the day seemed to fly by. Cara had put a ham in the oven for dinner and was just preparing the scalloped potatoes when she spotted a car pulling in the driveway. Karen and Jason had arrived. After wiping her hands on her apron, she scooped up Corby and hurried to the door. She was excited to have her family home for the holidays.

When she opened the door to greet her guests, she was surprised to see not two people but three standing at the door. Cara greeted everyone and brought them into the foyer before hugs were exchanged. She recognized the third person to be the young woman Jason had introduced her and Michael to during their fall visit to Vancouver.

"Merry Christmas," Cara said with a smile as she hugged the woman. "What a nice surprise to have you here. It's Julia, right?"

"Yes," the woman answered with a smile. Her green eyes were highlighted by the emerald coloured sweater she wore. Her long, dark curly hair was pulled back from her face revealing fabulous diamond stud earrings. "Merry Christmas. I told Jason he should tell you I was coming but he insisted on surprising you."

"Well that's a very nice surprise. I'm so glad to have you all here. Come in. I'll show you to your rooms so you can get some of the luggage out of your arms. I love your earrings Julia. They are beautiful."

"Oh, thank you," she replied rather shyly. "They were an early Christmas present from Jason."

"Wow, Jason you have amazing taste," Cara declared.

"Hey, what can I say? I grew up in a house with two women," he chuckled as he picked up the remaining luggage to carry to the bedroom.

Cara looked toward her mother for an answer to her questions but Karen just smiled and shrugged her shoulders. She knew that Jason had a girlfriend but there had been many and certainly never one he brought along to a family event. Cara liked Julia from the moment she had met her, she just never realized how much Jason obviously cared for her. She hoped this was as serious as she thought it must be. It would be nice to see him settle down and start a family of his own.

While everyone busied themselves with unpacking, Cara went back to the stove to finish making the potatoes. Karen took Corby along with her to unpack while Jason and Julia went to their room to do the same. Karen and Jason both kept slipping past the kitchen to pile gifts under the tree in the living room. Cara could not believe the mountain of presents that had formed.

Just as Cara began to set the table, everyone reemerged from their rooms to help put the meal out. The food was placed into serving dishes and Jason sliced the ham to put on a serving platter. Cara complimented the meal with a nice bottle of *Jackson-Triggs Proprietors' Grand Reserve* merlot. Karen praised her on her excellent choice of wine.

The conversation was relaxed and fun as the four visited, enjoyed the meal and enjoyed the antics of an ever-exploring Corby. He had already eaten his supper earlier, as he was accustomed to, and he happily busied himself making brave attempts at walking. If he was not pulling himself up on the sides of the furniture, he was pulling himself up using his mother's legs. Everyone enjoyed watching his efforts. Jason and Karen commented on his ever-changing development since they had last seen him in the fall.

For dessert, a chocolate mousse was served along with coffee. Suddenly Jason cleared his throat in an effort to interject the conversation. The three women all turned toward him and he smiled brightly.

"I have an announcement to make," he said as he placed his arm around Julia who was seated next to him. "Just to get right to it, I'm sure it is obvious to you guys that Julia and I have a serious relationship so it should come as no surprise when I tell you that I have asked Julia to be my wife. Believe it or not, she even said yes." Jason gave her a squeeze and kissed her on the cheek as she smiled brightly.

"Jason, I knew there was something up with the way you two were acting on the plane," Karen said with a laugh. "Congratulations. I'm so happy for you two," she said as she got up from the table to hug both of them.

"Yes, congratulations," added Cara. "That's wonderful news. Welcome to the family." She too got up to hug the pair.

Jason gestured quietly to Julia and she excused herself from the table for a moment. She went to the bedroom, returning shortly to display her hand to Cara and Karen. On the third finger of her left hand rested one of the most beautiful diamond engagement rings Cara or Karen had ever seen.

"That is gorgeous!" said Karen, admiring the ring.

"I'm impressed Jason," said Cara. "I thought you did well on the earrings but that ring is amazing."

"Thank you," said Jason. "Julia kept it well hidden during the flight. We wanted to surprise you guys."

The engagement ring was a *Simon G.* design in white gold which featured a one and a half carat round brilliant cut *Polar Bear* diamond surrounded by six marquise shape diamonds. The sparkle of the ring was radiant.

Jason and Julia explained how they were planning their wedding for the following winter in the Dominican Republic. They intended to invite their family and close friends and had estimated about forty guests would attend. Karen and Cara both agreed that it would be a wonderful event tied in with an escape from the cold winter.

As it was getting later, Cara excused herself to bathe Corby and get him into bed while the other three did the dishes. By the time Cara returned to the living room, Jason had started a fire in the large stone fireplace and everyone had settled around the warmth of the fire and the Christmas tree. A few more stories and laughs were shared before Karen and Julia both excused their selves and said goodnight.

Cara and Jason each poured a glass of wine and settled into the warmth of the living room. They always made time to talk alone which is what kept them so close even with the distance.

"Well sis," said Jason with a smile. "What do you think?"

"I think I'm so happy to have you guys here for the holidays and I also think you definitely surprised me with your announcement. I'm really happy for you guys; now I just have to get to know this girl who has finally captured your heart."

"You and Julia will be all good," said Jason as he sipped his wine.

"I think you're right. I'm glad you've found someone to make you happy and to share your life with. That's important," Cara finished the statement with more emotion in her voice than she had intended.

"Thanks Cara. Look, I know this still isn't an easy time for you so you can say no if you'd like. Cara, will you please stand up for me at our wedding?"

Cara jumped up from the sofa and hugged Jason hard, spilling some of the wine on his pants.

"Sorry about that!" exclaimed Cara. "You shouldn't keep giving me all of these surprises. I would be honored to do that for you little brother." Tears of joy streamed down her face.

"Thanks Cara. You really are one of my best friends."

The two chatted long into the evening about childhood shenanigans and little things their mother still did not know about. They laughed out loud until the last ember of the fire had died out completely.

In the morning Cara rose early to the sounds of Corby. She had his breakfast made when her mother emerged from her bedroom. Cara put the coffee on and began to fuss over a bigger breakfast for the group.

"Cara, don't worry about breakfast," said Karen. "We can have toast or cereal or something. There's going to be plenty of cooking to do over the next couple of days. Let's not make a big effort over breakfast."

"Are you sure?" said Cara as she set out the coffee mugs.

"I'm sure."

It's supposed to be a pretty decent day today," said Cara. "I'd like to take my horse out for a ride before we get into too much baking or anything this afternoon. Would you mind watching Corby for me?"

"Of course I can," said Karen. "Isn't it a little cold for riding?"

"It's already up to minus six and the sun is shining. It should be perfect."

Soon Julia and Jason came to the kitchen, helping themselves to coffee, juice and toast. After a relaxing morning Cara headed out to the field to catch her horse. The saddle horses were always kept around home and never taken out to winter pasture with the race horses. Garret always worried that the aggressiveness of the race horses would end up injuring a saddle horse.

Cara easily caught her horse, giving Garret's horse a scratch on the ears and a bite of oats before taking her horse to the barn. She considered selling Garret's horse as it was not fair to the animal not to get used, however she later decided against it. The horse was a quiet, older horse and soon Corby would be ready to ride. She thought the horse could be his.

Cara tied her horse in a stall before retrieving a brush. He happily ate his oats while she brushed his coat. She returned to the tack room to retrieve her saddle pads and saddle. When she lifted the saddle she grimaced a little. Garret had always saddled her horse for her. Every time she picked up the saddle, it reminded her more of his absence.

Before long the horse was saddled and they were on their way down the driveway. She pulled her hat down over her ears and pulled up the collar of her thick winter coat as she rode out of the yard. The sun was shining brightly but the air was still chilly.

Cara rode down to the winter pasture first. She and Garret placed a grain bin in the pasture a few years earlier and Michael filled it before the snow came. Cara rode up to the bin, dismounted her horse and opened the bin door just in time to hear the thunder of the hooves coming up the hill for oats. Cara scooped the oats from the bin with a large grain pail. She divided the feed into the feed troughs that lined the fence. When all the horses settled into their feasts, she took the time to look them over for any sickness or injuries. When she was content that all looked well, she remounted her horse and carried on with her ride.

The sun sparkled off of the fresh snow as Cara rode along. She admired the beauty of the snow sitting on the trees as she made her way down to the creek where she and Garret had been so many times before. She had not been to the creek in a long time; it always seemed to make her heart ache. As she looked across the sparkling water and the ice-filled banks, she did not hurt. For the first time in many months, she breathed in the winter air and tried to appreciate the life that was hers. Contentment seemed to be reaching out to her and she tried hard to reach back.

When Cara turned to ride for home she felt some peace in her heart.

Cara spent the next two days trying to get her mother not to fuss over more food than four of them would ever eat. She enjoyed the time with her family and took the time to get to know Julia. She seemed like a wonderful woman and Cara knew that she and Jason would be very happy. When Christmas morning arrived, gifts were torn open and smiling faces filled the room.

Cara chastised her mother for spending far too much on her grown children. Karen laughed it off while Cara admired her new cashmere sweater. Corby received more toys and clothes than he could possibly use. He overlooked the toys and contentedly played with the wrapping paper and boxes. Once the gifts were opened, everyone settled into the huge brunch that Cara had insisted on making since Karen and Julia had insisted on being in charge of Christmas dinner. By the time the day was over, everyone was exhausted and happy.

With Corby tucked into bed, the evening seemed quiet and suddenly Cara had a longing for Garret that she could not control. She watched Julia and Jason teasing one another in the living room as her mother sat in a corner chair relaxing with a book. Everyone seemed satisfied with their lives and Cara could not seem to find this. She felt the tears well up in her eyes as she grabbed her hat and jacket before heading outside to the barn. It did not take Jason long to notice her absence and the lights on in the barn.

"Mom, just let me go talk to her," Jason motioned to his mother to sit back down as he reached for his coat and gloves. "We knew this holiday would not be easy on her." Jason closed the door behind him and walked out to the barn.

Upon entering the barn, Jason saw the lights on in the tack room to his right. He knocked gently on the door before opening it. Cara sat on some horse blankets in the large tack room. Her eyes were puffy and red from crying.

"Hey you," Jason's tone was soft.

"I, I can't breathe Jason!" Cara gasped between cries. "I just can't breathe!" Her arms were wrapped tightly around her shins as she rocked back and forth on the pile of blankets and sobbed. "When am I going to just breathe again? When is life going to let me live again?"

Jason sat down beside her, wrapping his arms around her as she wept and asked questions aloud that no one could ever possibly answer. When she calmed down, she and Jason talked for hours about Garret, their life together and his death. It was the most Cara had spoken to anyone about what had happened. She felt so betrayed by the people she thought were her friends. She really did not feel safe telling anyone, other than Mary, what was really on her mind but she still held back somewhat with her.

Cara trusted Jason so deeply that she felt she could finally release the feelings she had been holding on to for so many months. When it came time to walk back to the house, she felt that she was getting herself back together. The release of all of that emotion felt so good. Jason wrapped his arm protectively around her shoulders as they walked. He felt so terrible about everything she had endured. He often wondered where she found the strength.

That night, as Cara slept she dreamed of Garret.

He was right there, like so many times before. She had spotted him riding his horse out in the pasture in the warm spring sun and he waved to her to come to him. Cara rode toward him on her horse, her heart pounding. There were no words when she finally reached him and they kissed passionately under the warm sun. Cara stopped the kiss just long enough to scold him a little for being gone so long.

"Everyone thinks you're gone Garret but I knew you couldn't be," Cara kissed him again through her tears. "I knew you weren't dead. You wouldn't just go when you know how much Corby and I both need you."

"Oh Cara, my sweet Cara," Garret cupped her chin in his hands as he spoke to her. "I've missed you so much honey but you know I can't come back. Cara, you have always had the strength in our relationship and in everything. You are the strongest person I know. I'm so proud of you for being such an amazing mother to Corby. I know this is a long journey but you're making it everyday my love."

"I just need you to hold me again," Cara sobbed as she reached for him.

"Sweetheart, you know all of those times when I held you, in fact it was you holding me," said Garret smiling at her, holding her tightly in his arms before once again capturing her with his powerful kiss. "I have to go my love but I needed to meet you here to tell you that I'm okay now and all I want in this world is for you to have an amazing life. Things don't always work out like we plan but sometimes I think there are plans for us that we just don't understand right from the start. I'll always love you Cara. Please stay strong for me and for our son. You can do this Cara. I have complete faith in you sweetheart."

"I can't do it Garret," she cried. "Please don't leave this up to me!"

"I love you Cara," Garret reassured her. "You're already on your way sweetheart."

As he spoke his last words, Cara noticed his face fading in the brightness of the sun. She tried to hold on to him but he was gone. In the distance she could hear the banging of the train as it made its way past their property.

Cara awoke to the sounds of pots clanging in the kitchen and the pounding of her heart. It felt as though Garret had really been there only moments before and somehow it gave her peace. She hugged his pillow tightly before climbing out of bed.

When Cara entered the kitchen her mother gave her a concerned look. She was not sure how things had turned out the night before as she did not wait up for her children. Cara looked happy and at peace which quickly reassured Karen.

"I'm okay Mom," she said as she hugged her. "Everything's going to be just fine."

Karen hugged her back tightly. She believed her daughter was going to make it through this pain; she just worried about all of the hills and valleys the path of grief takes. She was relieved to see that Cara was happy now, especially on the day she had to return to the west coast.

Shortly after breakfast it was time for Karen, Jason and Julia to pack up for their flight home. Cara truly seemed to be where she needed to be this time and parting was not quite as difficult. Tears were still shed but there was also the feeling of hope which was something Cara had not felt in a long, long time. Christmas brought far more than Cara could have ever wished for. Even with all that was lost, she knew she was still blessed to be surrounded by such an amazing family.

Chapter Twelve

The day after Boxing Day, Karen, Jason and Julia went back to Vancouver leaving the house quite empty and quiet. Cara mentally reviewed all of the events of the past year. She quickly determined that change was needed if she was going to move on with her life as Garret had asked her to in her dream. She knew that Garret would be in her heart forever but she also knew that she was developing the strength to keep growing away from her pain.

As soon as Corby finished his breakfast, Cara began to tackle her long to-do list. She tore down the Christmas decorations and cleaned out the closets, boxing up all of Garret's clothing to take to the shelter. She then packed up any of his other belongings that were not personal mementos, to be donated elsewhere. Garret's many racing awards and pictures were removed from the family room and put into storage in the basement to save for Corby.

With the removal and storage of items completed, Cara and Corby took a trip into the city to purchase bedding, new window treatments and a lot of paint. After her shopping was completed, she called Mary to ask if she could watch Corby for a few hours while she tackled some of the painting projects she had in mind. Mary happily agreed and Cara dropped him off on her way home.

"You seem pretty ambitious for a lady who just had a home filled with family all week?" Mary inquired.

"Yeah, well, I don't have much time between now and the start of school so I'd like to get a few projects done," explained Cara.

"That's a good idea. I wish I had your energy about now," Mary laughed.

"We'll see how far I get anyhow," said Cara with a laugh. "What I'm lacking in energy these days, I'm making up for with sheer determination. Watching Corby for me so I don't have him in the paint is a huge help."

"Anytime," said Mary as she took Corby from Cara. "You sound like a woman on a mission." She smiled warmly. She was impressed with the changes she was seeing in Cara lately. She really seemed to be moving forward. As far as Mary was concerned, it was time.

"Bye, bye," Cara kissed Corby and waved as she stepped back out the door. He was always content at the Hartman's home and waved to his mother with a smile on his face as he said "bye-bye". He was starting to pick up a few words and Cara was proud to say that "Mama" was one of them.

Since Cara had pretty well cleared everything from the family room earlier, it was easy to go to work preparing the room for painting. She chose a deep mocha as a feature wall for the room and a lighter taupe for the rest of the walls. The ceiling and the trim would be white and the drapes were a blend of chocolate and cream colours. Cara liked the warmth of the colours and eagerly went to work on the project.

As Cara prepared to start painting, she looked down at her watch and her wedding band. Deciding that she did not want to get paint on her jewelry, Cara went to the bedroom to remove her watch. She looked down at her wedding band one last time before carefully slipping it off of her finger. The ring had never been removed since her wedding day, when Garret had placed it on her finger. She swallowed a lump in her throat as she placed the ring with her engagement ring inside of her jewelry box. She had work to do and part of the work was continually trying to move on.

"Goodbye my love," Cara's voice cracked. "Until we meet again." She closed the jewelry box, patting the lid before she left the room. When she returned to the family room, she picked up a roller and began to paint, losing her thoughts in the rhythm of the roller.

Just as she completed the first coat of paint, the phone rang. It was Sharon, Garret's mom. It occurred to her when she saw the number on the call display that today was the day the McCormack's hosted their family Christmas party. Cara had completely forgotten.

"Hello," said Cara in a cheery voice as she picked up the phone.

"Hi Cara, this is Sharon. I was just making sure you hadn't forgotten about our little Christmas gathering today."

"Oh, no of course not," Cara lied. "I was just finishing up a few things here and then we will be right over."

"Okay, that sounds good," said Sharon. "We'll see you shortly then."

Every year, Edward and Sharon held their family Christmas gathering a day or two after Christmas so that their children and grandchildren could all attend.

Cara hung up the phone and called Mary quickly to advise her of the party that she had forgotten about. She then hurried to close up the paint cans and rinse out her brushes before dashing to her bedroom for a quick shower.

Mary brought Corby home while Cara showered. She dressed him in the clothes Cara had set out for him. Cara grabbed her royal blue cable knit sweater from her closet and a pair of her favorite blue jeans. By the time Cara had dried her hair, pulled it into a ponytail and dabbed on some makeup, Mary had Corby ready and waiting.

Cara hurried from the bedroom, suddenly stopping dead in her tracks. She could not bring herself to leave her wedding band in the jewelry box. Her hand felt naked without it and the rush of guilt she felt for taking it off overwhelmed her. She quickly retrieved the ring from her jewelry box and slid it back on her finger.

"Thank you Mary," said Cara as she rushed down the hall toward them in the kitchen. "I can't believe I forgot about their family Christmas!"

"Well, it's been a full holiday season for you," said Mary. "There was bound to be something you missed. I won't tell if you don't," she grinned.

Cara smiled at her friend as she pulled a container of baking from the freezer part of the refrigerator. As she arranged some goodies on a tray, she quietly thanked her mother for over-doing the amount of Christmas baking.

Cara and Corby were dressed in their winter clothes and ready to go out the door in record time, thanks to Mary's help. As Cara drove down the road to Edward and Sharon's, she pondered how she could have forgotten Garret's parents Christmas event. Nonetheless, they arrived at the house on time. Everyone was happy to see them. Sharon gladly took Corby from Cara's arms as she returned to the car to retrieve the tray of baking.

Garret's brother Robert and his sister Suzanne were both waiting at the door when Cara returned with the tray of baking. Suzanne took the tray of baking from Cara and hugged her with her free arm at the same time.

"It's good to see you Cara," said Suzanne. "Sometimes Edmonton is much too far away."

"Yes, it is," Cara agreed. "Corby and I have been meaning to come for a visit since the fall and we still haven't made it that way." Cara knew that was not the whole truth. She was not entirely comfortable being around Garret's family since his death. She loved them dearly but all of the reminders were painful. Now that she felt she was making an effort to move forward with her life, she made a mental note to spend more time with all of the McCormack's.

Robert gave Cara a huge hug once Suzanne had relieved her of the tray. The past few months had been especially difficult for him as he had worked with Garret and the horses so much. Robert still stopped in at the ranch for a visit more often than the rest of the family but Garret's death was still raw on his emotions.

"I'd like to help Michael with the horses this spring," Robert said quietly to Cara. "If he could use a hand, that is."

"That's very kind of you," said Cara. "I'm sure he'd appreciate your help a great deal. I'll let him know when he returns from his Christmas holidays."

"He's away right now?"

"Yes. I think he gets home today."

"Cara, why didn't you tell me? Who's been looking after the horses?"

"I've been taking care of them. It really hasn't been a big deal. In fact, I've kind of enjoyed it."

"You know if you need a hand you can always call," Robert said sincerely.

"I know," answered Cara. "Well, I guess we should get in there to visit with everyone," Cara smiled. "Merry Christmas Robert."

"Merry Christmas to you too."

All of the children were busy tearing open presents on the living room floor when Cara and Robert entered the room. Cara said hello to the rest of the family before kneeling down on the floor to help Corby with some of the wrapping paper on his presents. While the children played with their new toys, the adults visited and helped Sharon with the beautiful turkey dinner she cooked. It was a beautiful evening and Cara was glad that she had not missed it.

As Cara and Corby prepared to depart for home, Sharon packed up some of the leftover food for her to take with her. She said goodbye with a promise to visit soon. She knew that she had grown distant with Garret's parents and she vowed to turn that around immediately.

When Cara arrived back home she noticed the lights on at Michael's house. Her heart skipped a beat and it was only then that she realized how much she had missed him over the holidays. As she lifted Corby from the back seat, she found herself wishing that Michael would see that they were home and come up to the house for a visit.

Cara got Corby ready for bed as soon as they entered the house. He was a little cranky after all of the excitement and it was far past his bedtime. Once Corby was settled into his crib, she returned to the family room to admire her work so far. The room would require one or two more coats of paint but she could certainly see her vision coming together. Deciding that it was too late to start painting again, she put the kettle on for a cup of tea.

Just as she was settling on to the sofa with her fresh cup of tea, there was a soft tap at the door. To Cara's delight, it was Michael. Knowing that Corby would be sleeping, he quietly opened the door. By this time she was standing in the foyer and welcomed him in.

"Hey stranger," she said as he stepped on to the mat in the foyer, the snow melting from his boots in the warmth of the house. "How was your holiday?"

"It was nice," replied Michael. "It was very relaxing with a lot of talk thrown in about wagon racing."

"That's good," said Cara. "Is you family pretty excited about your new venture?"

"I think they are thrilled and nervous for me all at the same time," said Michael with a laugh. "They haven't spent a great deal of time around the racetrack since the days my uncle used to race."

"Well, that's good that they're excited and nervous," Cara laughed. "That's pretty much how they should feel. I've just made some tea. Would you like to come join me for a bit?"

"That sounds nice," Michael said as he removed his jacket and boots. As they entered the family room Michael looked around with surprise.

"Wow, someone's been busy over the holidays!"

"Actually, I just got started on this today."

"It's looking good. I like the colour."

"Thank you Michael. I just hope I can get everything finished and back in place before it's time for me to go back to work."

"You're pretty dedicated to things when you get on a project," said Michael sincerely. "I'm sure it won't be a problem for you."

"Well, I will take that as a compliment," Cara laughed as she sat down on the sofa with her tea. The furniture was all covered with old sheets to protect it from the paint. Michael took a seat on the sheet covered chair across from Cara.

They discussed their holidays and their families. Cara told Michael about Jason and Julia's wedding plans and Michael told Cara about his sister who was due to have a baby in May. When they had finished the pot of tea, they suddenly both became aware of the late hour and Michael said he should be going. She walked him to the door and said goodnight.

"Cara, I was just wondering what your plans are for New Year's Eve?" he asked as he grabbed at the door handle.

"Oh, I um, I don't imagine anything," she said. "I think Corby and I will just have an evening at home."

"Well in that case, I was wondering if I could make the two of you dinner and then we could ring in the New Year?" asked Michael. "I'd say I'd cook at my place but I imagine you will want to be able to put Corby to bed well before midnight so I'd have to borrow your kitchen as well."

"That sounds very nice Michael." She was both surprised and pleased at the offer. She had really hoped she would not be all alone on New Year's Eve.

"Okay. I'll bring the ingredients over on New Year's Eve day then," said Michael. "Goodnight Cara."

"Goodnight Michael." She locked the door behind him before turning to go to bed. She was already anticipating New Year's Eve and she scolded herself for making more out of it than it was. By the time she climbed into bed, she convinced herself that Michael was simply doing something nice for his friend and her child.

Over the next couple of days, Cara worked fervently to complete the project she had started in the family room. Before long, the painting was completed and the new drapes were hung. Garret's racing awards and chuckwagon photos were replaced with *Bernie Brown* prints; a western artist Cara became familiar with not long after moving to Alberta. The scenes of children with puppies and horses were Cara's favorites. The black framed prints were bold against the freshly painted room. The overall warmth of the room drew one in immediately.

Cara did not have the energy to paint another room however, after washing the walls she replaced the drapes and bedding of the master bedroom. The white islet bedding with matching drapes set a fresh, new tone in the room. The down duvet, once covered in a taupe fabric, now looked even fluffier tucked into the islet cover with matching pillow shams. When she had finished arranging the room, Cara stepped back to admire her work. She was pleased with the way everything had turned out.

Cara finished up with the house work for the day and turned her attention to Corby. She bathed him and gave him ample time to play in the tub before dressing him in his pajamas and feeding him his supper. She did not know what Michael's meal plan was but she was pretty sure it was not going to be something Corby was ready to eat.

When Corby had finished eating, she washed his face and hands and then let him toddle after her to her bedroom so that she could get dressed for the evening. She easily chose the new cream coloured cashmere sweater her mother had given her for Christmas and paired it with blue jeans. She chose some small silver hoop earrings and no other jewelry. She did not want to seem over done. She left her hair down and her waves of dark hair gently cascaded over her shoulders.

Just as Cara was applying a dab of lip gloss, she heard Michael's truck coming up the driveway. She quickly opened the door for him as he approached the house. His arms were filled with grocery bags.

"Happy New Year!" he exclaimed as she took some of the bags from his arms.

"Happy, almost New Year to you too," Cara laughed. "It looks like you've brought enough food to feed an army."

"I wanted to be sure I had lots of variety," said Michael. "I'll be right back. I've got a few more things in the truck that I need."

Michael returned to the house with three fondue pots in hand. He set the pots down on the counter and plucked Corby from his spot on the floor. He played with him until he had him giggling with delight before setting him back down to his toys.

"Fondue," said Cara. "I love fondue."

"That's a relief!" said Michael. "I was hoping you would approve. I know not everyone likes this sort of thing. I'm going to do meat and vegetables, cheese and of course, chocolate."

"That sounds wonderful Michael. I'll pick out some wine to go with the food."

"Already done," said Michael with a grin. "You just need to sit back and relax."

"That sounds easy enough," said Cara. She seated herself at the kitchen table while Michael took over the kitchen, preparing the food. Corby happily played at his mother's feet. He was now walking quite well and no longer stayed in one place for long. As Michael finished working on the meal, Cara took Corby to get him ready for bed. She was enjoying her evening so far. It was such a treat to have someone else working in the kitchen.

When Cara returned from tucking Corby into bed, the kitchen had been transformed. The fondue pots were set up on the table alongside of carefully chopped breads, meats and vegetables. The wine was poured in beautiful stem wear and a pretty arrangement of red and white roses, with red Hypericum berries and greenery adorned the centre of the table.

"This is perfect Michael!" Cara said admiring his work.

"Please, sit down," said Michael as he pulled her chair out for her.

They enjoyed the amazing feast as they visited throughout the fondue dinner. By the time they were ready for dessert, both decided they had already eaten far too much and tabled the chocolate fondue plans for later in the evening. After a quick clean-up, they retired to the newly decorated family room. Each savored a glass of wine as they relaxed in the new retreat. It was the prefect setting to open up discussions of things they had never talked about before.

Cara opened up the conversation by asking Michael about his childhood. She really did not know a great deal about his past or his family for that matter. She laughed hysterically as he described parts of his brief career in rodeo. He tried Boys Steer Riding when he was thirteen. His first ride out claimed the seat of his jeans which was somewhat humiliating. The third ride out, he broke his left arm and his mother put a halt to his career in rodeo right then and there. Later on, when his Uncle Bill invited him to travel along with him on the chuckwagon circuit, he became hooked.

They laughed and talked into the night until Cara suggested they get the chocolate fondue ready in time to ring in the New Year. She gathered the fruit from the fridge which had been previously cleaned and sliced, while Michael prepared the chocolate.

They enjoyed the fruit and sweet melted chocolate along with their wine as they continued their discussion of childhood antics. Cara suggested they turn on the television in order to witness the countdown. As the clocked ticked down on the screen, the crowds in downtown Calgary joined in the count.

"Four, three, two, one," Michael and Cara cheered along. "Happy New Year."

As *Auld Lang Syne* began to play, Michael kissed Cara softly on her lips.

"Happy New Year Cara," he said in a whisper.

"Happy New Year Michael." She kissed him back.

They smiled at each other. It had been a difficult year and it was finally over.

"Thank you for making my New Year's Eve a special one Michael."

"We have a long road ahead of us this year. I had to at least butter you up at the start of it," he joked.

Their laughter was interrupted by the sound of Corby's cries. His cries grew louder as Cara excused herself and hurried down the hall to his room. There she found her son, covered in vomit and sweating profusely. She quickly pulled his pajamas from him and carried him to the washroom. Michael, sensing that something was wrong, followed her to the washroom.

"He's burning up," she declared over his loud cries. She started the bath water for Corby and removed his diaper. Michael monitored the bath water while Cara rocked her son to comfort him. A few minutes into his bath, Corby began to calm down.

"Is there anything else I can do?" asked Michael.

"I don't think so. I'm going to bath him and give him some fever medication. Hopefully he will be fine after that. I think perhaps there has been too much excitement lately with everyone around for the holidays."

"I'm going to go then," said Michael.

"That's probably best," said Cara. "Thank you again for the evening." She continued to bath Corby, not really looking up as she said goodbye.

"Goodnight Cara." Michael quietly closed the bathroom door before walking to the foyer to retrieve his things. He hoped that Corby would be okay.

Following his bath, Cara rocked Corby gently back to sleep. The fever medication seemed to be helping. With her one free hand, she stripped the bedding from his crib, retrieved new blankets from the linen closet, made up the crib and gently laid him down.

It was past two o'clock in the morning when Cara made it to her bedroom. She was worn out. She was sorry to have ended the evening with Michael this way but she was sure he understood. She sat on the edge of her bed looking at their family photograph. She looked down at her wedding band and once again removed it, placing it in her jewelry box. It was a new year and she planned to be ready for the change that would come with it.

Cara did not see Michael much after New Year's Eve, other than on New Year's Day when he came to retrieve his fondue pots and a few other items. In a few days the holidays would be over and it would be time to return to teaching. She cherished the last bit of time she would have with Corby before he would have to return to the Hartman's while she worked. The Sunday before school would start again, she saw a truck pull into the driveway. It continued past her house and up to the barn. She watched as Darryl Baker got out and walked into the barn. She figured he obviously wanted to speak with Michael, although she did not think they knew each other well. A half hour later she heard the truck's engine again and watched Darryl drive back to the house, parking behind her SUV. As he ascended the sidewalk, she went to the door to greet him.

"Good afternoon Cara," said Darryl as she opened the door.

"Hi. This is a nice surprise. Come in. What brings you all the way out here? It's a little early for spring training don't you think?" Cara laughed while Darryl removed his coat and boots.

"So many questions," he joked. "I just thought it was a nice day to go for a drive and low and behold, I ended up at Spruce View."

"Well, I'm glad," said Cara. They hugged before he followed her into the kitchen.

"How was your Christmas?" she asked.

"It was quiet. I went home to see my family. Mom made a huge dinner the way she always does. It was nice. What about you?"

"My family came here for Christmas as planned. My brother brought his girlfriend and they announced their engagement. Corby got spoiled. We had a nice Christmas too."

Corby toddled across the room to where Darryl had taken a seat in the kitchen.

"Wow, the little man's walking now!" exclaimed Darryl.

"Yes he is. He had to get going so he could keep up with everyone during the holidays."

"I can't believe it. He was just a baby the last time I saw him."

"Well, time flies when it comes to kids growing up." She laughed. "Now then, can I get you something to drink?" Cara asked as she arranged some fresh muffins in a basket. "I can put on the coffee or boil the kettle."

"Just water is fine for me," Darryl answered. "These muffins look delicious."

"You just lucked out. I only bake when I'm not working." She filled a glass with water from the water cooler and carried it to the table for Darryl.

"Thank you," said Darryl as she sat down at the table.

Corby continued to walk around, stopping to play with toys or to stand near his mother while Darryl made funny faces to him. Corby laughed but he did not get brave enough to get too close to this stranger.

"I saw you were out at the barn," said Cara. "Setting up your rides for next year with the new driver?"

"No, not really," he grinned. "I just thought I should try to get to know the guy a little better before the season starts."

"That was nice of you."

"I guess I kind of thought with your partnership, maybe something was going on with the two of you."

"Oh, so you're getting on that band wagon now are you?" Cara's skin was flushed but her tone remained even.

"No Cara. Don't get the wrong idea. I figured if you were into this guy, I just hoped that he is a decent guy because that is what you deserve. He told me that there is nothing between the two of you other than business and there never will be. That pretty much cleared things up for me."

"He told you that hey? Well, he's right. It's a business relationship, nothing more." Cara was embarrassed only because she couldn't believe she was sitting there explaining her relationship status to Darryl. Since when did her love life or lack thereof, become the business of the entire NCA? She had never felt more uncomfortable talking to Darryl than she did right now. She passed him the basket of muffins and changed the topic of conversation as quickly as she could.

"So where's your girlfriend today? She didn't feel like taking a drive?"

"No. It was more like she didn't feel like being my girlfriend anymore."

"Oh. I'm sorry." Cara lied. She was pleased that bringing up his personal issues took the spotlight away from her.

"No big deal. I don't think we were exactly meant to be." His comments were nonchalant. It was the way most men acted when they were attempting to pretend they were not hurting. "Cara, I didn't come here to talk about me. Really I came here to see how you're doing. I know that it's been a long road for you and I just wanted to make sure that you know people still care."

"Thank you Darryl. I appreciate hearing that. We're figuring it out one day at a time." They finished their muffins and Darryl said that he needed to get going. She was not certain why but she felt somewhat relieved.

After showing him to the door and hugging him goodbye, Cara watched as Darryl drove down the driveway. She did not know what was more irritating; Darryl asking Michael about the status of their relationship or Michael making such a big deal out of denying it. They both knew nothing was going on so she could not understand his angst about it. He made it seem as though she were something forbidden. She was Garret's widow and somehow, getting close to her seemed to be the equivalent of getting the plague.

Her final hours of her last day off were spent cleaning house and fuming over people and their presumptions. She suddenly realized that what angered her most was Michael's denial of her. A true friend would have stood up for her, not cowered in a corner making excuses to people who did not deserve any answers.

She pondered how she would make it in this partnership with Michael if it meant once again being around the people of the NCA. She wondered who these people thought they were with their speculations. It sickened her and made her realize who her true friends really are. Since Garret's death, there were very few people left that she could turn to. She questioned why people could not just worry about their own lives and leave her alone. If it were not for Corby, she determined that she would probably have just gone to bed and stayed there for a year or so.

When evening came, Cara made no effort to invite Michael for supper as she so often did. She had Corby. He was her family and she needed nothing more. In the morning she was happy to return to teaching. The comfortable routine helped her to forget about all of the other aggravating factors in her life.

A full week went by before Michael knocked at the door. It was once again Sunday afternoon and Cara was busying herself with tasks around the house.

"Hello Michael," she said as she answered the door.

"Hi Cara," he said with a look of uncertainty on his face. "I guess you've been busy since school started again. I haven't really seen you guys around."

"Yes, it's been busy," she replied, knowing that he must realize she was trying to avoid him.

"Well, I was wondering if the two of you would have time to let me take you out to dinner tonight."

"I um," Cara stammered. She did not know if she should accept the invitation or not and then suddenly she found herself saying yes.

"Great. I'll pick you guys up around six then." He said nothing more before closing the door behind him and returning to the barn.

After he had gone, she wondered why she agreed to go anywhere at all. It just seemed that when he asked something, she could never quite say no. He had this pleading, childlike look that made it hard for her to do anything other than agree. She smiled as she thought back to New Year's Eve. He had gone to so much effort with the fondue and with making it a special night. He really was a genuine friend.

The dinner started out on a rather awkward note until helpful little Corby managed to reach from his highchair and flip Michael's steak-filled plate onto his lap. Cara could not apologize enough as she attempted to mop steak sauce from his shirt. Soon both went into gales of laughter. As it turned out, the dinner invitation was a beautiful first step toward a more solid relationship as spring training approached. When she was not teaching school and he was not working in the oil patch, the horses consumed the rest of their time.

Mary watched Corby while the training was going on. It was an interesting dynamic of people who came to help. Garret's brother Robert came to help as often as he could while Michael's brother came to pitch in when he was able. Cara worked well alongside everyone, the memory of Garret still burning strong in her heart. She was happy for Michael and all that he was accomplishing but it was not the same. As much as it troubled her, she came to accept that it never would be.

Early one Saturday morning in March, Michael brought in Fool's Gold. He was a new horse bought at a thoroughbred auction in Edmonton that winter. He was a big, strong four year old bay horse with a lot of attitude and strength that might work well on the pole of Michael's wagon. Just as Michael was leading the horse to the barn, Cara appeared from her house, ready to help before anyone else arrived.

The weather had been warm over the past few days leaving the barnyard full of mud. Cara frowned as she stepped carefully through the mud in her rubber boots. She did not want to slip in the big mess. When Michael slid open the large barn doors, Fool's Gold was startled by the squeak of the metal on the door runner. He pulled back abruptly, pulling Michael off balance. He did not want to let go of the horse for fear he would run and hurt himself. He fell backward into the mud, still holding on to the lead shank. When Cara realized what was happening she made a grab for the horse, catching him by the halter. The horse paused long enough for Michael to regain his footing. Fool's Gold flared his nostrils in fear but quickly calmed down as Michael talked to him in his deep quiet voice.

The incident was over in less than a minute, leaving Michael in head-to-toe mud. Cara contained her laughter right up until the horse was safely tied inside the barn. Morning training took a break while Michael proceeded to his house for some dry clothes but not before he had a chance to smear a little mud on Cara's clean face. A little mud never slowed her laughter down at all.

When the long morning of training was through, Cara went over to Mary's to pick up Corby.

"How are things going over there?" Mary inquired as she gathered Corby's things.

"Pretty good," Cara laughed as she relayed the story of Michael's morning incident.

Mary laughed. "Nice to see you having some fun with the training, even if it is at Michael's expense."

"Oh yeah, it was fun alright. Thanks again for watching Corby Mary."

"Anytime."

When they returned home, Cara could hear the phone ringing as she carried Corby inside. She picked up the receiver just before the call went to voicemail. It was Karen. She was thrilled to hear from her mother. It seemed as though it had been a while since their last long conversation. Karen asked about spring training and Cara filled her in on the ongoing antics of the training. When Cara inquired about Karen's catering business, the tone of the conversation seemed to suddenly change.

"Well," said Karen. "I have some exciting news."

"What is it Mom?"

"I've sold my catering business. The name, the equipment, everything."

"You're kidding me! I never thought I'd see the day. So I'm presuming, by the excitement in your voice, you have some plans in mind?"

"Well, I hope you're ready for this Cara. I've decided to take you up on your offer. Let me just get right to the point. I'm coming to Spruce View to stay. You're listening to the voice of the proud owner of Karen's Creations. It's an internet business I've started, selling homemade gourmet goodies. I'm already taking orders all over western Canada and I plan to expand," she explained. "I know that Michael occupies your other house, so I'm hoping it won't be a problem if I live with you and Corby while I look for my own home. My condo here is already sold so it's now or never."

Cara was flabbergasted by the huge amount of information she had just been given but at the same time, she could not be happier. "When can I be there to help you move Mom? I can hardly wait!" Cara laughed with delight and they discussed the plan in greater detail.

The following weekend Cara and Corby flew out to Vancouver using the tickets Michael gave her for Christmas. She helped her mother pack some things and get organized for the big move. Karen would be living in Spruce View with them by May.

Chapter Thirteen

March melted into April and Michael's training schedule began to get more hectic. He was working full-time with the horses now and would not be returning to his job in the oil patch until September. He was driving four teams daily and the energy he put into hooking, driving and caring for the animals was taking its toll on his body. He was almost thankful for the day of pouring rain that arrived. It meant there would be no training. The track was far too muddy. Once the chores were completed he worked around the barnyard for a while, fixing fence and cleaning up before going to his house to get warm and relax.

When Cara returned from work, she could see a dark figure along the fence in the pasture. It appeared to be a horse that was thrashing on the ground. She had not yet picked up Corby from the Hartman's so she quickly ran into the house. Pulling on her jeans and a t-shirt, she dashed back to the foyer. She put on her rubber boots and an old coat before running back outside to see if a horse was in trouble. He may have just been rolling, as horses often do but it was an unusual occurrence in the rain.

Not seeing Michael anywhere, she ran out to the pasture. The horse was still on the ground and appeared to be caught in the fence. She glanced back toward Michael's house, thinking that she should get his help but deciding against it. The horse had obviously been struggling for a while. She did not want to risk his further injury or even death while she tried to find Michael. She had helped many downed horses in her day and decided that this incident would be no different.

As she neared the horse, she realized that he had caught his back feet under a low wood plank on the fence. He must have been rolling near the fence or slipped on the muddy ground and caught his feet there. Most of the fence had been replaced by higher level lengths of pipe as it was a more horse-friendly material but some of it was still held together by older plank sections.

Cara first approached the thoroughbred gently, talking to him as she neared his head. She did not want to startle him and cause him to injure himself with his thrashing. The only way that she could see to slide the horse out from under the plank was to pull his tail so that his back feet could swing out. She had done this before when horses were caught up but it was no easy task for someone of her petite stature. She could only hope that the wet ground would help the horse slide more easily.

Cara had a firm grasp on the horse's tail before she pulled with all her might. She slipped on the wet ground, landing on her rear. The horse reacted violently under the plank and she could see that he was skinning the hide on his legs. She was now frustrated and thought she would give it one last try before going to search for Michael. With one final heave, the horse moved out from under the plank. In his eagerness to regain his footing, he struck Cara in the chest with his front foot as she slipped to the ground in the mud.

The world seemed to close in around her as she gasped for air. She rolled over to her hands and knees and pushed herself up. Suddenly Michael was there, helping her from the muddy ground.

"My God Cara," Michael exclaimed. "Are you okay? What were you thinking? You could've been killed."

"Calm down," Cara gasped. "He scraped me a little and winded me but I'm fine." She tried to put on a brave face as she wiped the mud from her face. She began to shiver in the rain as they looked toward the horse. The horse had galloped off immediately. It was obvious that he was not lame. The scraped hide on his legs could be tended to when he was brought in for feeding time.

"You should've called me," said Michael. "I was just in the house."

"I figured I could handle it and I did," she grinned at him.

"You handled it alright," he chuckled as he wiped some mud from her face. "Come to the house and at least get dried off. I can tell you're freezing. I've got my fireplace going."

"That sounds like a plan," said Cara.

The spare house was located between the barn and the main house. It was a rather quaint cedar house, tucked in amongst the pine trees. The covered veranda held a porch swing which welcomed people on warm, lazy afternoons. As they stepped into the house, Cara was immediately enveloped in the warmth of the smoldering fire that burned in the stone fireplace. The house was essentially one large room. It contained the kitchen, the dining area and a sitting area in front of the fireplace. The well polished old hardwood floor along with the Navaho print furniture gave the living area a cabin-like feel. A door to the left of the fireplace led to the bathroom. To the right of the fireplace, the door led to a small storage room. The bedroom was in the loft which overlooked the sitting room. A handcrafted rough pine railing partnered the staircase that ran along one wall up to the bedroom.

"Why don't you go into the bathroom and grab a towel from the closet. You can get dried off while I stoke up this fire," said Michael. "There's a robe on the back of the bathroom door. You're welcome to put it on while your clothes dry."

"Oh, I, um, I'm fine with just the towel," Cara stammered like a high school girl. She suddenly wondered what she was doing here at all when she simply could have made her way back to her house. Nonetheless, she found a fresh towel and tried to dry off a bit before returning to the sitting room. She looked around admiring the room. She had not entered the place since the day Michael had taken up residence there. She was impressed with how tidy he kept it.

As she sat on the sofa staring at the fire, Michael sat adjacent to her, trying to take his eyes away from her. Her wet hair clung to her neck and shoulders. The cotton t-shirt she wore clutched at her full breasts. He felt envious of both her hair and her shirt for the way they touched her skin. He again willed his eyes to turn away from her but suddenly found them pulling back. He had never felt so many things for any woman.

As a trickle of water ran down her cheek, he turned to her and wiped it away with the towel that was sitting on her shoulders. He gently released the corner of the towel and suddenly leaned toward her and kissed her. She kissed him back with an urgency she could not explain, allowing his tongue to explore her mouth completely. He tasted so good.

He dragged a feather quilt from the back of the sofa as he gently laid her down in front of the warm fireplace. The goose bumps rose on her skin from both the cold and her excitement. He quickly willed them away with the warmth of his lips. She again accepted his lips with a hunger she could not define. Michael explored her mouth gently and then more aggressively, desperately searching every place inside as though he might capture it in his memory forever. She moaned softly in approval as he gently grasped her bottom lip between his own before moving on to her beautiful neck, still damp with rain. Cara could not believe all of this was happening and still, she found herself giving into her every raw emotion and need.

Michael scooped Cara into his arms, carrying her up the stairs toward his bedroom. Still kissing each other hungrily, he gently set her down on her feet as they tore at each other's clothes. An aggressive tug on his shirt sent several buttons spilling to the floor. The shirt was quickly torn away revealing his strong, muscular build. Michael responded by peeling away her cotton t-shirt. The breasts he revealed readily rose and fell, awaiting their release from her bra.

Michael slowed his pace. He wanted to savor every moment. He gently laid her down on the bed before lowering his lips to her flat tummy. He softly kissed her skin before trailing to the edge of the waistband of her jeans which he playfully kissed and tugged at with his teeth. Cara responded to his every touch, longing for more. She arched her hips toward Michael and then sat up far enough to reach his shoulders with her hands. She pulled him toward her and fervently kissed his lips as she ran her fingers through the soft curls of his hair.

As he reached behind her, unclasping her burgundy colored lace bra she breathed softly into his ear and gently bit his neck. Michael moaned softly with pleasure as he pulled her bra away and dropped it to the floor. He cupped her breasts in his hands as he nibbled along her collar bone giving her new pleasure.

He pressed himself against her through his jeans as he pulled her toward him and just held her there, flesh against flesh. The sensation was amazing.

He smiled at her before he made his way to her waiting breasts. He welcomed each breast into his mouth tenderly while still caressing them with his hands. Her breasts responded to the pleasure, a pleasure that had been lost for so long. Slowly he moved away from her breasts and back to her moist lips. One hand gently grasped her chin as he used his free hand to undo her jeans. She slowly undid the buckle on his jeans before grasping at the button that held them closed. She could feel herself trembling now and she hoped that Michael did not notice.

Finally both were free of their jeans which were still damp with rain. As they looked deeply into one another's eyes, Michael gently slid his hands down the curves of Cara's beautiful body, admiring every inch of her in the dimly lit room. Cara was now aching with desire. She could feel her whole body craving him as she wrapped her legs around his back. He rocked against her gently as his lips moved along her neck and between her breasts. Slowly he slid his tongue along her hips before moving to taste the flesh along the inside of her thigh. She could feel her body pulse as his soft breath stimulated her aching mound. Cara moaned with satisfaction as her fingers clenched Michael's shoulders and he brought his lips up to meet hers. He entered her gently and they softly rocked as one, moving more quickly as their combined desires erupted. Cara exploded with pleasure as she pushed her pelvis against him in unending satisfaction. Michael rocked against her as he reached his own gratification. He never wanted to let go of her or of this moment, ever. When they were both spent, they held each other for a long time, enjoying the moment as they listened to the rain spattering on the rooftop.

Suddenly Cara leapt from Michael's bed, gathering her clothes as she went.

"Cara, what is it?" Michael asked with alarm. "I'm sorry if I've upset you. I thought this is what you wanted. I thought we were both ready for this."

Cara leaned down to Michael and kissed him hard on the mouth. "It's not that. This was wonderful. You are wonderful. I have a son to pick up, remember?" Cara smiled. She dressed quickly and left the room leaving Michael to swim amongst the haze of what had just happened between them. He rose from the bed and dressed. It was time to bring the horses in for their evening feed and he would need to check the legs of the horse that had been caught under the fence. He liked that this felt like a normal day. He hoped that he and Cara could spend many normal days together. He was not going to push this relationship forward but he certainly was not going to push it away either. It felt good. It seemed right.

Cara grabbed her keys from the house before returning to her vehicle to go pick up Corby from the Hartman's. She could not very well walk over there and carry him home in the rain. Visions of Michael and his touch on her body raced through her head. When she reached the Hartman's doorstep she was suddenly overwhelmed with guilt. She did not know what she was feeling not to mention what anyone else would think if they found out. Michael was a wonderful friend and an overall great person. He was the kind of person that everyone was drawn to. His quick wit, his sense of humor and his optimism made him easy to like. Even with all of these things, she wondered what people would think about the two of them together. She wondered what they would think about her with any other man.

"Hello Cara," Mary said as she swung open the screen door. "I saw you standing outside and you looked a million miles away." Cara tried to smile at Mary before suddenly bursting into tears.

"What is it hun?" Mary guided Cara into the kitchen where Corby was happily engulfed in his toys.

"I, um, well Michael, we," she stammered through her words. "I think we are more than business partners," she finally spilled out the words. "I just, I don't know what to feel. I don't know what others will think." Her thoughts came out all at once before Mary placed her hands on Cara's shoulders and brought her words to a stop.

"Cara, everyone loves Michael," Mary began with her usual soft, kind voice. "Look at the things that he does for you, for Corby. I mean the guy can hardly pass a shop that he isn't picking out some little toy for Corby and he would do anything for you at the drop of a hat. That's love my dear. Recognize it for what it is and stop all of this guilt. Stop pretending that you don't affect each other the way that you do. I know that you're afraid and I know that you still miss Garret. What you had with Garret was amazing. That does not have to be replaced. It is okay to love someone that true twice in a lifetime."

"I just don't know," the tears streamed down Cara's eyes as she spoke. "The good people of the NCA will be all over this one."

"Is that what matters here?" asked Mary.

"No. I mean, it shouldn't matter but these people have an interesting way of making one feel like hell over something that should be a happy thing."

"Well, I think it's time these people in glass houses worry a little more about themselves and a little less about you. Cara, you have been through hell and back and you have remained strong. After all of that, I don't think anyone has the right to judge you. It's time for you to open your heart to someone new. You have someone who loves both you and Corby. Do you really want to wonder for the rest of your life, what might have happened if you had not taken this chance?"

"No, I think I'm ready to take the chance," said Cara with a smile.

"That's more like the Cara I know," said Mary. "Only you and Michael can decide what the future holds. No one else has that right."

"Thank you Mary," said Cara drying the last of her tears. "I think I just needed to hear that from you." She hugged Mary and packed up Corby's things to return home. In her heart she knew that everything would be okay.

Michael and Cara spent the rest of spring training enjoying getting to know the more intimate sides of one another. They were subtle about their feelings for each other when others were around but they did not hide them entirely. It was a slow process that gave people the comfort they needed to accept this new relationship. Cara worried about how Garret's family would react and was pleased to have their acceptance when they became aware. She knew it was not an easy thing for them to see her in a new relationship but it did not prevent them from being happy for her either.

When May came, Cara's mother arrived from Vancouver as promised. She was not surprised at all to see this new bond that had formed between her daughter and Michael. She was pleased to see Cara healing and moving on with her life. She was happy to see that she had a second chance at happiness with someone who so obviously cared about her daughter and her grandson.

The new on-line gourmet goodie business had taken off and Cara helped her mother to pack boxes and ship orders in the evenings when Corby was asleep. It was a delight for her to have her mother back in her life and not an hour's plane ride away.

Jason and Julia called often to discuss their tropical wedding plans. They were excited about their winter nuptials. Cara did her best to help with the plans as much as she could. It would be a beautiful wedding. The date was set for the week before Christmas.

When the day finally arrived to return to Grand Rapids for the first race of the season, Cara felt that no amount of fresh air would relieve her of the anxiety she was feeling. She let the conversation she overheard between Barbie and Nicole at the winter ball get into her head. Perhaps they really did believe she was with Michael just to stay around the races. It seemed like such a senseless idea but it sickened Cara nonetheless.

With the help of her mother, Cara set up her trailer in Grand Rapids while Michael and his brother worked at the barns with the horses. Corby was now old enough to play in the sand with the other children. He was having a ball with the other children who had gathered.

Cara swallowed hard as her attention turned to the two women approaching her trailer. It was Barbie and Nicole. She told herself that no matter what the women had to say she would stand up for herself. She seated herself in a lawn chair to watch Corby play and she made no effort to acknowledge the women as they approached.

"Hello Cara," Barbie spoke first. "It has been a while."

"Hello." Cara said nothing more as she pretended to concentrate on Corby in the sand.

"You, um, you look good," said Nicole. Cara only nodded in response as she prepared to do battle as quietly as she could in front of all of the children.

"We don't mean to stand here stammering over small talk," said Barbie. "We are both her to apologize for last winter."

"Yes," agreed Nicole. "We never meant to hurt you that way. We aren't just here to apologize for what you overheard. We're here to apologize for saying it in the first place."

"I think we were jealous of your strength," added Barbie. "You are a strong woman and instead of being two people who should have realized how blessed they are to have a friend like you, we let the green-eyed monster raise its ugly head. We didn't even consider what you had been through or what it took for you to come to that ball in the first place."

"Ladies, it's been a long year for me," Cara spoke softy but looked at them intently. "I have had my struggles and I have found my strengths. It hurt me a lot to overhear the two of you but it wasn't the worst thing going on in my life at the time. I've just put it into perspective. Friendship can have its ups and downs at times. I don't want ours to be ruined over one incident."

"Thank you Cara," said Nicole and Barbie. The three women hugged and shared some tears before Cara invited them to sit down and enjoy the sunshine with her. It would take some time but their friendship would survive.

As soon as the women departed, Michael was at Cara's side questioning whether or not she was okay.

"I'm fine, really." Cara smiled at Michael. "You don't have to protect me. It's going to be a long summer if you're always coming to make sure no one has hurt my feelings."

"I know. I just thought I'd ask just this once," he grinned. "Darryl Baker was over to my barn this afternoon. He mentioned that it was nice to see you here, or rather, to see us here. He's going to outride for my first race tomorrow night."

"That's great Michael. He won't let you down. I'm sure of that." She paused before asking him the one big question that had been on her mind all day. "So I think we can handle all of this, hey?"

"Cara," Michael spoke her name in a whisper before bringing his lips down to kiss hers. "I think we're going to do just fine."

People seemed to be accepting whatever Cara and Michael had become more easily than either thought they would. Maybe just as Cara had, others realized life was full of uncertainty and change.

Michael parked his holiday trailer alongside of Cara's. They were working on big dreams together at a pace comfortable for both of them. Something special was in the air again. Cara had been afraid of that feeling for a long time but now she welcomed it back.

The pain and heartache of the past year was losing ground in the backstretch; the present glory of life was gaining with every stride; and the promise of their future was closing hard at the finish line.

Epilogue

"It's an exciting first night at the *Calgary Stampede* and for you folks listening at home, we'd like to draw you a little picture," radio announcer Dale Mallet's voice came over the radio for every racing fan that could not be at the races that night. "John, as the history buff of chuckwagon racing, I'll turn the mike over to you."

"Thanks Dale," said John Sherwood. "Tonight we'd like to tell you about a brand new page in *Calgary Stampede* history that's about to be written. It's been a long time since we've seen the blue and white diamond pattern of the McCormack racing team at the *Calgary Stampede* but tonight the late Garret McCormack's son, Corb will make his stampede debut."

"Yes, it's a beautiful sight," added Dale. "I can see Corb's mom in the grandstand off to my left. This is certainly a proud moment for her. Her husband, Michael DeWalt and her son Corb are both competing in this year's stampede."

"She does look excited Dale. As most racing fans will remember, Corb's Dad, Garret lost his life in a highway accident the day following his first ever *Calgary Stampede* championship some eighteen years ago."

"It was such a tragic loss for the chuckwagon racing community. We are all so excited and moved to see Corb out there tonight, proudly driving in his father's footsteps."

Corb drove his team up to his barrel for his premiere *Calgary Stampede* race. He was both excited and nervous but he pulled his team up and awaited the sound of the horn like a pro. Just before the horn, Corb was certain he felt a gentle hand on his shoulder reminding him that he could do it. As the horn sounded, Corb's team surged ahead, swiftly departing the barreling area. Corb smiled all the way around the track as a new generation of racing fans cheered him on to the finish line.